# THE POWER AND THE GLORY

# NEMESIS

## BOOK TWO

## CHRISTINE WASS

Romaunce Books

1A The Wool Market Dyer Street Cirencester Gloucestershire GL7 2PR
An imprint of Memoirs Publishing  www.mereobooks.com

978-1-86151-934-4

First published in Great Britain in 2019
by Romaunce Books, an imprint of Memoirs Publishing

The address for Memoirs Publishing Group Limited can be
found at www.memoirspublishing.com

The Memoirs Publishing Group Ltd Reg. No. 7834348

Typeset in 10/16pt Century Schoolbook
by Wiltshire Associates Publisher Services Ltd.

# CHAPTER ONE

"Thank you, Abeona!" Flavius Quinctilius Silvanus murmured a prayer of thanks to the goddess of outward journeys as the Caesarea Headquarters of the Governor of Judea loomed before him. To further prove Abeona had been lovingly guiding them, the weather had improved the further west they had travelled.

As part of Pontius Pilate's entourage, Flavius was relieved that the journey from Jerusalem to Caesarea had passed without event. He was also relieved to have a brief respite from the troublesome religious festivals held by the Jews. He would not have to return to Jerusalem until the spring, which was unfortunately when, so he'd been told, the most troublesome festival of all was celebrated – Passover.

Breaking their journey to Caesarea, the entourage had

stayed overnight at the Antipatras fortress. On arrival, hot and tired, they had all been glad of a good meal and a much-needed rest. The next day the cavalry from the garrison in Caesarea had arrived. Once Pilate, Flavius and the rest of Pilate's retinue were safely on their way with them to Caesarea, the escort from the fortress Antonia in Jerusalem, led by Prefect Alae Antonius, began their journey back to that city.

Flavius had mixed feelings about going to Caesarea. He was sure now that Pilate had guessed about his feelings towards Princess Farrah, who, just as their love had begun to blossom, had been kidnapped by the felon Eleazar ben-Ezra, and had purposely taken him away from Jerusalem and its bad memories. On the one hand Flavius thought a change of scene might ease his troubled mind; on the other hand, what if Farrah wasn't dead and was found and brought back to Jerusalem and he wasn't there to see her? Well, it was too late now. He was on his way to the coast, with new people and different things to discover.

Flavius did not know very much about Caesarea, as upon his arrival there the year before, he had cleared the port and gone straight to Antipatras, then continued his journey to Jerusalem to take up his position at the Antonia. If his duties allowed, he would make a point of discovering what the city was like.

Pilate entered the grounds of his residence as the rest of the party, including Flavius, followed the cavalry into the Caesarea garrison.

Flavius quickly settled into his role as temporary Senior Tribune at the garrison, which housed a contingent of the Tenth Legion and several cohorts of the Legion Sixth Ferrata, who were not only busy dealing with the problems on land but had to oversee the busy port area. Pilate too had to be guarded while he was in residence. With all of these duties to contend with, Flavius found little time to dwell on past regrets. His days were full but his nights were a torment, his dreams filled with sad memories.

Despite being busy, Flavius made time to enquire about the whereabouts of Julius' father, the Centurion Cornelius Vittelius, and was pointed in the direction of the Second Italian Cohort, also stationed in the Caesarea barracks. Flavius stood before the Italian Cohort officer in charge and presented his credentials. The officer gave a smart salute to his superior and led Flavius to the Centurion's quarters.

As Flavius entered Cornelius' room he saw the Centurion sitting reading from a scroll. When Cornelius looked up and saw Flavius standing there, he quickly put the scroll in a drawer of his desk, got to his feet and with a ram-rod straight back, saluted Flavius.

Flavius acknowledged the salute. "Centurion Lucius Cornelius Vittelius?"

"Yes sir."

Flavius took a moment to study the Centurion. He immediately saw the likeness between Decurion Julius, the young cavalry officer serving at the Antonia, and his father. He guessed Cornelius was in his early forties. His short dark hair was beginning to grey at the temples. He was almost as tall as himself, his body lean but muscular. His handsome face showed intelligence, his square jaw strength of character. With a distinct aquiline nose and high cheekbones, together with his famous name, he looked every inch the patrician, but given his rank, however prestigious, he obviously did not come from a present-day patrician family background. He hoped that when he knew the Centurion better, he might tell him of his origins.

"At ease, Centurion, this is not an official visit. I bring you news of your son." Flavius saw the Centurion tense. He quickly dispelled any concerns by saying "All is well with him." Cornelius visibly relaxed.

Flavius handed him the rolled scroll. "He asked me to deliver this letter to you." He handed the scroll over.

Cornelius took it, wondering how a Senior Tribune could know his son so well that he would carry a letter from him to give to a humble Centurion. "Thank you, Tribune," he said, trying to keep the element of surprise out of his voice.

"Well, Centurion, I'm sure you have many duties to attend to, as have I. Perhaps we can meet again when our duties allow."

Cornelius smiled. "It will be an honour, sir."

Remembering that this Centurion was a *princeps* – one of the *primi ordines,* the highly experienced backbone of the Legions – Flavius returned the smile. "The honour will be mine," he said.

Cornelius saluted and Flavius left the room. He quickly returned to his desk and sat down. He unfastened the leather tie, opened the scroll and read the news from his beloved son. As he read, a smile spread across his face.

When Flavius finally had some time to himself, he began to explore the city of Caesarea. He was filled with amazement. Seeing the buildings and architecture, it was difficult to believe that he was in an eastern province, albeit a powerful one, a long way from Rome. He had only seen the palace headquarters from a distance as his ship from Ostia, Rome's seaport, had neared the port almost a year ago. Close up, he was stunned by the marvellous construction of the building which was now used as the official residence of the Roman Governors of Judaea Province. Herod the Great had built the palace on a promontory with commanding views of the Tyrrhenian Sea. The magnificent harbour nearby, also built by Herod, was bustling with ships arriving from countries from all over the Empire, as it had been that day when Flavius' ship had landed. As he took in more of the sights, he began to appreciate how interesting this city was.

Two days before the Saturnalia, Flavius was on duty at the Governor's Palace. He was standing at attention in Pilate's austere office, watching as Pilate dictated letters to a scribe. The dictation ended and the scribe was dismissed.

Pilate let out a sigh. "Well that's the official business

over for today." He looked up at Flavius. "Tribune Flavius," he said.

"Sir." Flavius stood waiting for his next order.

"I'd like you to accompany me to my private apartments. My wife will be delighted to see you." Pilate got up from his chair and turned to go out.

Flavius was pleased. He had hoped to see Claudia Procula during his stay in Caesarea. He followed Pilate out of his office into a beautiful, frescoed corridor. They came to a heavy door guarded by two legionaries, who saluted as Pilate approached. Pilate offered a casual wave of his hand in reply and waited while one of the soldiers opened the door, then walked through. Flavius followed him. The soldier closed the door behind them and returned to his position.

They entered another world. Flavius marvelled at the luxurious, magnificently-decorated room, so different from the austerity of Pilate's office. Sunshine flooded in through the latticed windows placed high up in the walls, highlighting painted walls depicting scenes from *The Labours of Hercules* and casting patterns of dazzling light onto the mosaic floors and the marble statuary which stood on ornate tables scattered around the room. One statue in particular caught Flavius' eye: a beautiful piece of marble with carvings of hunting dogs bringing down a stag. It was superbly made; he'd seen nothing like it outside Rome.

Pilate saw Flavius' appreciative expression. "Yes, it is rather beautiful isn't it?" Pilate studied Flavius for a brief moment. "What do you think of Caesarea, Flavius?"

"What I've seen of the city so far, Lord Pilate, has taken me completely by surprise," Flavius answered. "Jerusalem's architecture is beautiful, but I had no idea a second city in this land could also be so inspiring and cosmopolitan."

"Yes. It is quite magnificent. When I attained the Governorship of Judaea Province, before I arrived in Caesarea and took up residence in the Governor's Palace, I was familiarized with some of this city's history. It was first built by the Phoenicians, along with a small port, and was called Strato's Tower. When the Divine Emperor, Augustus, gave this city and port to his friend, Herod, the so-called Great" – his voice took on a slight note of contempt – "Herod did a good job of rebuilding this archaic place into what you see today. Apparently, the Emperor was delighted when Herod renamed the area Caesarea Maritima, in his honour."

Pilate clapped his hands "Well, I think that's enough history for today, Flavius." A slave appeared. "Ask the Lady Claudia to attend me here," he said without looking at the man.

The slave bowed and hurried off to another part of the palace. In a short time Claudia Procula appeared. Tall, slim and elegant, she was dressed in a royal blue dress edged with silver, which complemented her light brown hair. Claudia walked over to Pilate, who took her hand and tenderly kissed it. He introduced Flavius.

"My dear, do you remember Flavius Quinctilius

Silvanus, the elder son of Senator Silvanus and my cousin Lydia Flavia? As you see, he is a Tribune now."

Claudia looked at Flavius and a deep smile lit up her face. "Of course I remember. How lovely to see you again Flavius. It has been a long time."

Flavius gave a brief bow. "Thank you, my lady."

"Well, I'll leave you two to catch up." Pilate kissed his wife's hand again. "I will see you at the reception, my dear." With a nod to Flavius he walked briskly out of the room.

Claudia sat down on a silken couch. Pointing to the couch opposite, she said "Please, sit down, Flavius" He did so. "Now tell me, how are things with your family?"

"They are all well, Lady Claudia. My mother is so proud of Governor Pilate." Was it his imagination, or did a frown briefly cross her face?

"How kind of Lydia Flavia." Her voice held a melancholy tone.

Flavius tried to hide his anxiety as he looked at her. He could see she was still a beautiful woman, but she was too pale. There were dark shadows beneath her eyes and the beginnings of worry lines around her small mouth.

Keeping his voice steady, Flavius said "Lord Pilate says that you are happy here in Caesarea. But you must miss Rome."

She looked wistful. "Yes, I do like it here; the sea breeze is very refreshing. I feel I can breathe here. Of course, I do miss Rome, but I hear it is not an easy city to live in at the present time."

Flavius wondered how much she knew about the unrest

in Rome caused by the Emperor's insistence on living on his island of Capri whilst in Rome, one would-be dictator after another plotted against him. He changed the subject.

"Jerusalem is not an easy place to live in either. We have had a lot of trouble with bandits and thieves lately." An image of Farrah flashed before his eyes.

"Jerusalem was never easy to live in. I have unfortunate memories of that city," Claudia said sadly. They were memories that would stay with her forever: of a disturbing dream leading her to warn her husband not to have anything to do with an innocent man on trial before him, a man from Nazareth. Her warning had been disregarded and the man had been crucified by the will of the conniving Temple authorities and a raging mob.

Flavius grew concerned as he saw her suddenly stare into the distance, her eyes taking on a haunted look. Whatever her memories of Jerusalem, they obviously deeply disturbed her. He leaned forward. "Lady Claudia, are you feeling unwell? Shall I call for a maidservant?"

She quickly snapped out of her reverie. "Thank you for your concern, but that will not be necessary." She smiled at him. "But how rude of me! You have not been offered refreshment, Flavius."

He shook his head. "I don't want to put you to any trouble."

"Nonsense. It's no trouble." She clapped her hands and the slave reappeared. "Fetch the Tribune some wine."

The slave bowed and left the room, soon returning with

a tray holding a silver pitcher and wine cups. He placed them on a table close to Claudia. "Shall I pour the wine, my lady?"

"No. That will be all for now." She dismissed the slave, who bowed and left the room. Claudia poured wine into one cup and handed it to Flavius; she declined to drink herself.

They chatted for a while about Flavius' family and the pleasant days of the past when they had all spent time together at family events. Then, giving her apologies, she got up from the couch. "I'm afraid I must go. I have to join my husband tonight. We are hosting a welcome party for a delegation of merchants from Cyprus and I must look my best."

Flavius stood up. "It has been good to see you, Lady Claudia."

She turned to go, then turned back again. "Flavius, I would like it very much if you came to our Saturnalia festivities."

Flavius was delighted. "It would be a great honour, my lady."

"Good. I'll ask my husband to give you light duties that day so you may be free to attend. A litter will be placed at your disposal." She saw Flavius's surprise and smiled. "We can't have a member of my husband's family walking through the streets at night."

Flavius gave a wry smile. He had been on duty out on those streets at night on one or two occasions since his arrival in Caesarea with, so far, no mishap, but then he had been wearing uniform and had been accompanied by armed legionaries. This time he would be expensively dressed and carrying costly presents. He knew she was right; it would not be safe. He bowed. "Thank you. That is most gracious of you, my lady."

"That's settled then. I will see you at the Saturnalia. Until then..." With an elegant wave of her small hand, Claudia turned and left the room.

Flavius felt more light-hearted than he had for a long time as he left the palace and returned to the garrison. It had been a while since he'd attended a Saturnalia party and he knew it would prove to be an excellent diversion.

# CHAPTER TWO

Had Flavius been in Rome on the day of the Saturnalia, he would have gone with his family to the Temple of Saturn, which stood in the Forum, to worship and make offerings to the god in remembrance of the 'Golden Age of Saturn' when there had been plenty for all and peace had prevailed. From childhood he had witnessed the Saturnalia festivities beginning with rituals and sacrifices. The statue of the god being hollow, it was filled with olive oil, a symbol of his agricultural functions, and his feet were bound with woollen strips which were unbound at Saturnalia. After the rituals, the Senators, who were obliged to be at the Temple ritual, dismissed the excited crowd who gathered in and around the Temple with the age-old cry of "Io Saturnalia!" This was the sign for the family gatherings and other more private parties to commence. As he had grown into manhood, the celebration after the rituals had become more enjoyable. After a celebratory meal with his family, Flavius would eagerly depart to parties given by his friends, where he would happily partake in feasting, drunkenness and playing pranks. More often than not he would meet a girl willing to participate fully in the Saturnalia celebration of sex, traditionally just for the procreation of children, but for Flavius and his young friends it was purely for pleasure.

Flavius was now a long way from the Forum and Saturn's Temple in Rome. Being on duty at the garrison, he got up early, just as the sun was rising, and made private obeisance to the god in the quietness of his quarters. He poured some olive oil over a small statue of Saturn he had purchased in the marketplace, intoning the sacred words. Lady Claudia had been successful in getting her husband to give Flavius light duties, which he carried out until the afternoon. After a short rest, it was time to get ready for Pilate's party.

Flavius knew that with the post-ritual party taking place at the Governor's palace, he would have to look his best. There were many slaves at the palace ready to attend to all of the senior officers' needs. He had been assigned an older man, originally from Gaul. Strong and muscular, the slave was skilled at his tasks. After Flavius had bathed in the luxurious palace bath house, the slave dressed him with special care.

Flavius wore his favourite tunic of deep red edged with

silver, with matching soft leather boots. He checked his leather bag, which hung from a thin silver belt encircling his waist. Inside the bag, wrapped in a gold threaded cloth, was a small, exquisitely-fashioned silver statuette of Saturn holding his customary sickle; similarly wrapped was a pair of beautiful silver earrings, the intricately carved drops being shaped in the form of the goddess Ops, the sister/wife of Saturn, who was the goddess of fertility and harvest. She was holding a carved cornucopia, the symbol of abundance and plenty. He had bought these, at great cost, from a prestigious silver merchant in the city, as presents for Pilate and Claudia Procula as befitted the tradition of giving silver gifts for the Saturnalia festival.

He wondered if Pilate would honour the other tradition of masters being slaves and slaves becoming the masters for the occasion. Flavius himself had given permission to his slave to join the party.

The litter bearers arrived. Satisfied that he was ready, Flavius called for the guards who would walk beside the litter to protect him on his journey to the Governor's palace. His slave would walk with them.

When he arrived at Pilate's residence he could hear, above the sound of pan pipes and drums, the excited voices and laughter of the guests. He stepped out of the litter, then dismissed his own guards and litter bearers with the instruction to stay in the area ready for his return to the garrison. He told his slave to go with the other servants and enjoy himself, but to stay sober. He watched as the slave moved away and joined the others, then he introduced himself to the guards on the front entrance of the palace, who saluted and stood aside to let him pass.

He entered a large courtyard which was surrounded on all sides by a roofed colonnade. Palm trees and shrubs scattered around the courtyard were decorated with silver stars, while swathes and garlands of greenery hung from the roof. In the centre of the courtyard stood a large fountain topped by a huge marble dolphin. Wine cascaded out of smaller dolphin-shaped water features placed on four sides of the fountain bowl.

A palace slave took a goblet and filled it with the flowing wine, then handed it to Flavius, who took it and drank from it. The man was truly a slave, Flavius had seen him working during his previous visit to the Palace. Obviously Pilate was not going to give up his position as master, even for the Festival.

He approached the door to the main reception area; an ornately-arranged green wreath hung over the door. He entered the room. Standing by the door were a young couple. He smiled at them, observing that the young man looked immaculate in a dark blue tunic. Judging by his smart haircut and his bearing, Flavius thought he must be a junior officer. The girl holding onto his arm barely reached his shoulder. Her golden hair was swept up in curls caught with a silver pin. The hairstyle complemented her delicately pretty face. Her slight frame was draped in a simple white gown with gold edging crossing over and under her small breasts. To Flavius she looked unspoilt, virginal. He guessed she was no more than sixteen or seventeen years old.

Seeing the young couple, Flavius wished Farrah was with him. Something in his heart told him to keep hoping. He would not believe she was dead until he saw her body. He tried desperately to banish the thought of her from his mind. To distract his tortured thoughts he looked around the room, seeing the tables and benches laid out ready for the feast.

He moved further into the room and saw that the senior members of Pilate's household, including some of his secretarial staff, were standing talking together in a corner. Close by were some junior officers he recognised from the barracks, while a group of young women were clearly appraising them and talking about them; they were laughing coquettishly and whispering from behind their hands.

Flavius' attention was drawn to a thin-faced, imperious-looking man who stood apart from the officers. He had seen that haggard face before, but where? He racked his brains trying to think, but no answer came to him.

A clash of cymbals announced the arrival of Pilate. The pipes and drums stopped and all chattering ceased as every head turned towards a doorway set in the painted walls. Pilate swept into the room with Claudia Procula by his side, her hand resting on his arm. Pilate was resplendent in a long tunic of light green edged with an embossed silver pattern. Lady Claudia wore a gown of emerald green encrusted with pearls. Around her neck was a collar made up of pearls and silver, with matching earrings in her ears. Her light brown hair had been hennaed into a fiery red. Flavius thought she looked magnificent.

Flavius watched as Pilate hesitated briefly and inclined his head towards a group of guests, who responded with light applause and deferential bows of the head. All but one; the tall, thin-faced man who had aroused Flavius' curiosity simply stared coldly at Pilate. For a brief moment Flavius thought he saw a look of surprise cross Pilate's face, followed by fear. He frowned, seeing a look of concern on Claudia Procula's face as she looked up at her husband. Pilate patted her arm as if to reassure her, then with a barely concealed effort, he regained his smile and moved on to acknowledge his other guests.

Pilate and Claudia stopped in front of Flavius, who inclined his head and returned Claudia's smile.

"We are so glad you could come, Flavius, aren't we Pontius?" Her voice was soft and melodious.

"Yes. Yes indeed," said Pilate.

Flavius could see that Pilate was troubled, but it was not his place to draw attention to the Governor's obvious discomfort. Instead he said blandly, "Thank you for inviting me, Lord Pilate." He presented the gifts to them. Pilate seemed pleased with his silver statuette, while Claudia beamed when she saw the earrings. They thanked Flavius for his thoughtfulness, then, with a brief smile, Pilate whisked Claudia away to meet a group of foreign guests. Perhaps, Flavius thought, they were the delegation from Cyprus.

Pilate was soon in animated conversation with the men, but Flavius noticed that he wore a taut expression, and would occasionally look across to the thin-faced man, who had not moved from his place. Claudia, meanwhile, had gone over to a group of older officers' wives and struck up a conversation with them.

Soon it was time for Pilate, Claudia and their guests to take their seats. First, Pilate went to a shrine set on a table in the corner of the room. The governor's chief household god was Mars. There was also a small statue of Saturn in deference to his festival. The prayers were said and the libation given. Then the host and hostess sat at the top table with Flavius and the top-ranking officers seated either side of the couple.

Pilate prayed again to the household gods, and then the first course was brought in by servants dressed in leaf-green tunics. The dishes were carried shoulder high and contained jellyfish and eggs and sows' udders filled with eggs and milk; they were followed by boiled chickens, their unplucked plumage dyed many different colours and fashioned into fantastic shapes. The next course consisted of platters of tender cuts of roasted lamb and dressed suckling pigs.

When all the preliminary courses had been eaten, the main course of the banquet was led in by flute-playing servants. It was carried in on a large square silver platter by four more servants, two on each side. The guests voiced appreciation and applauded as they saw the magnificent offering before them: it was a huge sturgeon; its open-mouthed head was supported by an ornate silver plinth with spikes on each side to hold the head still. The monster fish was surrounded by a selection of smaller fish and polished shells.

The banquet concluded with the serving of sweetmeats in the shapes of suns and stars, succulent dates and hot African sweet wine cakes served with golden honey. This whole feast was washed down with copious amounts of wine poured by young men dressed in silver-coloured tunics edged with embroidered dark green vine leaves. Some of the guests had now consumed far too much food and wine for their personal comfort, so they went outside to the vomitorium and used one of the feathers provided to tickle the backs of their throat in order to set off the process of clearing their stomachs. A short while later, they returned to the table and began to indulge themselves all over again.

After the feast, amidst much merriment, a troupe of energetic acrobats entertained the guests, followed by four jugglers; the entertainment finale was a wrestling match between two equally powerful opponents, the winner receiving a bag of silver coins from Pilate.

The entertainment over, Pilate and Claudia rose up from their chairs and with the Governor's permission, the guests began to leave the tables and retire to another reception room. Some of the officers settled down to play dice or board games. Flavius had disciplined himself not to eat and drink too much, as he did not want any reports of bad behaviour getting back to his father, but he could see that others around him were not so cautious. Raucous laughter rang out from the young officers; one of them began to lurch drunkenly across the room to where the group of young women stood. He grabbed a dark-haired beauty by the hand and led her towards a doorway leading into the garden area. The girl giggled and turned with a knowing look to her watching friends, who laughed and whispered amongst themselves. Flavius smiled to himself, this was one couple at least who would be fulfilling the true celebration of Saturnalia.

Flavius watched as Pilate approached the young couple he had first seen on his arrival and heard him say, "Ah Marcus, I need to speak with you." Pilate smiled at Marcus' companion. "You will excuse us, my dear." It was not a question, rather a statement of intention.

The nervous young woman bowed her head in reply. She watched as Pilate led the young officer away in the direction of his office. The thin-faced man's eyes followed them.

Pilate ushered Marcus into the room, entered and closed the door behind him. He could see that the young officer was a little afraid. Pilate smiled. "Don't worry my boy, you've done nothing wrong. On the contrary, I am very pleased with you. I have been watching you for some time and you show great promise."

"Thank you, Lord Pilate," Marcus said, visibly relaxing.

"As a result of your exemplary conduct, I offer you my Saturnalia gift: a place on my personal staff."

Marcus sharply drew in his breath at this surprising news. "I don't know what to say, my Lord. You do me a great honour."

Pilate waved his hand. "Nonsense, you have earned it. All I ask is that you are obedient to my will and give me your loyalty at all times, whatever the consequences."

Marcus drew himself up to his full height. "You already have my loyalty, Lord Pilate. I promise you my obedience too."

Pilate slapped him on the back. "Then it is done. Go and enjoy yourself, but don't get too drunk as I shall expect to see you outside my office early tomorrow morning."

Marcus gave Pilate the full military salute and with head held high, left the office. He made his way back to his companion and said proudly, "The Governor has just given me a position on his personal staff." He lifted her off her feet and whirled her around in his excitement.

When he put the breathless girl back down, she was beaming with delight "Oh Marcus, that's wonderful!" she gasped.

Before Marcus could continue, one of the other junior officers stepped forward. "I couldn't help overhearing your good news, Marcus. Well done. This calls for a celebration. You lot" – he called to some other young officers – "we're going to have a celebratory drink with Marcus. He's just been promoted."

A cheer went up and before Marcus could protest, he was hoisted up onto the shoulders of the largest of the soldiers and carried off.

Flavius watched the soldiers, amused. He didn't notice Marcus' pretty companion looking forlornly after the young, triumphant officer. His attention was taken by a guest whom he recognised as a leading Caesarea businessman. The man approached him and engaged him in conversation, telling him about the expansion of his wine business. Flavius was only half listening, as he wasn't the least bit interested in the man's business affairs, but he did catch a proud statement about the Governor being an important customer. As it was difficult to know who Pilate favoured in the commercial life of Caesarea, Flavius did his best to give the impression that he cared about what the merchant was saying.

Pilate left his office, turning to close the door behind him. When he turned around a shiver ran down his spine, for standing in the corridor looking straight at him was the thin-faced man. Pilate swallowed hard and murmured, "Calpurnius Aquila."

"Back into the office, please." Aquila's voice was hard. Pilate reopened the door. Aquila pushed past him and entered the room. Pilate followed him and closed the door behind him, fighting back anger at the man's audacity. He controlled himself, knowing he had to be careful. Some months ago, he had been astonished to hear that Aquila, a man who had once been the would-be dictator Sejanus' most notoriously merciless agent, had been pardoned by Tiberius and now worked for him as a state spy. How in the gods' names was this man still alive? By what cruel twist of fate had he somehow been allowed to change allegiance and plead loyalty to the Emperor, thus avoiding execution? More importantly, what was he doing here?

"When did you arrive in Caesarea?" Pilate asked through tight lips.

"A couple of days ago," came the reply.

"Why didn't you announce your arrival?"

"I wanted it to be a surprise." Aquila's skeletal face broke into a smile, showing bad teeth.

Pilate raised himself up "How did you get here from Rome? The shipping lanes are closed until the spring."

"I left Rome some weeks ago. I travelled before the shipping lanes closed for the winter, first to Lycia, then from there, by sea to Antioch. I made my way to the main fortress, where the Legate treated me as an honoured guest." Pilate caught the inflection in his voice at those last two words. "I stayed there for some time, catching up on all the news concerning this region." Aquila paused briefly as he saw a frown cross Pilate's face, then continued. "When it was time for me to leave, the Legate ordered some of his troops to escort me over the border into Samaria. They returned to the fortress, while I, disguised as a merchant, purchased a donkey and travelled the rest of the way here, where I found an excellent hostelry in the city."

If the mood had been different, Pilate would have laughed as he pictured this pompous, officious man riding on the back of a humble donkey.

Aquila looked Pilate up and down disdainfully. "If I were you, I would reprimand your gate guards, they are sloppy. I entered the city easily. I could have been anybody."

"When I find out who they are, they will be severely reprimanded." Pilate was feeling distinctly uncomfortable now. "How did you get past my palace guards tonight?"

"I showed them my official pass, signed by Tiberius. How could they refuse me?"

An official pass signed by the Emperor? Pilate's question had been answered. No doubt this schemer had somehow managed to convince Tiberius that he truly regretted working for Sejanus and was now the Emperor's most obedient servant. His well-known reputation for getting information out of people in the most horrific ways had no doubt persuaded Tiberius that his skills would be useful for state purposes. Worrying questions were going round in Pilate's head. Had the Emperor sent Aquila to check up on him? There was only one way to find out – ask him directly. "Why are you here?" he said.

Aquila nonchalantly began to chew on one of his fingernails, spitting a piece onto the floor. His manner became menacing as he stared at Pilate. "I'll get straight to the point. I'm on a fact-finding mission – the Emperor is not pleased with you. Remember, it was on the traitor Sejanus' recommendation to the Emperor that the role of Governor of Judaea was given to you."

Pilate tried not to laugh in his face. The traitor Sejanus? That was rich coming from a man who had served the monster faithfully, carrying out unspeakable punishments on those who opposed him.

Aquila sneered. "Well, like Icarus, Sejanus flew too close to the sun and paid for it with his life. Be careful you do not end up the same way." He moved closer to Pilate and said aggressively, "I must tell you that the Legate also is not pleased. I understand that acting on your request, he sent a Prefect Alae with his squadron of cavalry to the fortress Antonia in Jerusalem to help to find a criminal called Eleazar ben-Ezra, who is seemingly free to roam around plundering the countryside and murdering our troops." He drew himself up. "Because of your laxity, you could cause a major diplomatic incident. You know what I'm talking about, don't you?" Aquila looked directly at a now sweating Pilate "This business of Princess Farrah's abduction and probable murder, most likely by this same brigand." Aquila relished seeing Pilate's discomfort and hammered home his next statement. "You have made too many mistakes, mistakes that reflect badly on the Emperor. He can't afford an uprising here, or amongst our allies, and this latest error is the worst so far."

Pilate blanched. How had Aquila found out about the Princess? He had not reported the incident to the hierarchy in Rome and as far as he knew, the Sheikh had not been told. He dismissed the idea of Flavius or Drubaal telling anyone outside the Antonia. How, then? He frowned. There had to be a spy amongst his personal entourage or his soldiers at the Jerusalem garrison. But who could it be? He vowed silently to find out who the traitor was and have him killed.

Pilate swallowed hard. "I have not yet given up the possibility of finding the Princess, or the perpetrators of the crime against her. A body has not been found – there is still hope."

Aquila bared his teeth. Pilate took an involuntary step back to distance himself from the man's threatening air and putrid breath. "So far I have managed to keep this from the Emperor's ears, but one more mistake..." He left the rest of the sentence hanging in the air between them. "If you want to live to see another Saturnalia, this is what you will do. As soon as the festival is finished, you will continue to send out patrols. The Princess must be found – alive or dead. If she is dead, I will concoct a story to satisfy the Sheikh and King Aretas. If she is still alive we must hope she is so grateful to be rescued that she doesn't put in a complaint to Tiberius, especially as he has just bestowed on her the honour of Roman citizenship, marking his approval of the work she has done for Rome. Be warned, our beloved Emperor is not well, his mood is not good. It won't take much for his anger to destroy anyone who upsets him or threatens Rome or her citizens' safety. Do I make myself clear?"

Pilate's throat was too dry to speak. He nodded instead.

"Good. The Emperor's orders concerning the Princess' citizenship honour will be in the next dispatches you receive from Rome." Aquila moved away, much to Pilate's relief. "By the way," Aquila turned back and said smoothly, "I noticed Senator Silvanus' son at your reception." He paused for dramatic effect. "Look after the Tribune won't you? Remember the Senator was once a good friend of Sejanus. After a warning from me, Silvanus re-took his oath and swore his loyalty to the Emperor. He is, for now anyway, in favour at court, and we don't want any harm coming to his son." Aquila narrowed his eyes. "I don't have to remind you that it is only through Emperor Tiberius' good grace that you hold this governorship. Don't abuse your position – or his generosity."

Aquila's mood changed abruptly and he smiled a sickly smile. "I won't return to your lavish party. I need some sleep, so I will return to my accommodation in the city. However, I will continue to observe things here and write my reports accordingly until the morning after the Festival has finished. Despite the closed shipping lanes, I must return to Rome as soon as possible. This time it will be from Caesarea. I expect you to arrange a ship, a boarding pass and a first-class cabin to be waiting for me at the harbour." He saw Pilate's look of concern "Is that a problem?"

"It is rather short notice and a ship's captain willing to risk his vessel, his life and that of his crew, to undertake such a dangerous journey may be hard to find, but I know of a Greek merchant ship's captain who might be willing to help you, providing the price is right."

Aquila grimaced. "Tell him he will be well paid for his efforts."

"I will attend to it personally." Pilate went to his desk and took out a scroll. On it he wrote a personal letter to a captain he knew who he hoped would be willing to risk the voyage, especially for the chance to gain a large sum of money. He signed the scroll, drying the ink off quickly with sand from a small silver-topped jar on his desk, rolled it and sealed it with his personal seal. He called for a legionary, who appeared immediately. He handed the scroll to the legionary, saying "Take this to the Triton tavern, now! You must ask for a ship's captain called Demetrius. When you find him, tell him that he must contact me with his answer as soon as possible. Impress upon him that this matter is of the greatest urgency." The legionary grimaced at the prospect of going through Caesarea on the night of the Saturnalia when the streets would be filled with drunken men and possible danger. He would make sure he had other legionaries with him. He saluted and hurriedly left the room.

Pilate turned back to Aquila. "I know Demetrius, he can be trusted. I'm sure he will sail to Ostia when you are ready."

"He'd better, if he knows what's good for him," Aquila snarled.

"Where are you staying so can I deliver his reply to you?"

"The Cornucopia hostelry," Aquila replied. "I hope this Greek doesn't keep me waiting too long." With that, he turned and left the room.

Pilate collapsed onto his chair, sweat pouring down his face. He prayed to all the gods that Demetrius would do as he asked. A hopeful thought crossed his mind – perhaps the ship would sink in a storm, or perhaps the sea would be so rough that Aquila would suffer from violent sea-sickness for the whole of the journey. But this was not a time for wishful thinking. He knew his career, if not his life, was in acute danger. Breathing deeply, he tried desperately to calm himself before returning to his guests.

It was getting late; the local businessmen offered their excuses to Pilate and left. Not long after, the Cypriot delegation followed them. Pilate was drinking heavily, but still managing to maintain some vestige of dignity.

Claudia knew that something was dreadfully wrong with her husband, but she was afraid to ask. He had cheerfully gone to his office with the young officer but had later returned with a chalk-white face and a haunted expression. She also noticed that the thin-faced man had gone. She wondered if Pilate's discomfort had something to do with him. She hoped her husband would tell her in his own good time.

Flavius looked around the room. Most of the older officers were slumped on couches, obviously too drunk to stand; their wives were still gossiping amongst themselves, but were beginning to look the worse for wear. Some of the younger officers had disappeared with the remainder of the young women. The pretty golden-haired girl who had been with Marcus had gone too. Perhaps he had returned and taken her home whilst Flavius had been engaged in conversation with the wine merchant.

Flavius felt stifled by the oppressive heat in the room, and a little bored. He decided some fresh air would revive him. He made his way to the gardens. Images of Saturn hung from the branches of small fig trees. Glinting silver stars decorated branches of olive trees and thick bushes, creating a magical scene. As he passed by the bushes he heard an assortment of sighs, stifled feminine giggles and cries of fulfilled lust coming from behind the lush vegetation.

He walked down a flight of stairs until he came to the lower level of the palace. Filling most of the huge space was the magnificent pool built by Herod, its centre picked out by a large statue. The pool was surrounded by a colonnade with many rooms. Flavius saw a pile of men's and women's clothes haphazardly discarded on the marble poolside. Several drunken young men, singing ribald songs, shouting and laughing, were frolicking with young women in the pool. He decided not to order them out. Let them have their fun while they could. In this troubled land it might be their last Saturnalia.

Suddenly a young woman came running out of one of the lower rooms and ran straight into Flavius. She was completely naked. She looked up at him, gave him a sultry look, then continued running towards the pool, laughing and shrieking in mock horror as a young man, also naked, chased after her. Surprised, Flavius recognised him; it was Marcus. The young officer caught up with her, grabbed her around the waist, and amidst her shrieks and wild protests, pushed her into the pool. Plunging in after her, he covered her face and breasts with kisses.

Flavius wondered if Marcus' young companion had any idea what he was up to. He felt sorry for the innocent girl. He hurriedly moved on towards a deeper, walled part of the garden overlooking the sea below.

A slight but chill wind blew off the sea. The clouds parted in the dark sky above, allowing the Moon, the goddess Luna, to cast her shimmering path across the still waters. Beautiful marble statuary, placed in carefully chosen positions in the landscaped gardens, glowed in her light. Towering marble columns stood in lines like sentries watching over shrubs and trees which had also been decorated with silver stars and images of Saturn. The ornamental flower beds were dormant, waiting for the exotic spring flowers to emerge from their warm sanctuary beneath the black earth.

Flavius stood for a moment taking in the scene of beauty and breathing in the cool air. A sudden feeling of longing and loneliness hit him. A vision of Farrah standing on the rooftop of the house in Bethany, her luxuriant dark hair gleaming with blood-red highlights reflected from the setting sun, flashed before his eyes. How beautiful she would look in this moonlight. He sighed. Was his beloved Farrah really dead? Had the Antonia Commander, Quintus Maximus, been right to call off the search for her?

He was brought out of his reverie by the sound of a woman sobbing. He moved towards the sound and saw the young girl who had originally accompanied Marcus. She was sitting on a marble bench looking out to sea, tears flowing down her pretty face. Flavius didn't know whether to leave her to her sadness or to try to help her. She was obviously in great distress. He decided he could not leave her. He carefully approached the marble bench and saw her tense visibly, obviously afraid of him.

"I mean you no harm," he said. Embarrassed, the girl turned her face away from him. Flavius spoke softly, not wishing to scare the girl. "Please, I don't mean to upset you any further, but can I be of any help to you?"

"No you can't. No one can." The sobs came again.

"Will you tell me what it is that's upset you?" he asked kindly. She didn't answer. "Look, I only want to help you – if you will allow me."

The sobbing subsided. "It's Marcus – I don't know where he is."

Flavius knew exactly where he was and what he was doing, but he could not tell her. He had seen the adoring looks she had given the young man. He could not, would not, break her heart by telling her the truth. He knew only too well what it felt like to have your heart broken.

"I'm sure he can't be too far away," he said. He saw her shiver. "The wind's getting up, it's chilly out here. You don't want to get a fever, do you?" She shook her head. "Why don't you go back inside in the warm? I'll see if I can find Marcus."

She looked up at him, eyes bright with tears, her hair glistening like spun gold in the moonlight and said softly, "It is very kind of you to take the trouble."

"It's no trouble."

She smiled a sweet, sad smile and wiped away her tears, then she stood up, smoothed down her dress, took a deep breath to compose herself and made her way back to the palace.

As Flavius watched her go, a wave of anger swept over him. How could this Marcus treat such a sweet, innocent girl this way? If he did manage to find him, he would find it hard to be polite to the wayward young man.

He returned to the pool area and searched around. A few revellers were still romping in the pool, but Marcus was not amongst them. Perhaps he had returned to the palace, or was he in one of the rooms surrounding the pool with the naked girl he had been chasing? Flavius walked up the steps and made his way back inside. He saw the young woman sitting alone and approached her, saying kindly "I'm sorry, I don't know where Marcus is." He saw her look of hope fade and knew she was in danger of bursting into tears again.

There was a note of desperation in her voice as she said "Where can he be? Surely he can't have left me stranded here?"

She looked so forlorn that Flavius took pity on her. "Do you have any means of transport to get home?"

She shook her head. "No, I came with Marcus in his litter."

He smiled at her. "Then I will give you the use of my litter. Come, it's late. I think it's time you went home."

Surprise and a little fear showed in her face. "I meant what I said,' he continued. 'I do not wish to harm you."

He led her outside to the gatehouse, where his litter bearers were sitting around talking. "I want you to take this young lady home to her residence," he told them. They looked enquiringly at him. "Just the lady, I will make my own way home. You guards light the torches." The guards, who had been playing dice to pass the time, jumped to attention at Flavius' order. Taking the flames from a lit torch in a sconce on the palace wall, the guards did as ordered. Flavius pointed to two of them. "You will escort the litter. You," he ordered the two remaining guards, "will wait here." Flavius helped the girl into the litter, instructing the chief litter bearer "Take her wherever she tells you."

She looked at her saviour, slightly embarrassed. "I don't even know your name."

He smiled. "It's Flavius Quinctilius Silvanus."

"Well, Flavius Quinctilius Silvanus, I cannot thank you enough." She smiled in return.

He gave a mock bow. "I'm happy to be of service."

She instructed the bearers and guards to take her to her home address, an area a little way outside of the city along the coast road. With one last thank you to Flavius, she closed the litter curtains. The bearers lifted the litter onto their broad shoulders and exited through the gate, the torch-bearing guards walking in front of them.

Flavius returned inside and gave his thanks and farewells to Pilate and the Lady Claudia. Then, summoning his slave and the remaining guards, he made his way back to the garrison.

The legionary returned soon after with the reply from Demetrius. Pilate uttered a deep sigh and smiled with relief when he read the message from the ship's captain. Demetrius was indeed willing to risk the journey to take Aquila back to Ostia, the Roman seaport. Whatever price the abhorrent spy was prepared to pay for this would be up to him. All Pilate wanted was to be rid of Calpurnius Aquila as soon as possible. Tomorrow morning he would have the good news delivered to the Cornucopia.

# CHAPTER THREE

The day after the party, Flavius, along with other officers, accompanied Pilate and Claudia Procula to the chariot races at the Hippodrome. Flanked by armed guards, the party first went to the eastern stands, to a shrine containing four marble right feet which protected the strength, power and good health of those who worshipped there. Cut into the wall Flavius saw an inscription in Greek: 'MERISMOS' – the charioteer.

After giving due reverence and saying prayers, the party made its way to the Governor's balcony. Shaded by a woven awning and hung with brightly-coloured festive garlands, the balcony was positioned to catch the pleasant breeze coming in from the sea. Pilate seated himself in the middle with Claudia on his right and Flavius in a seat behind them.

Flavius looked at the layout of the stadium. A huge obelisk set on a stone foundation dominated the centre of the track. Large, gold-toned dolphins were set into a marble construction next to the obelisk; long ropes were attached to them which would be pulled to lower the head of each dolphin as each lap was completed. Twin towers stood proudly at each end of the track. Although not as magnificent as the Circus in Rome, Flavius admired Herod's worthy construction. He cast his eyes over the thousands of people already in their seats, noting that they ranged from the middle rank down to the lower classes. Any persons of influence were seated in the front rows or in balconies overlooking the track, though none were as grand as the Governor's.

Flavius knew that Pilate, being the public officer in charge of the Saturnalia for this year, had paid for all the games and public festivities out of his own pocket. It must have cost him a small fortune, but Flavius also knew that the Governor would have clients selling food and drink on his behalf, so he would recoup a small profit. Whether it would enhance Pilate's personal standing amongst the local people was another question. Judging by the lukewarm reception Pilate had received as he had entered the stadium, it seemed to Flavius to be unlikely.

Flavius turned at the sound of movement behind him and saw other officers of Pilate's staff, including Marcus, taking up their positions in the seats behind him. The young men looked up to the balcony above them and began to flirt with the beautiful girls sitting there. Following the officers' gaze, Flavius recognised some of the girls who had been at Pilate's party. He wondered what had happened to Marcus' pretty companion. Had they been reunited? Or had Marcus discarded her, now he had his new promotion?

His attention was taken up by one of the girls on the balcony; it was the one who had run naked into him by the pool as Marcus chased her. She was looking straight at him and smiled when she saw him staring. Her eyes held an unmistakable invitation, an invitation Flavius instantly recognised from his previous assignations in Rome. He briefly looked away, but aware that she was still staring at him, he found his eyes returning to the henna-haired temptress. A few months ago he would have taken her up on this blatant invitation without a second thought, but now... still, she was beautiful, in a gaudy way, with a body that held the promise of pleasure and after all, Farrah was probably...

His thoughts were interrupted by Pilate.

"You see the ten gates running parallel over there?" Flavius' eyes followed the governor's finger as he pointed to the head of the track. "When Herod built this stadium, he favoured ten racing teams, but we Romans, of course, prefer to watch only four. To us it is quality, not quantity that counts. Superb skill and courage is all."

Flavius nodded in agreement. Pilate studied him.

"Have you laid a bet, Flavius?"

"I've put a wager on the Scarlet team."

"The Scarlets?" Pilate pulled a face "Then you'd better be prepared to lose your money. You should bet on the Greens, the current champions. That's who my wager's with."

There was much joking and rivalry amongst the officers, their voices growing louder as they argued about which team would win.

All talking stopped as a fanfare of trumpets announced the arrival of the racing teams. A cheer went up from the crowd as the first team, the Whites, appeared, quickly followed by the Scarlet team, then the Sea Blues. The cheers grew louder as the Greens appeared. The charioteer acknowledged the crowd as he proudly drove his team of black horses around the stadium, and the horses picked up on the excitement and tossed their fine heads, their thick manes flowing in the breeze.

The Greens' charioteer stopped before Pilate and saluted him. Pilate raised his hand in reply. Flavius wondered how much Pilate had bet on the favourite.

The charioteer flicked the reins and the horses moved away. He made one final tour of the track, receiving the ovation of the crowd, then joined the other teams ready for the signal to begin the race.

The four teams, each with four horses, lined up side by side on the starting line below Pilate's balcony. The horses knew what they had to do and were champing at the bit, eager to begin the race. The Sea Blue charioteer fought hard to control his team from crashing into the Scarlet team's horses.

Pilate turned to Flavius, a note of excitement in his voice. "If there are to be any spectacular crashes they will happen down there where the track slopes at an angle." He pointed to the area of track directly below them. "These seats give us the best view of any action on the track."

The crowd hushed expectantly as Pilate stood up, held his arm aloft then brought it down sharply, signalling the start of the race. There was a tremendous roar from the onlookers as the charioteers cracked their whips and the horses were galvanized into action. The Greens streaked away, taking the lead immediately; the Scarlets were a close second. The team positions did not change throughout the second lap. By the third lap, the horses were positively flying. The Scarlet team was still lying second to the Greens, closely followed by the Whites. The Sea Blues were lagging a full length behind but were steadily closing in on the Whites.

Flavius was pleasantly surprised to see the skill of the charioteers and the quality of the horses; he had not expected to see such racing outside Rome. Towards the end of the fourth lap the Sea Blues were running neck and neck with the Whites. The roar from the crowd was deafening as the excitement mounted.

Halfway through the fifth lap, desperate to keep third place, the driver of the Whites misjudged the corner and careered into the Sea Blues. There came the terrible sound of wood and metal crashing together as the chariots collided, the impact causing the side of the Sea Blues' chariot to disintegrate. The wheel of the Whites' chariot slammed into the fetlock of the Sea Blues' outside horse, shattering the bone. Screaming in agony, the horse stumbled, then collapsed onto the sand, its weight snapping the harness. The Sea Blues' charioteer had no time to alter his path or to stop the chariot from bouncing over the stricken animal, and the impact hurled the charioteer forward onto the broken rail of the chariot. Terrified, the other three horses surged on, eventually breaking away from the smashed chariot, their tattered harnesses dragging on the track behind them as they frantically galloped back to the stables.

The chariot finally rolled to a stop. The driver, dreadfully wounded, lay sprawled over the car, fixed into position by the broken rail which had impaled his chest. The crowd rose up at the shocking spectacle, some cheering, others cursing and shaking their fists at the Whites' charioteer.

Pilate half rose out of his seat, while Claudia looked away at the sight of the broken and bloodied man. He sat back and turned to Flavius. "I told you this was the best place to see any action."

Flavius did not answer but watched as the track stewards frantically waved their flags to let the other teams know there was danger on the track. Stretcher bearers rushed out to retrieve the dying man, while others tried desperately to remove the remnants of the chariot and the badly-injured horse before the three remaining teams hurtled around the corner straight into them, causing even more mayhem. They had just reached the edge of the track when the three teams were upon them. Desperately trying to avoid the accident, the Greens' charioteer was momentarily distracted, and suddenly the Scarlets were galloping alongside him. Not wishing to lose his first place, the Greens' charioteer frantically whipped his horses, urging them to gallop even faster. Scarlets and Greens rounded the Spina together, barely leaving enough space between them to stop them from crashing together. One more lap to go.

The crowd was on its feet as the teams neared the finishing post. The Greens and the Scarlets were still neck and neck, but as the last dolphin was ready to be lowered to finish the race, with a supreme effort, the Scarlets edged in front. There was a tumultuous roar as the public, some adoring, others cursing their bad luck, acknowledged the Scarlets as the winners.

Pilate sat stony-faced as the officers behind him uttered words of sympathy to him and to each other; they had all backed the Greens. Flavius, having chosen the winning team, said nothing.

The charioteer stepped down from his chariot, threw his arms around each of his horses' necks in gratitude for their efforts, then, leaving them to the grooms to take back to the stables, he made his way to Pilate's balcony and bowed before the governor. Pilate half-heartedly congratulated him and handed him the Victory Palm. The man bowed again, then turned to face the crowd. He held the Victory Palm aloft and grinned as he took in their cheers.

As the charioteer made his way back down to the track, Pilate stood up ready to leave. He shuddered as he caught sight of a familiar face in the opposite balcony: Calpurnius Aquila. Aquila inclined his head towards him, smiling his death's head smile. Why hadn't he seen the spy before? The balcony was crowded; he must have been hidden behind someone else until the people in the balcony turned to chat to each other.

Claudia Procula rose up from her seat. Seeing the expression on her husband's face, she realised that something had suddenly upset him. Her eyes followed the direction of his glare and she saw, sitting staring at Pilate, the haughty man who had caused her husband's discomfort at their banquet.

Pilate was keen to leave the stadium. He quickly waved to the crowd and a horn salute sounded, announcing his departure. The crowd cheered their benefactor for an exciting race. Claudia placed her elegant bejewelled hand on her husband's arm and without a backward glance, they left the Hippodrome, closely followed by Pilate's officers.

Flavius had also seen the thin-faced man. Again the face nudged at his memory, but still he could not place him. Frowning, he followed the entourage back to the palace. He had no wish to embarrass Pilate any further, so he decided to collect his winnings later.

Pilate was sombre all through the party that night. Flavius was glad when the Governor announced he was tired and ended the reception early. It had been a busy day, and promised to be just as busy tomorrow with a visit to the theatre, followed by another reception at the palace, this time for the artisans of the City.

Flavius sat in the theatre watching *Andromache*, by the Greek playwright Euripides. He found the tragic story of the widow of the great hero Hector, killed in the Trojan War, heavy going and disturbing. Andromache's grief at the loss of her beloved husband only served to bring back his own heartache at the loss of his love. Only in deference to Pilate and Lady Claudia, who seemed to be enjoying the play, did he try to look calm and interested. He was grateful when the performance finished.

Pilate issued an instruction to Flavius and the rest of the usual entourage to take the rest of the afternoon off ready for the reception that evening. As Pilate and Lady Claudia climbed into their litter and were carried back to the palace, Flavius, Marcus and the other officers piled out of the theatre, straight into the path of Centurion Cornelius and a young girl he recognised as the one to whom he'd loaned his litter. Flavius stood back as Marcus smiled and bowed to her. She blushed prettily.

Cornelius' expression was bland. "We haven't seen much of you lately, Marcus."

"I don't have much time to myself anymore," he said. "With my new position I have to accompany the Governor everywhere. It's part of my duties now."

Flavius thought his answer was rather pompous for such a junior officer.

The girl looked shyly at Marcus. "It's my birthday tomorrow, I hope you have time to see me then."

"I've arranged to spend some free time with my friends." He saw her wistful look and felt guilty. He took her hand. "As it's your birthday I will come and see you. When the Saturnalia is over, I will visit you more often, I promise."

His friends called out to him, "Hurry up, Marcus!"

With an apologetic smile to her and a brief nod to Cornelius, he rejoined his friends, one of whom said rather loudly, "Let's go to Marcella's. I've heard she has a new Egyptian girl. Apparently, she's quite athletic." A guffaw of laughter greeted this statement. Without a backward glance, the young men went off, laughing and boasting about how they would fill their time at Marcella's until the reception that evening.

Flavius realised by the frown on Cornelius' face that he had heard the proposal. It was obvious the girl too realised the meaning of the officers' boasts. He saw her distress. It was well known that Marcella ran the most expensive brothel in Caesarea, one much used by carousing, wealthy young officers. Flavius stepped forward, hoping to lighten the mood. As Cornelius saw him he stood straight and saluted. The girl looked down coyly, obviously not wishing the Tribune to see her unhappiness.

"At ease, Centurion. We are not on duty now. Were you in the theatre?" Flavius asked pleasantly.

Cornelius relaxed. "Yes Tribune. An early birthday treat for my daughter, Julia Cornelia." He pointed to the girl. "I thought my daughter would like to experience the powerful storytelling of one of the greatest of Greek writers."

Flavius nodded. So the young girl he'd loaned his litter to after the party was Cornelius' daughter and the much-loved sister of the Decurion Julius. He looked straight at Julia. "Did you enjoy it?"

Aware of his gaze, she looked up at him, her eyes sparkling with unshed tears, her voice trembling. "Oh yes, Tribune. I thought it was wonderful."

Flavius smiled at the girl, wondering how Marcus could treat her so indifferently.

Cornelius spoke gravely. "I would very much like to thank you for my daughter's safe return from the Governor's reception the other night, Tribune. I don't know what she would have done without you."

"I was glad to be of service."

"If it is not an imposition, sir, as a small token of gratitude, would you please come to our home tomorrow to celebrate Julia Cornelia's birthday? That is if you have the time."

Flavius was surprised at the request, but he liked the Centurion and did not want to disappoint Julia any further after Marcus' hurtful behaviour, so he said "I will only have a few hours free before I have to attend Pilate's reception tomorrow tonight, but, yes, I would be delighted. If you will tell me where you live I'm sure I can find the way."

Cornelius gave directions to his house, which was along the coast road not far from the city. Watched by Flavius, father and daughter got into their hired litter and were carried off. Flavius would make sure he had the time to visit them for Julia's birthday celebrations.

# CHAPTER FOUR

Deep in the Judaean hills, in the caves of Eleazar ben-Ezra's winter camp, Farrah was sleeping fitfully, too cold to settle. She sat up with a start as a series of screams, followed by the chilling sound of whimpering, echoed around the cave walls. She got up and went to investigate. Following the desperate cries, she came to a small alcove and looked inside, where she saw Anna in a squatting position, being supported under her arms by her man, Isaac. It was obvious to Farrah that Anna was in the throes of childbirth and that all was not well. She liked the couple and admired their faithfulness to each other. They were different from the other members of ben-Ezra's gang, who swapped partners when they felt like it. She decided she must help them.

Rachel too had heard the cries and had come to

investigate. Rachel placed her lit torch in a sconce on the wall, then dropped to her knees in front of Anna.

"It's taking too long. Come on Anna, push!" came Isaac's worried cry.

Farrah entered the alcove "Let me help her."

Rachel looked up and seeing Farrah, she scoffed, "You? What do you know about giving birth?"

"I know enough. Let me look and see what is happening." She could see Rachel was sceptical and snapped, "If you want to save Anna and the child, let me look!" Her voice took on a firmness that made Rachel move away, leaving room for Farrah to investigate the cause of Anna's distress.

"Rachel, take the torch and hold it so I can see." Farrah's tone was commanding, which annoyed Rachel. Farrah grew angry at the woman's hesitancy. "For Anna and the child's sake, do it!" she ordered. Isaac uttered threats to Rachel if she didn't obey. At that Rachel reluctantly complied and took the torch out of the sconce.

"Hold the torch here," Farrah instructed, pointing to where its light would give her the best view of Anna. Farrah could see what the problem was at once: this was going to be a breech birth, making it more difficult. "Anna, please do as I say," she said, then to Isaac, "Isaac, help Anna to lie down on the ground." Anna grimaced, pain ripping through her body, as Isaac gently helped her to lie down on the hard earth.

Without taking her eyes off the suffering woman, Farrah said, "Rachel, keep holding the torch where it is." To Isaac she said calmly so as not to add to the man's worries, "Isaac, try to keep Anna as still as possible." Isaac did as he was told. He gently supported Anna's shoulders and whispered words of encouragement to her. Farrah could see the baby's buttocks slowly emerging. She supported them, then gently manoeuvered first one leg out, then the other. Anna let out scream after piercing scream, biting her lip, drawing blood, the pain becoming too much for her.

Ruth too had been woken by the screaming. She stood in the entrance of the alcove shuddering with fear as she watched Anna and her mistress struggling to bring a new life into the world. Was this what she would have to endure when her time came? She could stand it no longer and left, weeping and covering her ears, vainly trying to block out the screams and moans of the unfortunate woman.

Farrah turned the baby as gently as she could, then managed to ease out a tiny shoulder, quickly followed by the second. She supported the little body, then gently pulled until the baby's head appeared. The birth completed, Farrah held on to the infant to stop it from falling onto the hard ground. The screaming stopped and the sound of a baby's mewling filled the alcove. Farrah said briskly "Rachel, give me your knife."

Rachel bristled. "Do you think I would give you a weapon so you can use it on me?" Farrah repeated her request in a firm voice. "Give me your knife, I have to cut the umbilical cord." Rachel understood then and drew out the knife she carried at her waist. Farrah cut the cord, tying the end securely, then handed the knife back to Rachel and looked up at her. "Rachel, fetch water and some cloth," she said. Rachel didn't argue but left the alcove, soon returning with a bowl of water and some woven material.

Farrah cleaned both mother and baby as best she could using some of the material and the water. "Give me your shawl," she said to Rachel, who, stunned by Farrah's handiwork, meekly took the woollen shawl from around her shoulders and gave it to her. Farrah wrapped it around the tiny mite and handed the baby to his weeping mother, "You have a very handsome son," she said.

Too exhausted to reply, Anna smiled in relief and reached out to take Farrah's hand in gratitude for all she had done to help her and her new-born son. Isaac beamed with pride and kissed his wife's forehead, then said "We will name him Asher." Anna nodded in agreement. Farrah uttered a deep sigh of relief; both mother and baby had survived the ordeal. Emotionally drained, but satisfied with her work, she sat back on the ground.

Rachel stared open-mouthed at Farrah. "Where did you learn to do that?"

Farrah smiled. "I helped my mother to give birth to my sister." She frowned at the memory. "I've also seen a birth like this before." She saw Rachel's inquisitive look and explained. "Amongst my people we have some very skilled midwives. When I was growing up I used to watch them at work, it always fascinated me. I remembered how one of them helped one of our women in the same predicament as Anna to give birth safely."

Rachel stood up. "Well, seeing that you know what you are doing, you can stay with Anna while Isaac and I go and tell the others the good news."

Rachel and Isaac hurried out of the alcove and Isaac called out in a loud voice, "I have a son!" He was greeted by the others with raucous laughter and many slaps on the back, before quickly returning to Anna and their newborn child. He looked up at Farrah and smiled. "Thank you," he said. It was all he could find to say before his adoring gaze returned to his family.

When ben-Ezra's woman, Rebecca, heard about Farrah's part in the birth, she cursed out loud. So the captive was proving to be useful as well as beautiful, and some of the gang were beginning to take to her. Anger and jealousy engulfed her. She must make sure that ben-Ezra sold Farrah as quickly as possible.


Flavius knew that Saturn would relish the exercise. He tried to ride out with him whenever his duties allowed, but for the past few days, because of the Saturnalia festivities, Saturn had been cooped up in his quarters at the garrison.

Saturn's thick black mane danced in the sea breeze as his long legs strode along the coast road, covering the distance to the house of Cornelius with ease. Flavius too was delighted to have the mild wind blow in his face; after enduring so many parties in stuffy rooms filled with heavy perfumes, it cleared his head and enlivened him.

The Centurion's house came into view and within a

few moments, he arrived at the small, neat, white-painted villa. A manservant came out of the villa ready to take the visitor's horse. He was followed by a smiling Cornelius, who said jovially "Welcome, Tribune. Thank you for coming."

Flavius smiled as he climbed down from Saturn and handed the reins to the servant. "I am pleased to be here."

Cornelius invited Flavius to enter the small atrium. He followed close behind. "My daughter will be so pleased to see you," he said, then beckoned a servant to him. The small, stout woman bowed before her master. He looked down at her and smiled.

"Martha, will you get some refreshment for our honoured guest, please?"

"Yes sir." She bowed again and scurried out of the room.

"Are you always so friendly with your slaves, Cornelius?"

"We don't use the word slave in this house, sir," came Cornelius' quick reply.

"But surely, Rome is built on slavery. It is part of our heritage," Flavius countered.

Cornelius was not at all embarrassed by his guest's inquisitive stare. "Martha is my cook and housekeeper. She also looks after Julia when I'm on duty – as once she did my wife." He hesitated for a moment as the memory of his beloved wife's face flashed before him. He regained his composure "Martha has been with this family for years and is a very trusted servant. We are lucky to have her."

"I see." Flavius checked himself; he was a guest in this house and did not want to appear rude or intrusive. How people chose to treat their staff was their concern and nothing to do with him.

Martha arrived back in the room carrying a tray holding wine and a goblet. She set the tray down on a small table, then stood in the corner of the room awaiting further instruction. Cornelius poured the wine and handed it to Flavius, who drank deeply, grateful to wash the dust of the sandy road from the back of his throat. He put down the goblet and said, "Where is the birthday girl?"

"She's in the garden with some of her friends. If you will follow me, sir."

Cornelius led the way out into the small garden. There, sitting on a silk-cushioned stone bench set amongst exotic flowers, sat Julia. She seemed happy surrounded by her friends. Her face lit up as she saw Flavius, and she rose up to greet him. Some of her friends smiled and whispered amongst themselves, wondering who the handsome stranger was.

"Thank you so much for coming, Tribune. It is very kind of you," she said shyly.

"I'm glad to be here." He smiled at her, noting the blush spreading across her face.

She pointed to the stone seat. "Please sit down, Tribune."

He sat down, aware of the curious looks Julia's friends were giving him. Julia sat down again, but not too close to the important visitor.

Flavius looked around the garden. Memories of a different garden in another place at another time came flooding back to him. He forced himself to concentrate on the here and now. "I'm sorry, I didn't have time to buy you a birthday present."

Julia, overcome with shyness at the closeness of the most handsome man she had ever seen, said "I didn't expect..."

Cornelius noticed his daughter's embarrassment and sat down on an adjoining seat. He looked directly at Flavius. "How are you enjoying Caesarea, sir?"

Flavius smiled. "It's certainly refreshing, and warmer, after Jerusalem. I'm amazed at the quality of the architecture here and the entertainments on offer. It's like a smaller and more exotic, version of Rome."

Cornelius nodded, stroking his chin. "Yes, Herod did a good job. It's a wealthy place too. You can get almost anything you want from the merchants here. Of course, the Roman Governor of the Province being housed here has certainly helped to bring in traders eager to make money off him – and us." He laughed.

"Julius told me he and Julia Cornelia were born here. Have they ever visited Rome?"

"No. I've tried to give them a simple life, especially after their mother..." Cornelius stopped.

Flavius saw a cloud cross his face. It was obvious that Cornelius and his wife had been devoted to each other. Losing her must have been devastating to him.

Cornelius, embarrassed that his emotions had got the better of him, pulled himself together and said, "Are you married, sir?"

Flavius shook his head.

"Is there someone waiting for you?" Cornelius asked tentatively, hoping he wasn't being too forward.

"There was." Now it was Flavius' turn to look uncomfortable. "She went away."

Julia stared at him, a puzzled look on her face. Who would leave such a kind and handsome man? Embarrassed when she saw Flavius returning her stare, she turned her face away and resumed conversation with her friends. Fortunately, one of Julia's companions changed the awkward atmosphere by telling a tale that brought forth gales of girlish laughter.

The afternoon passed pleasantly. Julia began to relax and stopped blushing when Flavius asked her about her hopes and aspirations. He was astounded when she told him that she was betrothed to Marcus and that they were to be married soon. After what he had witnessed at Pilate's party, he wanted to warn her about her intended husband's behaviour, but how could he? He would not be responsible for shattering a young girl's dreams; it was all too plain that Marcus could do no wrong in her eyes. He wondered if he should speak to Cornelius, then decided it was none of his business. Surely, the Centurion, a long-serving soldier and a man of the world, would see through the young officer and stop the betrothal before it was too late.

At that moment, Martha came out into the garden to announce Marcus' arrival.

Cornelius had had a sleepless night worrying about his daughter's future with Marcus. At first, when Marcus had asked his permission to marry Julia, he had been concerned, not knowing whether to give his permission or not. He had deferred his answer while he turned the positive and negative aspects of Marcus becoming his son-in-law over and over in his mind. On the one hand he showed promise as a future excellent officer who should easily be promoted, especially as Pilate had chosen him to join his personal staff – and he came from good stock, being the heir to a wealthy Equestrian family estate just outside of Rome, meaning Julia would never want for anything as far as money and comfort was concerned. On the other hand, he knew the young officer was a product of the times: hotheaded and too easily led astray by his dissolute friends. He also seemed to be filled with dreams of power. This could cause Julia hurt.

And yet – he had cast his mind back to his youth, remembering how his beloved wife's family had at first treated him. She had come from a patrician family background. He was related to the ancient, patrician gens Cornelia, and although one branch of the family still had some power, even recently producing a Consul in Rome, with the demise of the Republic, his side of the family had subsequently fallen on hard times, forcing him to make his own way in the world. His adored wife, Helena, had disobeyed her family to marry him, a struggling junior Centurion, some twenty-three years ago. He smiled at the memory of their wedding day. How happy they had been. Should he prevent his daughter from enjoying that same happiness? Even so, he'd found it hard to forgive Marcus for the way he'd treated Julia recently. He decided it was time to tackle him about his behaviour before it was too late.

Cornelius went back into the house, followed by Martha. He stood before a door leading into a side room, then gave Martha instructions: "Show Marcus into this room, Martha. I wish to speak to him in private."

Martha bowed, then fetched Marcus and asked him to enter the room where Cornelius stood waiting.

Cornelius looked into the young man's face. This was going to be tricky, given that the younger man was a senior officer, but he decided it had to be done. He got straight to the point. "Marcus, are your intentions towards my daughter honourable?"

Marcus briefly looked away, surprised and embarrassed by the question. He turned his face back to Cornelius "Yes, they are."

Cornelius spoke in a stern voice. "Then don't you think it's about time you moderated your wild behaviour and showed my daughter you actually cared about her?"

Marcus rubbed his forehead with his fingertips, trying to find the right words "I apologise for my recent behaviour. I promise I will distance myself from my friends and try to be worthy of Julia's love."

Cornelius nodded. He was glad Marcus had not pulled

rank on him. He could see the tension on Marcus' face and asked, "Is there something else?"

Not meeting Cornelius' eyes, Marcus replied in a low voice, "I have been ordered to return to Jerusalem with the Governor for the Passover. I'm afraid the wedding will have to be postponed until I return." He looked at his future father-in-law and saw the barely-controlled look of frustration on the Centurion's face. "I'm sorry, but as part of Governor Pilate's staff I must obey," he mumbled. "Will you tell Julia, or shall I?"

Cornelius let out a deep sigh "I think you should tell her. It's the least you can do." He called for Martha, who came bustling in. "Fetch my daughter here."

Julia came into the room and looked anxiously at the two men she loved. "Father, what is it?"

Marcus, who had retreated into a corner desperately wondering how he could tell her his news, stepped forward. She smiled when she saw him and went to him. He took her hand. Cornelius left them together, as he didn't want to be present when Marcus explained his position. Outside the door he heard an anguished cry, then the sound of crying. He thought his heart would break.

Eventually Julia came out and collapsed in her father's arms, sobs wracking her body. Marcus followed. Cornelius cast him a withering look and growled, "I think you had better leave." Without argument, Marcus turned and left the villa.

Julia went to her room, too embarrassed to face her

friends. Cornelius asked Martha to go to her and offer comfort as best she could, then returned to the garden, made an excuse about Julia suddenly being taken ill and asked the guests to leave. Julia's friends were bewildered. As they left the garden they whispered amongst themselves, wondering what could have gone wrong in so short a time.

Flavius, bemused by the sudden turn of events, made his way out to the front of the villa, where he saw Marcus about to mount his horse. He went to him, his voice hard as he said "What's happened? What did you do?"

Surprised, Marcus turned and saluted. "Tribune, I didn't know you were here."

"I was invited." Flavius frowned. "Has Julia's sudden illness anything to do with you?"

"Unfortunately sir, I have just had to tell my future bride that the wedding will have to be postponed. As part of Pilate's staff, I'll be accompanying him back to Jerusalem." He saw his superior officer's stern look. "I had hoped to be stationed here permanently, but if I want to rise in my career I must go where the Governor directs. Perhaps when he returns to Caesarea…"

Flavius felt an anger rising in him that he had not experienced for some time. This selfish, arrogant little nobody had chosen to humiliate the sweet Julia, today of all days, and in front of her father and friends, an action he could not forgive. He wondered how Julius would feel when he heard the news. He was growing to detest the young officer more and more and couldn't resist saying,

"And have you also said goodbye to the girl I saw you with at the Saturnalia?"

He could see that the barb had struck home. Red-faced, Marcus looked at him "Sir, I don't know what you mean. I had been celebrating and I was drunk, I don't remember the girl."

"Really?" Flavius gave him a hard stare. "I suggest you hurry back to your duties. Now!"

Marcus saluted, then mounted up and rode away without looking back. Flavius watched him through narrowed eyes, barely hiding his disgust.

Cornelius came outside in time to see Marcus depart and saw the look on Flavius' face.

"I gather Marcus has told you about his plans, sir." Seeing Flavius nod, he changed the subject, embarrassed. "Thank you for bringing me the letter from my son. He tells me he has been kept busy at the Jerusalem Garrison. I'm not surprised. It's been many years since I was stationed there, but I remember there was always some kind of trouble or other in that city, be it religious disturbances or terrorism."

"I can assure you, Cornelius, nothing has changed there." Flavius hoped that Julius had not mentioned ben-Ezra and Princess Farrah. Knowing the Decurion, he was sure he could be trusted to be discreet and keep the matter to himself.

Cornelius continued, "He speaks very highly of you, Tribune. He says you defended him when a senior officer was bullying him."

Flavius saw the look of concern on Cornelius' face. "Don't worry, I took care of the bully." Deep down, now that he was not in Jerusalem to look out for Julius, he wasn't sure Antonius would leave the young Decurion alone. He hoped that Julius would heed his advice and go to Centurion Sextus if the Prefect did ill-treat him again.

"There's a bully in every legion, sir. I would love to have that man in my cohort, senior officer or not. I cannot tolerate men who abuse their position." Cornelius looked stern for a brief moment, then regained his usual good-natured expression. "I would very much like to see you again before you leave for Jerusalem, Tribune."

Flavius smiled. "I would like that too."

Cornelius returned the smile. "I'd hoped you would. I'm sure Julia will be pleased to see you before your return." He could see the Tribune was anxious to be on his way. "But I am keeping you from your journey, sir. Thank you again for visiting us."

Flavius took his leave and rode back to the garrison to prepare for yet another of Pilate's tedious receptions.

Flavius entered the Palace reception area and looked around to see the henna-haired girl watching him. She smiled at him. He smiled back and she moved towards him.

"Did you enjoy the races?" She lifted her heavily-kholed eyes up to Flavius. Before he could answer, she purred, "I enjoy the excitement of the chase."

Flavius stifled a smile. Looking at her, he was sure she did indeed.

She suddenly ran her hand over her forehead and swayed. "It's so hot in here. I'm sorry... I feel a little dizzy" Flavius put out a hand to steady her. She turned her face to him as if to kiss him. Flavius tensed. "I think you should sit down," he said. He led her to a vacant couch and summoned a slave to bring her wine.

"How can I ever repay you?" She looked up at him coquettishly.

Flavius knew this game only too well. He knew what her repayment would be. Would he take her up on her offer? Why not? He hadn't bedded a woman since he'd left Rome and a few moments of pleasure gained from a casual liaison might ease the anguish in his heart.

"Oh, I'm sure I'll think of something," he said, smiling.

The girl stayed by his side for the rest of the evening, and when the party ended, Flavius offered to escort her home. In the litter she told him her name was Lavinia and that she was the elder daughter of an important official based in the city. When they reached her house, she invited him in.

"But your parents..." began Flavius, worried that he might be caught as he had been when he had had his unfortunate dalliance with Senator Virilis' daughter, Marcia, back in Rome, and Virilis had caught the pair of them frolicking in her bed. After Virilis' complaints and threats to his father, Senator Gaius Quinctilius, it had been the final straw as far as Gaius was concerned and had led to his decision to have his son join a Legion. He had ended up in Jerusalem as a Senior Tribune in the Tenth Fretensis cohorts based at the fortress Antonia, a decision which had changed his life.

Seeing his hesitancy, Lavinia shook her head. "There's no need to worry about them, they've gone to another banquet and they're staying there all night. My younger sister is only ten years old, so she will be tucked up in bed fast asleep by now. The door porter will not tell my parents, he values his position here and I know too much about his outside activities."

Flavius was curious as to what these outside activities were, if the daughter of the house could use them to blackmail him into turning a blind eye to her behaviour.

"In any case," she continued, "my parents will believe my word against his. Nessa, my faithful servant, will still be awake." She saw Flavius' raised eyebrows. "But don't worry about Nessa, she's very discreet and she's never told tales on me before."

As Flavius and Lavinia entered the house, Nessa appeared out of a side room. When she saw her mistress with her handsome companion, she smiled.

"Go to bed, Nessa," Lavinia said quietly. "I won't need you again tonight."

The servant nodded knowingly, then turned and went back into the room, closing the door firmly behind her.

Lavinia took hold of Flavius' hand and led him into her sumptuously furnished bedroom. She undid the golden clasps on the shoulder straps of her dress, letting the dress fall to the floor before stepping out of it. Taking the gold pins out of her hair, she shook her head until the curls tumbled down over her shoulders. She moved closer to Flavius and slowly began to undress him. She looked at his naked, muscular body approvingly, then sank down onto her red silk-covered couch and held out her arms to him.

He eagerly joined her there and took her into his arms. The smell of her perfume was overpowering, intoxicating his senses. He closed his eyes, feeling long-dormant sensations course through his body, imagining... He kissed her lips and her neck and his hands caressed her silken flesh. Filled with passionate longing, he murmured huskily "Farrah!"

He felt Lavinia's body suddenly stiffen and heard her sharp voice say, "Who is Farrah?"

The spell was broken. He opened his eyes and looked at the bemused girl. It was not Farrah's lustrous black hair spread out over the pillow, not her beautiful face looking up at him and not her lips he had kissed, nor was it her voluptuous body he had caressed. Shame engulfed him. The memory of Farrah's beauty and grace was still too fresh in his mind. He felt he was betraying her and their fledgling love. His voice was choked with emotion as he said, "I can't do this." He got up and moved away from the couch.

"What's wrong? Do I not please you?"

Flavius flinched at the clipped voice. He had to say something to appease her. "Lavinia, you are very beautiful and any man would jump at the chance to be here with you like this. It's just..." he took a deep breath "I'm in love with someone else."

Hurling curses at him, she picked up an alabaster jar standing on a small table close by and threw it at him. "Get out. Get out!" she screeched.

Flavius ducked as the jar flew past his head and smashed into the wall behind him, the perfumed oil it had contained running down the painted plaster onto the tiled floor. He picked up his clothes and quickly dressed himself. Once dressed, without looking at her, he said "I'm sorry." Then he left the house, leaving Lavinia pummeling her pillow with anger and frustration.

The Saturnalia festivities came to an end, and the weather was dull and blustery as Calpurnius Aquila boarded a merchant ship waiting in the harbour. Pilate had kept his word. The Greek captain, Demetrius, acknowledged the spy with a nod and a grunt. Aquila was shown to his cabin by a swarthy sailor as the captain prepared to set sail for Ostia. Aquila smiled to himself. He had always disliked Pilate, deeming him to be an upstart. When the time was right, he would bring the upstart down. When he returned to Rome he would have much to report to the Emperor.

Adolfo was worried. What had happened to the cloaked man? This was the second month he had returned to the papyrus merchant in Jerusalem to pick up fresh scrolls without seeing him. He had walked down the same alley where he usually met up with the man, but he had failed to appear. Over the past weeks, the man had given him many secret scrolls to slip into the dispatch bag carrying Pilate's official communications to Rome, which he had methodically done, so where was he now? Perhaps the man had left Jerusalem without telling him, just as he had done a few years earlier. He frowned. If the man had gone, had his hope of the promised reward of status and wealth gone with him? With that dismal thought, he made his way back to the palace of Herod Antipas and to the chief scribe, Scribonius.

Flavius felt relief now that the festival had ended and life had returned to normal at the Caesarea barracks. He had become somewhat bored by having to be with most of the same company every night, and glad that he'd managed to remain relatively sober throughout the numerous parties thrown by Pilate and other dignitaries housed in the city. There had been one awkward moment when he had run into Lavinia on the last night of the Saturnalia festivities held at the palace. He had hoped she would not cause a scene about their encounter, but then he thought that she would not want it known that a man had resisted her charms. Fortunately, he'd been right and she had just cast a scornful look in his direction, turned away and gone off with one of the young officers. Deep down he still felt a sense of guilt and betrayal. There was a chance that Farrah was still alive. Until he saw her dead body laid out in front of him, he would hold on to that hope.

Nine days into the New Year came the celebration of Janus, the two-faced god. This particular god was even more relevant to Flavius at this unsettled time, as the two faces of Janus shown on sculptures represented him looking backwards, as though to the past, on one side and on the other to the future. Flavius made offerings to a small statuette of Janus, depicting the god holding in his right hand a staff to guide travellers along the correct route, and in his left hand a key with which to open gates. In Rome, the temple priests would dedicate spelt grain mixed with salt to Janus, and a traditional barley cake. Flavius made do with offering a libation of wine and a barley cake bought in the city, and prayed to the god with heartfelt pleas that this year might be more fortunate.

Later that day, Flavius took traditional presents of dates, honey and figs to Cornelius' home, where he and his gifts were warmly welcomed.

# CHAPTER FIVE

The days passed slowly for Farrah, with each day seeming like the last. Trapped in the warren of caves, she knew neither the hour nor the month, only that her incarceration seemed endless. The supplies had begun to dwindle, so she was racked with hunger and thirst. To help pass the time she had watched Anna sing softly to her little boy as she nursed him. When Rebecca wasn't watching, Anna would smile at her. Miriam kept her distance, but would glance across at Farrah and Ruth to make sure they were all right. Farrah had also watched the other women as they repaired garments and chatted amongst themselves.

She was fascinated to see the way they found ever more inventive ways of cooking the remaining meagre rations, in the desperate hope of keeping starvation at bay until the weather changed. But mostly, she tried to stop herself from wondering about Flavius. Was he well? What was he thinking and feeling about her disappearance? She was sure that having no news of her, he must think her dead, and had probably forgotten about her and found a new love. The thought made her depression worse. To keep her sanity, she tried to block him from her memory, but it was so hard to forget the image of his handsome face and hard, muscular body, and his tenderness as he'd enfolded her in his strong arms and enraptured her with his kisses. She would never forget him as long as she lived. As long as she lived – just how long would that be, as a slave? Perhaps it would be better if she did starve to death.

She dug her long, unkempt fingernails into her palm, drawing a little blood. The pain pulled her up. What was the use of torturing herself? She had to resign herself to her fate.

Shivering, she wrapped a coarse woollen shawl around her thin shoulders and looked at Ruth, who was slumped by a small fire in the middle of the communal cavern. She was glad that so far, Ruth had managed to hide her growing belly from Rachel by wearing a larger dress given to her by Miriam.

Rachel entered the cave and looked straight at Ruth. "Why are you wearing that, it's not the dress I gave you?" she snapped.

Miriam thought quickly. "Ruth badly soiled her own garment when she suffered from sickness, so I've burnt it. We don't want disease spreading to us all, so I've given her something of my own."

This did not satisfy Rachel. Looking more closely at Ruth, she narrowed her eyes and said "Sickness? You're pregnant. Is it Abraham's child?"

Ruth shrank back from the woman's gaze, fearful of what she might do. She shook her head and said, "No, I must have been pregnant before I came here." She saw Farrah's questioning gaze. "My lady, I'm sorry. The father of my child is Boraz."

Farrah knew it was a lie, but she went along with it to stop Rachel from hurting Ruth. "Did he know?" she asked innocently. Ruth shook her head. "No. He was killed before I had the chance to tell him." She feigned tears of sorrow at her supposed lover's death.

Rachel stood with her hands on her hips and stared at Ruth. "I don't believe you," she said.

Miriam stepped forward. "It's true, Rachel. Ruth told me all about it just after she came here. I thought it best to keep quiet in case ben-Ezra wanted to get rid of her. As it is, surely he could sell her and the baby? Two for one?"

Rachel grimaced at Ruth. "If I find out you are lying and Abraham is the father, I will kill you."

"You will do what?" It was Abraham's voice. Rachel turned to see him standing in the entrance to the cavern. He strode towards her and taking her roughly by the arm, he swung her round to face him. Putting his face close to hers, he snarled "If you lay a hand on the girl, make no mistake, it will be you who will die."

Rachel cowered before him. "I'm sorry, I was just jealous, that's all."

Abraham let go of her arm. "I heard what was said. Miriam is right, ben-Ezra could make double the money when he sells her. I'll go and tell him about the child. Now, we will hear no more on the matter."

Farrah had silently thanked Miriam. It seemed she was the only friend they had.

Later, away from the women, she asked Ruth if the father of the baby really was Boraz. The young girl looked at her mistress and said earnestly, "I swear to you, my lady, Boraz has never touched me. The child is Abraham bar Saraf's. He raped me many times when first we came here." Farrah nodded. "You did well to blame Boraz, Ruth. It has saved you from Rachel's jealous anger."

Days passed by. Farrah was relieved that ben-Ezra had mostly ignored her, although whenever Rebecca was not around she would catch him giving her sly, lustful looks. For the past few days, he and Abraham had kept apart from the others. Farrah wondered what their whisperings were about and what they were planning. Today Abraham had been sent outside by ben-Ezra to test the weather.

She looked up as Abraham entered the cavern. He looked at the gathering and said, "The clouds are beginning to thin. There's still a chance of rain, but we can't wait for the weather to improve, we need fresh food now. Tomorrow I'll take a couple of men and go hunting. Spring is coming, so the animals will be looking for fresh water."

There was a look of relief on all their faces when, later the next day, Abraham and his two chosen hunters returned to the cavern each with a dead mountain goat slung around his neck, and the pronouncement that three more goats had been left inside the entrance to the caves. Isaac went with the two hunters to retrieve them, while Abraham went searching for ben-Ezra to give him the good news.

He found him in an alcove with Rebecca. At first the bandit chief cursed his second-in-command for interrupting his lovemaking, but when Abraham told him about the goats, he left Rebecca and went to inspect the animals. Food that would fill their hungry bellies was more important than a woman, especially one he could have any time he liked.

Later, everyone, including Farrah and Ruth, ate their first meal of fresh meat in days. With reasonably full stomachs, they all settled down contentedly; all except for Farrah and Ruth. The two women cast anxious looks at one another, realization setting in: if spring was fast approaching it would soon be time for ben-Ezra and his gang to leave the caves and for them to meet their fate.

Farrah saw silent tears begin to flow from Ruth. The poor girl had to face childbirth on top of everything else. Her pregnancy had progressed, but Farrah worried that with the privations she had suffered these past months, she would not be strong enough to bear the rigours of giving birth. She remembered only too well the agony her mother had suffered when struggling to give birth to her little sister. Then she remembered the wretched little waif Ruth had been when her uncle Ibrahim had brought her to their house in Bethany. She must have endured unimaginable hardship throughout her childhood, yet she had survived.

Farrah felt a sudden confidence that whatever problems life threw at her, Ruth had the ability to overcome them. She, on the other hand, had been brought up to a pampered existence, and it would be so much harder for her to bear. Desolation overcame her. She lay down on the floor and cried herself to sleep.

# CHAPTER SIX

In Damascus, several weeks had passed since Ananias had led Saul from the lodging house in Straight Street and taken him to the house of Jonathan, a cloth merchant. At first Jonathan had been shocked and afraid to see the persecutor of the followers of Jesus standing on his doorstep, but Ananias had assured him that Saul had been baptized into the faith and no longer wished to harm the converts. It had taken a lot longer for Jonathan's wife, Calisto, to feel comfortable in Saul's presence, but accepting Ananias' reassurance, eventually she too was happy to have him share their home.

As Saul got to know Jonathan better, he asked him about his background. He was dumbfounded when Jonathan said, "My parents originally came from Jerusalem, but they were fearful of the Roman occupation of the region, so they moved to Alexandria, where I was born. They were homesick, so they returned to Jerusalem when I was a young boy. My family and I belonged to the Synagogue of Libertines."

Saul blanched. Members of the Synagogue of Libertines had helped him to put an end to Stephen. He forced himself to concentrate on what Jonathan was saying.

"I was good friends with Stephen of Alexandria," Jonathan went on. He took a deep breath as the memory of Stephen's cruel death came back to him. "When you began the persecution, Calisto and I left Jerusalem. We came to Damascus as Calisto has some relatives here. They don't know we are followers of Jesus." He looked directly at Saul, then continued: "I didn't think I could ever forgive you for what you did, Saul, but in those days you were blind to the truth."

Saul bowed his head and tears began to form. "If only I could go back to that time and treat the Lord's followers in a different way. I will never forgive myself for persecuting them."

"Well, Saul, things are different now, your eyes have been opened. If the Lord can forgive you, then so must I."

Tears flowed down Saul's cheeks as Jonathan grasped his arm in newfound friendship.

Through Jonathan, Saul made friends with other new converts. Every week, these new friends would come to Jonathan's house to listen to Saul and pray together as a group. They were mesmerized by what Saul had to say and marvelled at his tale of conversion on the Damascus Road. Truly, they told him, he had been chosen by the Lord for some great purpose.

Saul had visited the synagogue a few times and listened to the Pharisee, whom he thought of as a holy man. On this Sabbath, as he sat amongst the synagogue congregation, he decided it was time for him to speak openly about his experience.

Jonathan stood at the back of the synagogue. He grew tense as he saw Saul rise up, go to the front of the building and stand beside the Pharisee. He saw the Pharisee's quizzical look as Saul bowed to him and asked if he was allowed to speak to the congregation. Jonathan knew the Pharisee to be a kindly soul and wasn't surprised when he indicated that he would allow it.

Saul looked around at the assembly, took a deep breath, and began.

"My brothers, friends. I bring you good news. The Messiah you have waited for has come." He saw the confused expression on the faces of the congregation as they looked at him, then at each other. "The Messiah is Jesus of Nazareth. The authorities had him crucified, but he rose from the dead three days later and is in Heaven with God, his Father."

The members of the congregation began to murmur amongst themselves, but Saul carried on relentlessly, "I have proof of this. I was a cruel man, responsible for much suffering to Jesus' followers." He hesitated for a brief moment. "Even the death of the man called Stephen, for which I am heartily ashamed. Despite all of my grave sins, the Lord forgave me, for when I was travelling along the road to Damascus, He appeared to me in a vision and spoke to me. Afterwards I lost my sight for a time and was plagued by nightmares, all of which I deserved. Then my sight was restored and I could plainly see, physically and spiritually. Now I stand before you proclaiming Jesus as Lord and the Son of God."

One man stood up and pointed at Saul, then turned to the others and said "Is this not the man who has tried to destroy those who speak in the name of this Jesus? Did he not come to Damascus to arrest the Nazarene's followers here? Was he not to take them back to Jerusalem to face the High Priests and the Sanhedrin?"

His questions were answered by a unanimous "Aye!" Another man protested against Saul, saying loudly "Go and get those men sent by the High Priests to take hold of him and take him back to Jerusalem. We don't want anything to do with his blasphemous talk."

Saul's voice rose above the clamour. "I speak the truth. You must believe that Jesus of Nazareth is the Messiah..."

His words were cut short as uproar ensued. Jonathan knew he had to get Saul away before the congregation took him. He rushed forward, grabbed Saul by the arm and pulled him forcibly through the synagogue. As they made their way to the door, some of the men lashed out angrily at Saul, their fists connecting with his face and body. The shocked Pharisee raised his hands heavenwards and intoned prayers for forgiveness for the sacrilege done in that holy place. When Saul and Jonathan reached the street, Jonathan let go of Saul's arm and yelled "Quickly, follow me!"

One of the mob ran to fetch the High Priests' men, led by Elias, as some others struggled through the congregation and followed after Saul and Jonathan, wanting to lay hands on Saul and hold him until he could be arrested. Jonathan and Saul could hear angry voices some way behind them, but they were too quick for their pursuers. With Jonathan leading, he and Saul ran as fast as they could until they reached an alleyway. "Quickly, down here!" he shouted.

They ran as fast as they could down a series of interlinked alleyways until they had left the confused followers behind, and wondering how they had vanished so quickly.

When Jonathan knew they were no longer being followed, he stopped at a house and knocked on the door. As he and Saul were getting their breath back, the door opened and a young woman appeared.

"Jonathan?" The woman was startled at seeing Jonathan's look of desperation and his companion's bruised and bloodied face. "Quickly, come inside," she said without hesitation.

Saul looked around the room and saw an old man sitting in a chair.

The old man raised his head and called out. "Who is it, Alitza?"

The young woman immediately went to him. "It's all right father, it's Jonathan. He has a friend with him."

The old man turned his head, clearly having difficulty in locating where the visitors were. Saul guessed that he was blind.

"My friend here is Saul of Tarsus." The old man draw back in his chair, and Jonathan saw a look of fear on his face. He swiftly said in a calm voice, "He means you no harm. We came here as we didn't know where else to go." He quickly explained to them what had happened in the synagogue and why Saul's face was injured.

Marvelling at the story, Alitza went over to Saul. "Is it true? Are you now a convert?" she said. She looked into his eyes and saw the zeal there, but it was not a destructive zeal; rather an inner light.

Saul tried to smile but winced with the pain of his injuries. "Yes, it's true," he said. "I know now that Jesus is the Messiah, the Son of God."

Alitza turned to her father and said, "I believe him, father." When the old man smiled she turned back to Saul and said "You are welcome here. Let me bathe your face, you have some nasty cuts and bruises."

Alitza fetched a bowl of water and a cloth and pointed to a chair next to a table. "Please sit down," she said. She placed the bowl and cloth on the table while Saul sank wearily onto the chair.

Jonathan sat close to Alitza's father and asked "Joseph, are you well?"

"Oh, the usual aches and pains that come with old age," replied Joseph, smiling, "but I feel all the better now that I know Saul is no longer our enemy."

Jonathan grimaced. "That's true, but there are still those servants of the High Priests who won't rest until they drag us to Jerusalem in chains."

"Saul's name will now be at the top of their list," Joseph said wearily, "and if the Lord appeared to Saul, then he is a very important man and must be kept safe at all costs. He is welcome to stay here with us. No one will know. Why should they? I am a worshipper in the synagogue who sits quietly at the back, I would have been there today if I hadn't been feeling out of sorts. I wouldn't have been missed, as members of the congregation rarely come to visit me." He heard a soft cry from Saul and turned towards him. He guessed Alitza was cleaning his wound.

Everyone froze at the sound of knocking. His voice shaking, Joseph called out "Who's there?"

It was a great relief to all when a voice replied "Ananias. Please let me in."

Jonathan opened the door and Ananias walked into the room. He looked at the wounded Saul and sighed. "So it's true. It was you, Saul, who caused the rumpus at the synagogue."

Saul looked contrite. "How did you find out?"

"Convert witnesses came to me and said that as they

were walking down the street they saw you and Jonathan running out of the synagogue and heard the threats of the congregation who followed you." He spoke gravely. "Saul, it is obviously not safe for you here in Damascus. Perhaps you should leave the city and move on somewhere else."

"I can't. There is so much more for me to do here."

Jonathan broke in. "Ananias is right. It is far too dangerous here for you now."

"But the word of the Lord is like fire within me, how can I not do as He commands?" Saul argued.

"You can do nothing for the Lord if you are dead, Saul." Ananias' voice was conciliatory. "There are many people in other places who have not heard the story of the Lord Jesus, why don't you travel there?"

Saul uttered a deep sigh. "The Lord will tell me when and where to go."

Ananias did not answer but blessed the gathering, and deeply troubled, left the house.

When Elias heard about Saul's speech at the synagogue and his subsequent escape, he was livid. From now on, he, and the High Priests' guards, would look in every synagogue in the city until Saul was found.


When Quintus Maximus read the order from Caesarea that the search for the missing Princess Farrah had to resume, despite there having been no sighting of her for months, he slammed his fist down onto his desk in frustration. Trying to contain his anger, he called Julius and Antonius to his office and told them the situation.

The Prefect stood with a set expression on his face. Julius' expression was at first one of surprise, for surely without sight or evidence of her for so long, she must be dead or out of the country, making the order futile. He took care to keep his thoughts to himself and adopted a bland expression. He realised that however futile the search seemed, Governor Pilate had ordered it, leaving the Commander with no choice but to obey it. The next day the combined cavalry rode out to begin scouring the surrounding countryside.

A few days later, Julius and his men rode into the fortress Antonia after yet another failed mission. He went straight to the Commander and gave him his report. Antonius had returned with his men earlier after combing a different area, and reported that they too had found no new evidence of the Princess' whereabouts.

Alone in his office, Quintus sighed. The same questions had buzzed through his head since he had received Pilate's order: why had Pilate suddenly ordered the search to resume? He couldn't afford to waste valuable manpower on such a hopeless task. Surely Pilate must realise that very soon the Passover Festival would be upon them and the fortress would have all the trouble which that brought with it to contend with too. He placed his head in his hands in utter frustration.

Julius was making his way to his quarters. He removed his helmet and wiped the sweat off his forehead with his hand.

Antonius came out from behind the workshop area and blocked his way. His face was twisted in anger as he snarled at Julius.

"You son of a bitch! If you'd done your job properly in the first place I could have stayed in Syria with my easy duties and my woman. Instead, I have to stay here in this stinking city and begin the futile search for that stupid whore all over again!"

Looking around to make sure no one was watching, he threw a punch at Julius, who managed to duck out of the way. Julius wasn't so lucky the second time and the Prefect's fist connected with the side of his head, making him reel. Antonius was about to hit Julius again when his raised arm was grabbed from behind. He was forcibly spun round to be faced by a furious Drubaal. He tried to back away, but Drubaal held on to him with an iron grip. Antonius gave up the struggle, knowing he had no chance of beating a man who stood head and shoulders above him and was much more powerfully built. Instead he spat out, "What do you think you're doing, you Carthaginian scum? Let me go, slave. I will see to it that you are crucified for this!"

Drubaal continued his hold on the Prefect's arm and gave him a penetrating look, then twisted Antonius' arm away from him. Antonius let out a howl of pain. "Why, you..." Before he could finish, Drubaal's sheer strength brought the Prefect to his knees. Foul-mouthed expletives and threats burst out of Antonius' mouth.

Puzzled by the howl and the shouting, some legionaries came out of the workshops to investigate. When they saw the hated Prefect's predicament no one went to help him; rather they stood sniggering at the scene.

Drubaal bent lower and put his face close to Antonius. "Leave the Decurion alone!" He let go of the Prefect's arm and watched as Antonius struggled to his feet clutching his painful arm. Drubaal walked across to Julius, who stood open-mouthed watching the scene unfold before him. He was concerned at the bruises quickly developing on Julius' face. "Are you all right, Decurion Julius?"

Julius was worried for his friend "I'll be all right, but I'm concerned for you. You were very brave to come to my defence and I thank you, but Antonius is not one to cross. Your life is in danger."

Drubaal smiled. "I have been in danger many times, Decurion Julius, but I'm still here." He turned and started to walk away.

Antonius roared to the watching legionaries, "Don't just stand there, you fools. Grab him and take him to the Commander."

Two legionaries stepped forward and grabbed Drubaal. In spite of their hatred for the Prefect, they had to obey his orders. Drubaal made no move to fight them, as he knew he was in trouble and did not want to make matters any worse. They led Drubaal to the Commander's office with Antonius following close behind, still rubbing his aching arm.

Julius watched sadly and shook his head. Drubaal was in desperate trouble. He knew what the punishment was for a rebellious slave, and it made him feel sick. He blamed himself for not being strong enough to stand up to Antonius. The Prefect had made his life a misery for weeks. If only he had gone to Centurion Sextus and reported it, as Tribune Flavius had advised, Antonius might have been stopped and none of this would have happened. Instead he had been fearful that the Commander would not believe him and Antonius would then treat him even worse than before. So he'd stayed quiet, but at what cost? What would he say when Tribune Flavius returned? How was he going to explain Drubaal's inevitable execution?

When he had first obeyed the Tribune's request to visit Drubaal, Julius had been dubious that the Carthaginian would want to speak with him and he was right, but he had persevered. After several visits he could see that Drubaal was slowly beginning to realise that he was genuinely trying to befriend him and began to be more relaxed in his company. Over the weeks the two had formed a close bond; now that bond would destroy the brave but foolhardy Carthaginian giant. Julius wanted so much to help his friend.

He came to a decision. He would act like a man and go to the Commander and explain how Drubaal was only trying to protect him, in the hope that he would be believed. He quickly made his way to the Commander's office.

Flanked by the two legionaries, Drubaal stood proudly before Quintus Maximus. Antonius stood to the side. He'd been aware that some legionaries had witnessed the scene and had not helped him. He would deal with them later. Meanwhile, he was not going to let the slave get away with humiliating him. He would make sure the Carthaginian paid with his life.

Julius entered the Commander's office, saluted and stood to attention. "Commander, sir! If I may be allowed, I would like to speak in defence of Drubaal."

Quintus nodded. It would be good to hear both sides of the story. "When Prefect Antonius has finished, you may put your side of the story. Proceed, Prefect."

Quintus sat stony faced as Antonius recounted the saga. Julius thought he was exaggerating the facts somewhat to make Drubaal's actions appear much worse than they had actually been. Antonius finished his diatribe by saying, "The slave is guilty beyond doubt, Commander. These two legionaries here witnessed the assault."

Julius stole a glance at the faces of the two legionaries, who were trying hard not to sneer at the exaggerated tale. He then stepped forward in an effort to defend the slave by telling Quintus about Drubaal's intervention into the beating he was receiving at the hands of Antonius. He felt the Prefect's eyes boring into his back.

Having heard the two statements, Quintus sat back in his chair. Rumours of Antonius' rough treatment, not only of Decurion Julius but of other legionaries, had been spreading around the fortress for some time. At first he had not believed them, thinking it was mischief-making amongst those who did not like the Prefect's strict discipline. Now he had just heard a first-hand account backing up those rumours, from a Decurion who had always done his duty, however unpleasant, without argument and had never been insubordinate. He could also see a vivid bruise beginning to appear on the young officer's face. In view of this, he decided to keep a closer eye on Antonius in future and to not so quickly dismiss any more rumours concerning him.

As far as Drubaal was concerned, he was perplexed as to what to do. The slave belonged to Sheikh Ibrahim bin Yusuf Al-Khareem, a powerful ally of Rome, who was also the uncle of the missing Princess; on the other hand, the scene had been witnessed by the lower ranks and if he let the slave go unpunished, it would be bad for discipline amongst the troops.

He made up his mind. The security of the Antonia had to come first. Drubaal must not be seen to be allowed to get away with his attack. However, he had no intention of having the slave executed, because for that he would face the wrath of Pilate. The slave would be punished, but he would call a halt to the punishment before the slave was too badly hurt.

His voice rang out: "This is purely an internal matter and punishment will not take place in public but within the confines of the fortress. Now, take the slave back to the dungeon. He will be punished tomorrow!"

Filled with despair for his friend, Julius forced himself not to speak out at the injustice of the order.

Antonius stepped forward and said, "I demand that he be publicly crucified, Commander."

Quintus stared at the Prefect. "You demand?" his voice was controlled, but there was no mistaking his anger at the Prefect's request. "Remember, Prefect Antonius I am in command here. The slave's punishment is my decision and mine alone. You are dismissed."

Tight lipped, Antonius stared straight ahead, barely concealing his annoyance at being slapped down by the Commander. "Yes, sir," he said. He saluted and turned to go out, giving Julius a sideways look of hate as he passed him by.

Drubaal narrowed his eyes at Antonius, but said nothing as the legionaries led him away.

# CHAPTER SEVEN

A grim-faced Centurion Sextus stood ramrod straight, with his vine stick held firmly under his arm, in front of the assembled cohorts lined up on three sides of the parade ground. A smirking Antonius stood before his squadron of North African Light Cavalry. He stared at Julius, who refused to acknowledge him. Julius' men lined up behind him were looking straight ahead, with barely-disguised disgust written on their faces.

Quintus came out of his quarters and took up position in front of all the troops. The mid-morning sun had not yet reached full power, but it still generated enough heat to send sweat running down the soldiers' faces and bodies beneath their helmets and armour. Behind the cohorts, the civilians who worked for the Romans at the Antonia, had gathered to watch the punishment. Quintus had ordered that all except the medical staff who were needed by their patients should witness the proceedings. It was the only way to his mind that he could control those who might have ideas about rebellion, even those amongst his own rank and file.

Drubaal was led out onto the parade ground by two legionaries. At first he shaded his eyes until they adjusted to the bright sunshine. He stood proud and tall and did not flinch when he saw twenty legionaries who stood in two parallel lines of ten facing each other, with an assortment of wooden staves and clubs in their hands.

So this was his reward for helping his master, the Sheikh, in his tireless efforts for the Emperor. Bitterness overwhelmed him. Rome had not helped his mistress either. He briefly bowed his head at her memory and intoned a prayer to his gods that she would be found safe. For himself he cared not. He was only a slave in the eyes of Rome, and this to them was a fitting punishment. He gritted his teeth. He would not show fear to the watching barbarians.

Quintus raised his arm, then let it drop, the signal for the punishment to begin. Rough hands took hold of Drubaal and propelled him forward between the lines of waiting men.

Drubaal knew his only chance was to run as fast as his feet would carry him. He instinctively covered his head with his arms in an attempt to protect his skull from fracture, and tucked his chin down towards his chest, hunching his shoulders, trying to make himself as small as possible. He tried desperately to dodge the clubs and staves as the legionaries brought them down one after the other onto his body and head. Drubaal clamped his teeth together in an attempt to stop himself from screaming in agony; only his superior strength stopped him from crumbling.

A sudden clamour arose from the back of the parade ground. Quintus turned his head to see what the noise was and saw one of the gate guards running towards him. Irritated by the interruption, he turned on the guard. "What is it?"

"Sir." The guard saluted "The Sheikh is outside the gate, he has armed men with him."

In a startled voice Quintus said, "How many men?"

"Eight, sir."

Quintus knew a man of the Sheikh's rank travelled everywhere with an armed entourage and eight was within the permitted amount of armed men allowed in Roman territory. They did not constitute a threat of war. Still, he hesitated. How could he explain his actions against Drubaal to the Sheikh?

"Commander, sir, he demands to be let in," the guard said urgently.

"Then let him in," Quintus snapped at the guard, who beat a hasty retreat back to the gate. Quintus ordered the punishment to stop immediately. The legionaries put down their staves and clubs as the Sheikh rode into the fort, his eight armed guards following him.

Sheikh Ibrahim climbed down from his white Arabian stallion and strode towards the Commander, his armed guards, now dismounted, walking behind. Filled with horror, he took in the situation and glared at the Commander, protesting loudly, "What is happening here? What are you doing?"

Quintus stared at the Sheikh. He resented being spoken to in this manner in front of his men, but the Sheikh was a relative and close friend of King Aretas, the ruler of Nabatea. If he so chose he could appeal directly to Pilate, or worse, Aretas himself. Rome held a treaty with Nabatea as one of her main importers. The country's network of caravan trading routes provided Rome with asphalt, spices, silks, jewels; all things that Rome needed. If the Sheikh did complain and the king decided to cease trading between Nabatea and Rome, the Emperor would get involved. Extra trouble he did not need. He could do nothing but take full responsibility for his actions and hope he could worm his way out of the mess.

Drubaal tried desperately to walk away from his tormentors, but he was overwhelmed by pain. His legs buckled and he fell face forwards onto the hard ground.

Sheikh Ibrahim winced at Drubaal's obvious agony. He called forward two of his Nabatean guards and told them to help the slave to his feet and support him. The guards moved towards Drubaal, glaring at the legionaries who had been put in charge of the punishment detail. Defiantly, the legionaries glared back at the Nabateans, then looked to the Commander for further orders. Quintus wanted no further trouble and ordered that the Sheikh's men take the Carthaginian to the hospital, together with the two legionaries who had led Drubaal out, as an escort. The punishment detail then stood back and let the Nabatean guards help the semi-conscious Carthaginian to his feet. Drubaal, supported by the Nabatean guards, was returned to the hospital he had so recently left.

Quintus turned his attention to the Sheikh "What are you doing here, Sheikh Ibrahim?"

Sheikh Ibrahim looked straight at the Commander and said in a clipped voice "I wish to see my niece. Where is Princess Farrah?"

Quintus swallowed. "Come with me and I will explain everything," he said. He was not looking forward to explaining the shocking abduction of the Princess to the already angry Sheikh. He dismissed the legionaries and civilians, gruffly telling them to go back to their duties.

Ibrahim ordered the Nabatean guards to remain outside as he followed Quintus into his office.

Antonius guessed who the protester was. As he marched his troops away he felt angry and frustrated that the slave's master should suddenly appear at the very pinnacle of his revenge. He had grimaced and bitten his lip, trying to hold his temper as the Commander had let Drubaal be helped to his feet by the foreigners. He made a vow that he would avenge this miscarriage of justice one way or the other – and soon.

The still angry Sheikh sat down in the proffered chair and said testily "Now, what is it you have to explain to me?"

Quintus sat down heavily in his chair, trying desperately to find the right words. He could not meet Ibrahim's eyes as he asked, "Sheikh Ibrahim, have you been to Bethany?"

Ibrahim nodded, his face grim. "Yes, it is why I am here. I returned to my house to find the whole place had been ransacked and ruined. It was obvious some kind of an attack had taken place. I came straight here hoping to find my niece safe and well. Drubaal is here, so I take it my niece and the rest of my servants are also here with you?"

Quintus stayed silent.

Ibrahim persisted "Where is she?"

Quintus hesitated for a brief moment, but knew he had to tell the Sheikh the grim news. He took a deep breath, then told him about the terrible events of the night his house had been raided, the murder of his legionaries, who he'd sent there to protect the Princess during the Sheikh's absence and the death of the servant Boraz, adding that it was his men who had found the badly wounded Drubaal and brought him back to the garrison hospital to be cared for. He struggled to find the right words, but finally said "I am afraid your niece and her servant have disappeared. It is my belief that they have been kidnapped."

The older man fought back tears as the story unfolded. Then anger took over. "Who is responsible for this?"

"We are certain it is the work of a criminal called

Eleazar ben-Ezra. We have been after him for some time for acts of terrorism and murder."

Ibrahim blanched at the thought that his beloved niece had been captured by the murderer of his brother Hassan and nephew Kadeem, Farrah's father and brother. By now ben-Ezra might well have killed her too.

"I assure you Sheikh Ibrahim, my cavalry officers and their men are searching tirelessly for Princess Farrah," Quintus went on.

"And?" Ibrahim asked expectantly.

"I'm sorry, so far we have found no trace of her whereabouts."

Quintus felt sorry for the Sheikh and tried to reassure him that everything was being done to find her, but he could see his words were falling on deaf ears.

Leaning forward, Ibrahim said "You said that Drubaal was badly hurt in the battle and you helped him to recover here?" Quintus nodded. Ibrahim continued coldly "Why then did you bother to save his life – only to punish him so cruelly now?"

Quintus was taken aback by the question. In answer he blustered, "I was left with no choice. He was witnessed attacking one of my senior officers. I had to be seen to be doing something. I cannot let rebellion in any shape or form go unpunished. Rest assured I had no intention of executing him."

Ibrahim gave him a withering look. "And what will you do with him now?"

The Commander rubbed his chin. "He has left me in a very difficult position."

Ibrahim narrowed his eyes. "Then let me help you to overcome that difficulty and stop what could be a serious diplomatic incident from escalating. I have no desire to return to the ruined house in Bethany, so I suggest that I stay here and keep Drubaal under my strict supervision. Then, when Pilate returns to Jerusalem, we can give Drubaal a chance to put his case before him."

Quintus seized the chance to resolve the awkward situation. It would give him time to properly question those who had witnessed the slave's assault on Antonius. He had been wondering why the legionaries had not come to the Prefect's assistance at once but had stood by watching the assault without interfering. He decided he would get to the bottom of this unpleasant episode before Pilate returned to the city.

"Yes. I will agree to that," Quintus said, nodding, "but you must give me your full assurance that he will not leave this fortress until he appears before Pilate."

"I give you my word he will not leave this fortress. On the matter of my niece, it is imperative that she be found, alive – or dead." A look of pain crossed Ibrahim's face. "Therefore, I offer you my guards to help you in your search for the Princess. I mean no disrespect to you Romans, but my men are expert trackers and highly skilled in both mountain and desert warfare. What do you say?"

Quintus frowned. He had noticed the lethal curved

swords and daggers carried by the Nabateans and had no doubt they were fearsome fighters, and he could do with all the help he could get, but they could not be seen to be armed with such weapons inside the fortress.

"Agreed, but they must hand their weapons in to my armoury until needed," he replied. He saw the concerned look on the Sheikh's face. "It is a requirement I must insist upon."

Ibrahim sighed. "Very well. They will not like it, but I will explain your order to them."

Quintus stood up. "I will see to it that you have suitable quarters for your stay here and give orders for accommodation to be found for your guards."

Ibrahim rose from his seat. "Thank you. The news of my niece's disappearance has upset me greatly and the rigours of the journey here have made me very tired. I should like to rest. But first, I will visit Drubaal in the hospital."

"Of course." Quintus immediately sent out orders that accommodation should be made ready for the Sheikh and his entourage as soon as possible. The obviously distressed man needed to rest and recoup his energy.

Once alone, Quintus decided to use the one man he could trust implicitly to watch Antonius and report back to him any evidence of bullying or general misconduct by the Prefect. If enough evidence was found, then he would bring it to the attention of Pilate. The Governor had asked for Antonius to be brought to Jerusalem, it was up to him to decide what to do with him.

He opened the door of his office and barked out orders to the legionary standing at attention outside in the corridor: "Find Centurion Sextus and bring him here. Now!"

Julius was speaking quietly with the Chief Medical Orderly. "How serious are his injuries?"

The surgeon's face was grim. "Frankly I am amazed at seeing Drubaal back in hospital again so soon. He's only just recovered from his previous injuries." He shook his head. "The man is a magnet for trouble."

"What are his chances?" Julius was extremely worried for his friend. A lesser man might well have succumbed to such a vicious beating.

"It seems the Sheikh arrived just in time. He's a strong man, and he will recover quickly. He has a couple of broken ribs, a broken left arm and a badly bruised right wrist, lacerations and deep bruising to his legs and most of his body. Fortunately his arms saved him from a cracked skull." He smiled, seeing Julius' worried face. "Don't worry, Decurion. Drubaal has the strength of ten men. It will take more than a few bruises and broken bones to finish him off." With that he turned and walked off to attend to a patient with a badly-cut leg.

Julius was relieved. He made a move to Drubaal's bedside, but then he saw the Sheikh enter the hospital and walk towards him. Before the Nabatean could ask about his servant's health, Julius forestalled him and told him what the orderly had said. The Sheikh's expression was grim, and Julius knew that no amount of apologizing would satisfy him, but he had to try.

"Sir, I am sorry that Drubaal is injured," he said. "I must take responsibility for placing him in danger. It was me he was trying to defend."

Ibrahim stared at Julius. "I think you had better explain why my servant endangered his life for you, Roman."

Julius hesitated, fearing there would be reprisals, but finally, at Ibrahim's insistence, he explained his deep friendship with Drubaal and why the Carthaginian had come to his rescue.

Ibrahim was incredulous. "If this Prefect has done these things, why does he go unpunished?" he asked.

"Because he is clever. Tribune Flavius Silvanus tackled him once when he saw him ill-treating me, but he is not here at the present time, and since then Antonius has made sure there are never any witnesses to his abuse. It was Tribune Silvanus who asked me to keep an eye on Drubaal during his absence – that's how we became friends."

The Sheikh started at the familiar name. He knew that the bond between Farrah and Flavius was strong. When he had seen them kissing in the garden of the house in Bethany, he had been deeply concerned. After the cruel deaths of her parents, brother and baby sister, he had grown very protective of his niece. She had suffered so much, and he had told Flavius that he would not stand idly by and see her hurt again. But this was not a matter of a broken heart. This was out of his hands; he had no control over her fate. If she had survived her capture, only the gods knew what was happening to her now.

He grimaced. "Is Tribune Flavius Silvanus part of the sorry tale concerning my niece too? Could he not have defended her?"

Julius shook his head. "No, sir. At the time he knew nothing about it. He was with the Governor when your house was attacked."

"You say the Tribune is away. A pity, I should very much like to speak with him."

"He's with the Governor in Caesarea," Julius replied. "They are due back in Jerusalem in a couple of weeks' time ready for the Passover Festival."

Ibrahim nodded. "I take it the Governor is fully aware of the situation?"

"Yes sir, as is the Tribune. It is the Governor who has given the order for the search to continue. Every day our troops are scouring the countryside looking for the Princess." Although in his own mind the search was futile, he could not take away the last vestige of hope from the older man. "Rest assured, sir, we have not yet given up hope of finding her."

Ibrahim nodded. "The Commander has given his permission for me and my guards to stay here. They too will be joining your legionaries in the search. Together we may have more success. Now if you will excuse me, I wish to see Drubaal."

Julius nodded, then left the hospital.

Ibrahim looked with pity on Drubaal who was propped up in bed. His swollen, blackened eyes were closed. A soothing salve had been carefully smoothed over the extensive cuts and deep bruising on his upper torso. He was heavily bandaged across his stomach and broken ribs. His broken arm was encased in wooden splints covered in bandages stiffened with starch made from wheat flour which had been soaked in boiling water and left to dry.

Aware of a new presence, the slave painfully opened his eyes. When he saw his master, tears began to roll down his cheeks.

"Master..." his voice was no more than a croak "I have failed you... my mistress..."

"Hush." Ibrahim spoke gently. "The Commander has told me everything. He said you fought to within an inch of your life to protect my niece. For that I thank you." He looked away momentarily, afraid he would give in to his grief. Then, gathering himself together, he said, "I am staying here, along with my guards. Together with the Romans we will find her. You just concentrate on recovering; I have great need of you my friend. Now try to rest. I will see you again soon."

Overwhelmed by his master's forgiveness, with tears rolling down his battered cheeks, Drubaal watched his master walk away. He felt despair sweep over him as he saw the Sheikh's shoulders hunched through weariness and worry. A fierce love for the older man engulfed him. He prayed to his gods that his bones would quickly mend so that he could avenge his master and help to hunt down the criminals who had spirited his mistress away.

# CHAPTER EIGHT

Pilate spoke to Flavius in his office. "Now that the shipping lanes have reopened, I think the new Senior Tribune will be arriving from Rome on one of the first troop ships," he said. "However, when he arrives, although your stint as temporary Tribune will end, I would like you to stay on as my staff officer. What do you say to that?"

Flavius was taken by surprise. He knew his tour still had some time to go before his army duties were finished and he could return home; it also meant he would have to return to Jerusalem with Pilate ready for the forthcoming Passover Festival, a place that held so many bad memories for him. But he knew he had little choice but to agree with Pilate's proposition, so he replied, "Thank you Governor Pilate. I am grateful for your offer, it is an honour to be chosen."

Pilate smiled. "Good, good. That's settled then."

Flavius saluted. "I'm sorry, sir, but it's time for me to lead the patrol to the harbour. A merchant ship is due to arrive from Sicily shortly."

Pilate waved his hand. "Of course. You are dismissed."

Flavius saluted again, then went off to organise his men.

Flavius stood talking with the Harbour Master, Laurentius. Since he had come to Caesarea, he had struck up a friendship with the retired Marine Centurion. Laurentius liked the Tribune, but he was always conscious of the difference in rank and treated Flavius with respect. The two men would often speak of Rome. Laurentius had never been there, so he relished Flavius' description of the imperial city. He had been born and bred in a southern coastal region, so he had always loved the sea. He had joined the navy as a junior marine as soon as he was old enough, then worked his way up to become Marine Centurion. When his career was coming to a close, he had been given the choice of retiring with honour or taking on the exacting job of Master of the Harbour in Caesarea. Laurentius knew he was still strong and had many good years before him, so he had gladly accepted the latter. He was flattered to be considered and vowed to do the job zealously and with pride. He had been at the harbour for three years now and had kept to his vow. He was well thought of amongst ships' captains and legionaries alike, being known as a fair man but one who would stand no nonsense.

Laurentius looked out to sea and saw the merchant ship come into view. "Ah, there she is, the *Eurydice*. If you will excuse me, Tribune." He saluted Flavius, then went off to oversee the landing of the small craft which would carry the goods to shore from the merchant ship, as she was too big to enter the harbour.

It was some time before Flavius was free to ride out to Cornelius' house. Cornelius was pleased to see him, although Flavius could see the effects of pain and disappointment etched on Julia's pretty face. It was obvious to him that Marcus' actions had caused her great heartache.

He accepted food and wine from Martha and stayed for a few hours, talking of Julius, life at the Antonia and his future in Rome.

Cornelius looked at Julia lovingly. "It is my hope that one day Julia will travel to Rome and see her mother's birthplace," he said.

Flavius smiled at her. "If you do, when my duties in the Legions have ended, you will be most welcome to visit me and my family," he said. However, he wasn't sure he wanted Marcus to be with her.

Julia smiled wanly. "Thank you, that is very kind of you."

He turned to Cornelius. "And what about you, Cornelius? Will you ever return to Rome?"

Cornelius smiled. "I have often thought about it. Perhaps when I retire from the Army..." He got up from his seat, "Now if you will excuse me for a moment, I need to ask Martha to bring us more wine." He left the room, leaving Flavius and Julia alone.

Flavius looked intently at Julia. "Has Marcus been to see you?" he asked. She nodded. "And is all well between you now?" He knew it was really none of his business, but he had grown to like this family and wanted to return to Julius with good news. And despite himself, it had grieved him to see this lovely young woman so heartbroken.

"Yes, all is well. I've told him I understand he has to put his duty to the Governor before all else and I've agreed to wait for him. He has assured me that we will marry when he returns from Jerusalem."

"I am glad for you."

Cornelius came back into the room. Martha followed him, holding a flagon of wine, and general conversation resumed. Flavius stayed for a little longer, then, after farewells and well wishes, he returned to the garrison. Soon it would be time to prepare for the return journey to Jerusalem.

# CHAPTER NINE

Now that the weather had turned, Abraham bar-Saraf and his chosen men had been able to hunt more easily and bring back a good supply of fresh meat. With ben-Ezra and the members of his gang no longer suffering from hunger, the general atmosphere within the cavern complex improved considerably.

With fresh meat inside her, Farrah hoped to put back some of the weight she had lost during the lean, rain-filled winter months. Ruth's pregnancy had progressed without any further problems. Miriam had continued to secretly look after the young girl and make sure she steadily regained her strength by eating properly, ready to face the rigours of giving birth.

Farrah's body and long hair were encrusted with dirt after months of not being able to bathe. She longed to feel clean again. When she mentioned this to Miriam, the elder woman smiled.

"Now that the flood waters have gone, there are rock pools amongst the cliff hollows," she said. "You could wash yourself and your hair."

Farrah's face lit up, but then she frowned "How can I do that? I don't know where these pools are, and in any case, would ben-Ezra let me?"

"We will soon be on the move. I'm sure he will want his trophy looking her best if he wants to get a good price at the slave market." Miriam stopped as she saw the distress on Farrah's face. "I'm sorry. I didn't mean... look, I will go to ben-Ezra and ask him if you may bathe."

A little later, ben-Ezra stood leering at her, then said abruptly "Get up!" He roughly pulled her to her feet. "Miriam tells me you want to wash yourself." He looked her up and down. "Yes, you could do with cleaning yourself up." He called to Miriam, who hurried to her master's side. "Take her to the nearest rock pool and see that she washes herself thoroughly. I want her looking her best when I hand her over to the slave-trader." With that he turned away.

Farrah shielded her eyes against the sunlight, so long withheld from her, as she came out of the warren of caverns into the daylight. Her eyes gradually adjusted to the light and she breathed in deeply. It was the first time in months she had breathed fresh air. Miriam led her carefully across a narrow path, hewn out of the massive rock through centuries of changing weather patterns and strong desert winds, mindful of the long drop to the rocky earth below. One slip would mean certain death. They came to a small natural bowl in the rock where the rainwater had collected. "You can wash yourself here," said Miriam.

Farrah hurriedly took off her rough garment and stood naked and shivering in the cool air, then carefully immersed herself in the water. A shock ran through her body as the cold water covered her. She splashed around for a moment to get used to it. After a while she began to enjoy the feel of the water on her skin; it exhilarated her. She washed the accumulated grime off herself and out of her hair as best she could with her bare hands. She didn't care that there was no expensive perfumed ointment to rub over her body; she just relished the feeling of being clean again.

She had her back to the pathway and did not know that someone was watching her bathe. She stopped washing herself when she heard a rough voice say "Leave, Miriam!" and turned her head to see ben-Ezra looking at her.

Miriam hesitated for a moment, looking first at Farrah, then back at ben-Ezra, fearful of what he might do to Farrah. But without taking his eyes off Farrah, he snarled at Miriam, "I told you to leave!"

Afraid of his anger, Miriam scurried back to the cave, leaving Farrah at the mercy of the bandit chief.

Ben-Ezra laughed as Farrah crossed her arms over her body to try to hide her nakedness. He removed the belt holding his sheathed dagger and put it on a small rock nearby, then took off his tunic and laid it on the stony path, followed by the removal of his loincloth, which he casually dropped onto the path. He reached down, grabbed Farrah under her arms and hauled her out of the water. She kicked out wildly with her feet, but he was too strong for her. He pushed her down onto the tunic, then fell on his knees beside her. She struggled to free herself, but his hands held her down. "Don't fight me," he growled.

Rebecca had seen Miriam leave with Farrah and watched as ben-Ezra had followed them. When Miriam returned alone, she became suspicious and decided to investigate. Casting Miriam aside, she left the cave and made her way along the narrow path. Hearing ben-Ezra's voice, she hid behind a rock and listened.

Ben-Ezra's eyes moved over Farrah's naked body, his unquenchable desire for her tormenting him. He spoke huskily. "I have tried to stay away from you, but even after weeks of imprisonment, you are still so beautiful. I want you so much. I must have you." He kissed her, forcing her unwilling mouth open to receive his probing tongue. He began to paw at Farrah's body, his excitement rising at each touch.

Rebecca ground her teeth in anger as she heard a stifled scream followed by the sound of ben-Ezra's grunts as he made love. That sound was all too familiar, but this time the woman was not her. She was consumed by jealousy.

When ben-Ezra had sated his lust, he lay down beside Farrah. Farrah fought to control her disgust. Hoping to save herself from further abuse, she said calmly, "Why don't you leave me alone? You have Rebecca. She too is beautiful. Is she not enough for you?"

He laughed. "Yes I have, but her beauty is no match for yours. She tastes like coarse wine compared to the sweetness of your honeyed lips. She has been well used by many men. She is damaged goods. You, the fabled Al-Maisan, lusted after by half of the men in Jerusalem, even by Herod Antipas – and the Roman," he sneered as he said 'the Roman' "you were untouched, pure. It was I who turned you into a real woman." He propped himself up on one elbow and fixed his eyes on her body as his fingers stroked her chilled flesh. "I have been thinking for some time. I can make money on your servant, she's pretty enough and if her baby survives... well, that gives me double the price. But I have changed my mind about you. You belong to me. I will not sell you – I will keep you for myself. In my hour of victory I want you at my side as my woman."

That statement filled Rebecca with a deep anger. He had promised that she would always be at his side. Now he was intending to replace her with this woman, this Al-Maisan.

Farrah suppressed a shudder at the thought of the dire future before her if she was forced to live with this barbarian. She stifled her panic as ben-Ezra leaned over and kissed her again.

Rebecca emerged from behind the rock, rage overwhelming her as her eyes took in the naked form of ben-Ezra kissing her rival. She could no longer control herself. She let out a cry of fury, then withdrawing her dagger, she rushed over and lunged at Farrah.

Startled, ben-Ezra turned and slapped Rebecca's hand aside before the knife reached a terrified Farrah. He jumped up and wrested the knife out of Rebecca's hand, throwing it to the ground, then gave her a vicious slap across her face, snapping her head back. She propelled herself forward and raked her nails across his throat, drawing blood. He roared in pain and in a blind fury punched Rebecca in the face. She fell to the ground, blood spurting from her broken nose.

A furious ben-Ezra turned to the cowering Farrah and growled "Get dressed!" He quickly put on his clothes, fastened his belt with its sheathed dagger then picked up Rebecca's dagger as Farrah hurriedly dressed herself. Grabbing her hand, he led her back inside.

He saw Miriam standing on the far side of the cavern talking with Ruth. Dropping Farrah's hand, he rushed over to Miriam, snarling "You bitch! It was you! You told Rebecca!" He grabbed her arm. Ruth tried to defend Miriam, but ben-Ezra roughly pushed her aside.

"I swear I said nothing to Rebecca," Miriam wailed, struggling to get away from him.

"How else would she know where I was?" Ben-Ezra increased the pressure on her arm, making her cry out.

"She must have seen you follow Farrah and me outside, then when I returned alone, she guessed that…" Miriam didn't finish her sentence. A maddened ben-Ezra drew his dagger and plunged it into her body. She screamed, clutched her stomach and fell to the floor. Farrah and Ruth rushed to her side. Ruth, with tears of shock and horror rolling down her face, tore off a piece of her dress and tried to staunch the flow of blood.

Shocked, Farrah looked up at ben-Ezra. "Why have you done this? Why would Miriam tell Rebecca? She owes her no loyalty."

"She was lying. She must have told Rebecca." He wiped the blood off his dagger and replaced it in its sheath. "I intended killing Miriam anyway; today, tomorrow. Who cares? She'd outlived her usefulness and had become a burden to me. Don't waste your time with her. She's not worth it." He turned and walked away, leaving Farrah and Ruth trying desperately to help the stricken woman.

In her pain, her vision beginning to cloud through loss of blood, Miriam reached out and took hold of Farrah and Ruth's blood-soaked hands. They leaned closer to hear her pain-racked gasp. "Do not grieve for me. I have so longed to be reunited with my husband. Soon we will be together again." The effort to speak took its toll and Miriam closed her eyes, exhausted.

Rachel looked at Miriam and sneered, "Good riddance," then said, "what did he mean, she must have told Rebecca? Told her what?" She looked around "Where is Rebecca?"

"She's outside by the rock pool," said Farrah angrily. Rachel marched off towards the pool. Farrah looked at Ruth, who was inconsolable. She took Miriam's cold hand into her own and whispered words of comfort to the dying woman. Miriam was the only one who had shown any kindness to her and Ruth.

Rachel was shocked when she saw Rebecca crouching by the pool, tears streaming down her face. She was washing away the blood which flowed from her broken nose with the cool water. Rachel went to her and knelt by her side. "Rebecca, what's happened to you?" she said. Using the hem of her skirt, she gently wiped Rebecca's face.

Rebecca looked at her through swollen and fast-blackening eyes and gasped, "Eleazar did this to me."

Rachel was astounded at the answer "Eleazar? But I thought he loved you. Why would he do this?"

Rebecca grimaced with pain as she answered. "Because I caught him having sex with that foreign slut. I wanted to kill her, but he stopped me." She pointed to her still-bleeding nose.

Rachel tried to comfort Rebecca as best she could, but she had seen Eleazar ben-Ezra's temper get the better of him before, and again just now with Miriam, for whom he cared nothing. But with Rebecca? She had been his woman for a long time.

"He did this to you for the sake of a slave?" she said. Rebecca nodded. Rachel was lost for words. What was going on?

Now that his hot temper had cooled, ben-Ezra was worried. He knew he was in danger of losing Rebecca and more importantly, of losing her brother's support, which was vital to his plan. Somehow he had to make it up to Rebecca. He went back to the rock pool to find her.

Rebecca became aware of ben-Ezra staring at her. She turned her head and looked at him, her eyes filled with hatred. She rose to her feet and spat out, "What do you want?" She backed away as he moved towards her, arms outstretched. "Don't touch me!" she snarled through tight lips.

Rachel grew agitated. Should she stay and try to protect her friend or leave before ben-Ezra turned on her too?

Rebecca solved her dilemma by saying, "It's all right Rachel. Go back inside."

Rachel beat a hasty retreat, leaving the pair alone.

"Rebecca..." his voice was husky "I'm sorry. I didn't mean to hurt you."

"Go away!" She dabbed at her nose. "You said terrible things about me, unforgettable things. You made love to that – that whore. How could you do this to me after all we've been through together?"

His face was a mask of contrition. She let him move closer and reluctantly let him take her into his arms.

"She is like a sickness, a sickness that will be cured when she is sold," he said.

"I heard you say you were going to keep her." She pulled back from him, searching his face for his reaction. His expression became guarded. He had to convince her for the sake of his plan that she was his only love.

"I promise you Rebecca, it was only words uttered in the heat of the moment. You are my only love and I will not go near her again."

She knew he was lying, trying to placate her. She would never forgive him for the things he had said and done. For the time being she had to fool him into believing that she had forgiven him, but later she would have her revenge.

She smiled painfully. "I would kiss you, but my nose..." She dabbed at her nose again, wiping away a droplet of blood.

He breathed a sigh of relief as she laid her throbbing head against his shoulder.

It took some time for Miriam to die, and Farrah and Ruth refused to leave her side until it was over. Farrah helped Ruth to her feet. "Miriam was a kind friend to me," said Ruth through bitter tears. "She helped me. Why did she have to die like that?"

Farrah could not find the words to answer her. Instead she placed a consoling arm around Ruth's hunched shoulders and led her away from the bloody scene. Anna and the other women turned away, avoiding Farrah's eyes, and got on with their tasks.

Farrah returned later and asked Rachel what would happen to Miriam's body. "The chief will order some of the men to take her outside to be left as food for the wild animals," replied Rachel. Seeing Farrah's stricken expression, she shrugged, and added "She can't stay here and we can't take her with us. What else can he do?"

Farrah wanted to hit Rachel for her callousness. Miriam had been a kind and decent woman who deserved so much better. She controlled the anger building inside her and with a supreme effort, walked away from the gloating woman.

A little later Isaac and Reuben carried the lifeless form of Miriam out of the cave and threw her body down into the ravine below.

That night ben-Ezra slept alone. Sleep eluded Rebecca. She lay on her pallet mulling over the day's events. Ben-Ezra had been the love of her life; he had rescued her from her brother's cruel clutches. She'd thought that she was his one true love, until today. Her love for him had died the moment she'd heard him say he would throw her aside for the foreign slut. When he had hit her, it had been the final straw. Her heart was now hardened against him. She would seek a way to gain revenge. Her head still ached intolerably, but she forced herself to think of a plan to bring him down.

# CHAPTER TEN

Cornelius was in a happy mood as he walked through the
Caesarea marketplace. He had twenty-four hours' leave
from his duties at the fortress barracks, giving him time
to purchase a suitable wedding present for his adored
daughter Julia. It was only a short time now until the
Jewish Passover. Cornelius knew that very soon Governor
Pilate would be leaving Caesarea and travelling to
Jerusalem for the festival, and when that had finished, the
Governor would return to Caesarea, bringing Marcus back
with him. Marcus had reassured him that upon his return,
the marriage ceremony would go ahead.

Cornelius stopped before a shop selling fine quality
marble statues. One small figure caught his eye. It was
beautifully crafted and fashioned in the shape of the
goddess Venus accompanied by the winged god Eros. He

entered the shop. After studying the statue to make sure it was perfect, he asked the shopkeeper the price. The portly shopkeeper smiled ingratiatingly and quoted a price. Cornelius knew it was too high, but he loved the statue and knew Julia would too. It was the perfect wedding present, so he paid the merchant the price quoted and asked him to wrap it up. The shopkeeper smiled again and bowed, saying that he had a good eye and that the statue was a wonderful choice, then he wrapped the statue carefully to protect it. Cornelius left the shop with his precious package safely hidden in the leather bag slung across his shoulder.

As he walked through the marketplace he saw a small group of people standing in a sheltered corner. A man was speaking to them. As he passed by, he heard the man say something about "the Son of God, the promised Saviour." Intrigued, he stood at the back to listen. He caught the words: "Sacrificed himself for us" and "the Redeemer". The man stopped speaking and some of the group went to him, their faces beaming; the rest turned and walked away, shaking their heads. Curious, Cornelius decided to stay and speak with the man. The last of the group dispersed and the man turned to walk away, but Cornelius stopped him.

"Wait, please. I would like to speak with you." The man turned to face Cornelius, who went on, "I heard some of your story. You are obviously not a Roman, so I wondered how you knew so much about the god Mithras."

The stranger studied the Roman's face intently. "No, I

am not a Roman, and I was not speaking of Mithras. I was telling the group about Jesus, the Messiah."

Taken aback by the man's answer, Cornelius said, "But you were speaking about things connected to Mithras. I don't understand."

The stranger smiled. "You Romans have your legends. I speak of reality: I speak of the one true God and His Son, Jesus, our Lord."

Cornelius stepped back, his body suddenly rigid. "I am a Senior Centurion, and I would advise you to be careful in what you say. If you are preaching some kind of sedition, I will have you arrested."

The stranger stared him down before speaking. "Friend, I am no threat to Rome," he said. "The Lord Jesus never spoke against Rome, and neither will I. I have done nothing wrong except tell a story of love to those who would listen." He smiled. "Please let me go on my way in peace."

Cornelius let him go. He stood watching as the man walked away and thought about his words. He had always been interested in philosophy and was widely read in both Roman and foreign works. In fact he had read many scrolls copied from the religious history of the Jews. For a while now, he had given money to the local synagogue; from time to time he had even stood in the synagogue doorway listening to the Pharisee as he read from the Jewish Holy scrolls and had been fascinated by what he had heard. It had helped him to understand a little better the conquered people he lived amongst.

He remembered one of the teachings read out by the Pharisee. It was a quote from the Prophet Isaiah, something like: '...for unto us a child is born, unto us a son is given: and the government shall be upon his shoulder: and his name shall be called Wonderful, the Mighty God...' Intrigued, he had found a scroll containing this prophecy and bought it. When Tribune Flavius had come to his office, he had been reading the scroll, trying to understand the Prophet's words as he foretold the birth of a saviour sent by their God to save the Jewish Nation from their enemies, but had put the scroll back into the drawer of his desk for fear of being caught and misunderstood. Was the 'given son' this Jesus the man spoke of? If it was, that name had not appeared in any of the text. He would make it his business to find out who both the stranger and Jesus were. Pondering on the matter, he made his way home.

Philip hurried away from the marketplace. Over the past few months he had gained many converts for the Lord in Caesarea without attracting any trouble from the authorities. He hoped it would remain so. It had been a worrying moment when the Roman had unexpectedly joined his little group. Only moments before his arrival, some new converts had joined the cause; he hoped he had not put their lives in danger. Yet the Roman had not had him arrested; rather he had noticed a spark of interest in the man's eyes. Perhaps they would meet again, hopefully next time on friendlier terms.

# CHAPTER ELEVEN

Since he had been attacked at the synagogue, Saul had not returned there. Instead, he had divided his time between the homes of Jonathan and Calisto and Joseph and Alitza. Converts would come to those houses to hear him speak. But he wanted to spread the Word to a wider audience. Having been stopped from doing so dismayed and frustrated him. There was so much to do.

He had spent a restless night at Jonathan's house, tossing and turning on the sleeping mat Calisto had provided for him, anxious about what he should do. The Lord's command burned within him, but if he was not allowed to speak in public about the Lord Jesus, he would fail to deliver His message. He wrestled with the problem for a while, then made up his mind. Nothing and nobody was going to keep him from spreading the good news.

After a breakfast of goat's milk, bread and honey, Saul told Jonathan he was going to see Joseph. Jonathan nodded, adding "Remember Saul, you must take care."

Saul smiled, then left the house. As he walked, he whispered "Forgive my half-truth, Lord." He kept to the alleyways, avoiding the main roads in case he should be recognised. To keep half of his story true, he called in on Joseph and Alitza to make sure they were well.

Joseph was alone. He struggled to the door, calling out "Who's there?" When he heard Saul's voice he unbolted and opened the door, saying "Please, come in and sit down, Saul."

Saul did so. Looking around he said "Where is Alitza today?"

"She's looking after a friend who's sick," Joseph replied, sitting down heavily in his chair.

Saul decided to broach a subject he had been waiting to ask about when he knew Joseph better. "Tell me, my friend, did you ever meet Jesus?"

"Meet? Unfortunately not. When He rode into Jerusalem before Passover, Alitza and I were offering sacrifices in the Temple. We heard shouts of 'Hosanna to the Son of David'. We wondered what was going on. Then we heard someone say, 'It's Jesus.' We had heard about the miracles Jesus had performed and how He'd raised His friend, Lazarus, from the dead. There were so many other stories concerning Him and now, here He was, in Jerusalem. We were so excited. Then we heard the commotion. Someone shouted 'Jesus is overturning the money changers' tables and setting the sacrificial animals free.' Well done, I thought. We have been cheated for so many years."

"And did you get the chance to speak to Him?" Saul asked.

"No, He left the Temple area rather quickly. But, the next day, He returned to the city and we heard He was preaching in the Temple Precinct. We went there to hear Him. Alitza wanted to take me to Jesus and ask Him if He would restore my sight. There were so many people crowding around Him, we couldn't get near." He smiled. "No matter. What we heard was enough, it changed us forever. His words were as a balm to our souls." He grew serious. "For so long we Jews have suffered under the yoke of Rome. There is no hope of escape from their cruelty, but Jesus' words showed us there was another kind of freedom: freedom within our hearts and minds. If we repented and turned our faces to God, lived a just life truly believing His promises, then a better Kingdom awaited us."

Saul could see by Joseph's expression that he was reliving those past days. He himself had heard about the raising of Lazarus and the other miracles, but at the time, as a young student Pharisee, he had dismissed them as ruses to gain the popularity of simple-minded people. Over the years, there had been so many pretenders claiming to be the 'Messiah' and all had met a violent end. At the time, he was not surprised that Jesus Himself had met the same fate.

"When we heard He had been arrested and put on trial, we couldn't believe it," said Joseph, his voice tinged with sadness. "Then came the news that He had been crucified. We refused to believe it was over. Surely such love could never die. A few weeks later, we discovered that Jesus' Disciples were preaching that He had been resurrected from the dead. Something must have happened to make them even think about saying such a dangerous thing. Then came reports that they were openly speaking in the Temple Precinct and at the Pool of Siloam. If it wasn't true, why would they endanger themselves?" He took a deep breath. "We began to hear rumours about the High Priests plotting vengeance on those who believe in Jesus."

"Is that why you came to Damascus, to escape them?" Saul felt a wave of guilt go through him.

"Yes. So too did many of our friends, including our old neighbours Abigail and Simeon. Then the stories began about you. News of Stephen's death and of the terrible persecution you were conducting against the converts came to Damascus, told by visiting Jewish merchants. That's when we first met Jonathan and Calisto. Jonathan was one of those merchants who decided to make a new home here. When we heard you were on your way to Damascus, we were afraid you would arrest us and have us killed too." He sighed. "We felt safe here, but we know now that the High Priests will never give up their relentless persecution of the followers of Jesus. If only they could see the truth as you have."

Saul felt uncomfortable and decided to make an excuse to leave. As he stood up, Joseph said in a kindly voice: "You will always be welcome here, friend Saul."

As Saul left the house, he felt deeply ashamed. These were good people, as he was sure were many of the others he had terrorized and imprisoned. Now, weeks later, Joseph and Alitza had forgiven him and had made their former persecutor welcome in their house.

Walking along the road, he suddenly saw some patrolling Damascus Guards coming his way. He quickly hid in a doorway until they had passed by. Then, making sure the road was clear, he walked on.

Elias was walking through the marketplace, as he did every day, searching for Saul of Tarsus. He stopped at a merchant's stall pretending to look through the merchandise like any other would-be buyer, but all the time he was watching out for Saul and listening to snippets of conversation. Standing close by, two women, one young, the other older, were looking at another stall. They were speaking in hushed voices, but Elias had superb hearing and caught some of the conversation between the two women. What he overheard made him smile grimly. He caught Saul's name. As the two women parted he heard the older one say in a normal voice, "I hope Joseph is well, Alitza." Then the reply: "My father is very well, thank you Abigail. Do come and visit us. You know where we live: it's the house with the black door in Spice Street."

Elias watched as the women walked off in different directions. He had three names and an address. Surely the Pharisee or someone from the synagogue would know who these people were. When he knew, he would take action. He hurried off in the direction of the synagogue.

Saul walked to a different part of the city and entered the synagogue for that district. He listened attentively to the Pharisee as he read from the scriptures and intoned prayers, then, when the Pharisee had finished, Saul decided it was time for him to speak. He looked around the room, wondering what his reception would be. He did not have long to wait. As soon as he began to tell of his conversion and his belief that Jesus was the One mentioned in the old scriptures, the atmosphere changed.

When he spoke of his intention to spread the good news of the risen Jesus, the congregation reacted angrily. One of them cried out, "This is the blaspheming trouble-maker we have been told about." He was answered by a chorus of "Blasphemer!"

The Pharisee approached Saul and said sternly, "You are a disgrace! Leave this Holy place!"

On the Pharisee's instruction, Saul was bodily removed from the place of worship and once outside, vicious blows were aimed at his face and body. One man swore as he ripped Saul's headdress off and violently punched him in the side of his head.

The High Priests' agents, who happened to be passing through that side of the city, saw the disturbance and were curious to know what was happening. They approached the scene and asked a member of the congregation, who replied, "This man Saul is a blasphemer and a liar. We don't want him in our synagogue". Alerted by the name, they looked at the man lying in a heap on the ground being kicked and punched and saw that it was indeed the one they had been searching for. They wrestled the angry men off Saul and seized him. He would have been arrested there and then, or beaten to death, had not the Damascus Guard patrol marched around the corner opposite the synagogue.

Seeing the disturbance, the guard officer leading the patrol shouted at the mob, but they carried on beating Saul. The officer ordered his men to draw their swords and at his order, the patrol moved forward. Realising their own lives were in danger, the mob, including the Jewish agents, dispersed and ran away, leaving a battered Saul lying on the ground.

The Damascus Guard officer looked down at Saul and said in a gruff voice, "I don't know what this is all about but I would advise you to go home immediately, while you still can."

Saul breathed a sigh of relief. The guard obviously did not know who he was. He winced as he looked up at the officer and tried to stand. His legs were like jelly. He was grateful when the officer proffered a hand to help him up. "Thank you," he struggled to say through swollen and bleeding lips

"Now, be off with you before I change my mind and have you arrested for causing a disturbance," said the guard.

Saul wanted to say, "What about the men who assaulted me?" but he thought better of it. Instead he nodded and slowly made his way back to Jonathan's house.

Jonathan was appalled at seeing Saul in such a state and when Saul said it had been a Guard patrol that had saved his life he grimaced. "That's it! You must leave Damascus. It's bad enough the Jewish authorities are after you, but now the Damascus authorities have got involved too. You were lucky the guard officer didn't know who you were. You may not be so lucky next time. It's too dangerous for you now, and for us too. We'll make a plan to get you out of the city."

Saul frowned. "How? Every gate's being watched, how can I escape?"

Jonathan thought for a moment. "I'll speak with Joseph and some of our other friends. Together, we will find a way."

The next morning Alitza answered a knock on the door, thinking it was Abigail come to visit her. She was thrown aside as Elias, Jacob and some of the Temple guards burst into the house. Joseph was pulled roughly out of his chair as Jacob grabbed Alitza and roughly held on to her.

"By order of the High Priests in Jerusalem, you are under arrest. You're coming with us." Elias crowed proudly.

As they left the house, a gruff voice said "Who are you? What are you doing?"

Elias turned in shock to see an officer of the Damascus guards looking at him, his armed men arrayed around him.

"This is Jerusalem Temple business and none of yours," Elias said defiantly.

The officer smiled grimly. "I am Azif, Captain of the Damascus Guards. What goes on in this city is my business. You are coming with us." He waved dismissively to the Temple guards. "Go away! You are not needed." The guards, outnumbered, did not argue and walked away.

A little later, Jonathan went to Joseph's house. He knocked on the door, but there was no answer. He knocked louder and the door swung open. He entered the house, wondering why there was no one at home. He looked around and saw overturned chairs and a broken table. The garment Alitza had been sewing was discarded in a heap on the floor. Who had done this? It could not have been a burglar, for they had nothing of any value to steal. Dread ran through his veins. Had they been arrested? He looked down the street carefully, and satisfied that no one was watching, he fled from the house.

The Governor of Damascus sat on his official chair in the audience chamber of the Governor's residence. Standing before him was Captain Azif, with his guards surrounding him, while Elias and Jacob waited at the back of the room with their prisoners Joseph and Alitza. The Governor called for the prisoners to be brought up. Elias and Jacob ushered them forward. The Governor stared haughtily at the old blind man and the beautiful young girl.

"I understand from this man," he pointed to Elias, "that both of you have been charged with blasphemy and that you are friends of Saul of Tarsus, who has been spreading lies about a traitor called Jesus of Nazareth. What have you got to say for yourselves?"

Joseph knew their situation was grave, but he answered proudly with no fear in his voice, "Yes, we are followers of the Lord Jesus. Have we done you harm or caused harm to anybody else, sir?"

The Governor narrowed his eyes "Every word you speak is harmful. Don't you realise that ideas such as yours can lead to insurrection? I have already been informed about the disturbances in the city synagogues." He looked at Elias. "Who is this Saul of Tarsus I hear so many complaints about?"

Before Elias could answer, Joseph intervened. "He spreads the news of love and forgiveness, Governor, as directed by our Lord and Master. It's something we try to follow."

The Governor bristled. "The only lord and master in Damascus is the King of Nabatea, King Aretas. We have enough of our own deities without adding a troublemaker's twisted view of yet another new religion to the list. He looked sternly at Elias and Jacob. "I'm told that these men have been sent here by your Jewish High Priests to search for people like you, arrest you and take you back to Jerusalem." He grimaced. "Well, let me tell you, your High Priests have no jurisdiction here."

Elias protested, "But, Governor, all synagogues come under the jurisdiction of the Temple in Jerusalem, it is the High Priests' right to ensure..."

"Silence!" The Governor glared at Elias and shouted, "King Aretas graciously allows the synagogues the freedom to practice your religion here in his territory. If I report to him that your religion has begun to cause trouble in Damascus, he will shut the synagogues down and have all Jews removed from his Kingdom." He turned his attention back to Joseph and Alitza. "As the King's representative, I am in charge here. I have the power to arrest you, or set you free. So if you know the whereabouts of Saul of Tarsus, you must tell me where he is."

Joseph did not like to lie, but knew that in this case he had to for Saul's sake. He shook his head. "We have not seen him for some days, sir. We don't know where he is."

"You had better be telling me the truth old man, or it will be the worse for you."

Alitza raised her beautiful eyes and looked directly at the Governor. "Sir, my father is telling the truth. Please believe us when we say we truly mean no harm to you, the King or anyone else. We just wish to live here peacefully. My father is blind and reaching the end of his life. Have you ever had cause to arrest him for a disturbance or for not paying our taxes?"

The Governor knew he had never seen the two prisoners before. He would certainly have remembered the girl, as she was stunning. He rose out of his chair and stepped towards Alitza, looking her up and down appreciatively. "Such a young beauty as you should not be bothering her pretty head with religion. You were made for much better things."

Joseph pulled Alitza closer to him. "Have pity, sir. She is all I have. Please don't harm her."

"You dare to speak to me like that?" The Governor lashed out and slapped Joseph across the face. Joseph reeled from the impact. "I am the authority here and I will do as I please. Now, I will ask you for the last time, where is Saul of Tarsus?"

"I repeat sir, we do not know where he is, or even if he is still in Damascus."

"Then you leave me no alternative." The Governor motioned to one of the guards standing at attention nearby. "Take the girl to my private rooms." He called another guard and pointed to Joseph. "Take this old man to the cells. Give him a small portion of bread and enough water every day to keep him alive. I don't want him to die too soon."

"Father!" Looking back once, she sobbed as the guard led her away.

The Governor beckoned Elias and Jacob forward. "From now on you will work for me. Forget your priests in Jerusalem. If you make any further arrests, you will bring the criminals here to me. Is that understood?"

"Yes, my Lord," Elias replied, his voice quaking.

Alitza was taken to the Governor's private quarters and left with his female servants, who would prepare her for the Governor's pleasure. As Joseph was roughly led to the cells below the audience chamber, he uttered whispered prayers, not for himself but for his daughter, who he knew would soon be savagely used.

Joseph's right hand wrist and right ankle were chained to the wall. The position of the chains meant he was unable to sit or kneel. His old legs were weak and he wondered how long he could stand before his body gave up. His blindness prevented him from seeing his surroundings, but every so often, his ears picked up the sounds of anguished cries. He wondered who was making those agonized sounds. He hoped they were not from other converts. His body might be weak, but his spirit? Never. He would pray and ask the Lord to forgive the Governor. After all, didn't Jesus forgive His tormentors, even as He suffered unspeakable agonies of torture and death on the cross?

Alitza sat on a silken couch in the Governor's private bedroom, fear coursing through her body. The servant girls had told her how lucky she was to have caught the Governor's eye, but she did not feel lucky. They had bathed her and washed her hair in scented water, then massaged her body with expensive oils until her skin shone. Lastly they had applied perfumes to her neck and breasts, their fragrance so strong they had given her a headache. After this she had been dressed in a blue silken robe, her face had been painted and her hair dressed in an elaborate style. It seemed to her that the servants had prepared her as a sacrificial gift to one of their idols.

She suddenly froze as she saw the Governor framed in the doorway. He clapped his hands and the servants giggled, bowed and left the room.

He approached the couch, saying appreciatively "You are so beautiful, my dear." He sat by her side. She moved along the couch away from him. He slid alongside her.

"Now, now," he said silkily, "there's no need to be afraid. I am told I am a competent lover. I'm sure we will enjoy each other."

Horrified, Alitza cried out "You will never possess me. What you are doing is a sin."

The Governor laughed out loud. "A sin? Who says so? Surely not your Lord and Master? Anyway, who cares what He would think, the man's dead. He can't save you now, my beauty." She screamed as he moved closer to her, breathing heavily. As his hands touched her, she fainted with shock. Furious, he said "What's this? Don't think you can fool me. I will have you!" He lunged at her.

When Alitza regained consciousness she looked around the room. The Governor had gone. At first she was mercifully unaware of what had happened to her. She wondered why she felt such a nagging pain inside of her, then looked down and saw blood on her dress and on the couch. She cried out in anger and humiliation as she realised it was her blood. Desperate tears began to fall, and she vowed he would never touch her again.

It was two days later that he returned to her. She steeled herself for what she was about to do. As he moved to touch her, she got up and moved to the other side of the room.

"Ah! Playing games are we, my sweet?" He laughed and followed her. "Is this to heighten my desire for you? When I catch you I promise you, you won't be disappointed. I know I won't be. I understand that the first time for a woman, especially one as young as you, can be awkward, but we are surely past that now. This is where pleasure will take over from pain and fear." He reached out to her and she backed away from him. He grew angry "Don't try my patience, I don't have time for this!"

His frustration and anger grew as she continued to move away from him until, his patience spent, he caught up with her and grabbed her by the throat. His eyes narrowed as she continued to defy him. "You will submit to me."

"You could have let my father and I live a quiet life worshipping the Lord Jesus, but you cannot bear the thought that the love of Jesus far transcends your own vile ways," she replied. "You have mocked the Lord, but I forgive you for what you have done to me, and I pray the Lord will forgive you too." Alitza looked into his maddened eyes and said defiantly "I will never give myself freely to you."

The Governor was beside himself with rage. He shouted, "Then I will take what is mine!"

He threw her to the floor, placing his forearm over her

throat so she could not escape. As he reached the heights of passion his arm pressed down more heavily. Oblivious to everything except his own pleasure, he did not realise that he was crushing her windpipe. At last, passion spent, he said, "There, that wasn't so bad was it?"

There was no answer. He looked at her; there was no movement. He removed his arm from across her throat and realised what he had done. He stared at the lifeless body for a moment, then stood up and adjusted his clothing. He called for a guard.

The guard entered the room, trying to keep his eyes from the obviously dead girl laying on the ornate floor.

"Get another guard, fetch a large piece of cloth and come back here," the Governor said sternly.

The guard saluted and soon returned, holding a large piece of material, together with a second guard following on behind. The Governor barked out "Get rid of this corpse! And say nothing about this, or else!" Then he turned away as together, the guards wrapped Alitza in the cloth and carried her out of the room.

The Governor sighed. What a pity she had been so difficult. He would have enjoyed making love to her for far longer, or at least until someone else caught his eye.

With that thought he left the room and returned to the audience chamber, ready to meet with a delegation of merchants from Arabia.

When Joseph heard his cell door being opened, he thought it was the guard bringing his daily ration of bread and water. He was growing weaker by the day and ever more worried about what was happening to his beloved Alitza. But it was not the guard's voice he heard.

The Governor stood before the old man, holding a perfumed cloth to his nose. He wanted to give his message and leave as soon as possible, as the smell of the cells always made him nauseous. His voice was cold as he said, "Your daughter is dead."

Joseph could not speak, so great was his shock.

"Have you nothing to say, old man?" He laughed cruelly "Don't you want to know how she died?"

Joseph found his voice. He spoke through cracked lips "What did you do to her?"

"She disobeyed me and I couldn't have that, so I killed her. She seemed to think more of this Jesus you worship than anything I could offer her. She could have had riches, you know. I would have showered rubies and emeralds on her to enhance her beauty. Instead..." – he shrugged – "a great pity that." He turned away, eager to be gone, but a last cruel thought struck him. He wanted to see the old man utterly destroyed. "Oh, by the way. I enjoyed her twice. She was not a virgin when she died. I know how that must upset you to know that, especially a man of your beliefs."

With a wave of his perfumed hand, the Governor said "Goodbye, Joseph. I shan't see you again. You will be joining your daughter soon and maybe you'll both be with your *Lord*." He spoke the last word with sarcastic emphasis. His laughter rang through the dungeon.

When the Governor had left the cell, Joseph broke down in tears. He had nothing left to live for now. Through his tears, he prayed, "Please Lord Jesus, accept my dear Alitza into your loving care." Suffering grief, shock and with a worn-out body, Joseph knew he would not last much longer.

Outside the dungeon, the Governor issued orders to his guards. "Find Saul of Tarsus and bring him to me. When I have finished questioning him, you will kill him."

Elias had been busy. He had been watching every day in the marketplace for Abigail to return. When she did, he would follow her to her home. Today was his lucky day.

He watched as she purchased her goods and then, keeping his distance, he followed her. Now he knew where this friend of Saul lived, he would return with some guards and arrest her. How grateful the High Priests would be when he led these foolish people back to Jerusalem in chains. He did not know that the Governor had no intention of returning the converts to Jerusalem and had his own plans for them.

That afternoon, Elias and the Damascus guards descended on Abigail's house and forced their way inside. Elias rubbed his hands together in satisfaction, for there were several people sitting together there. Taken by surprise, Abigail's husband, Simeon, muttered, "Save us, Lord Jesus!" That was all the proof Elias needed. "Take them to the Governor," he ordered.

In his cell, Joseph heard a commotion and women screaming. He heard a guard's rough voice and other voices pleading for mercy coming from the corridor outside of his cell. Was that Alitza's friend Abigail? And Simeon? There were several other voices he recognised. So they had been discovered and arrested too. Would this persecution never end? Some of them were young and had their lives before them; he knew he was dying and would soon be free of this horror, but those poor souls... he wondered what would become of them.

He raised his eyes heavenward and prayed: "Lord, there is so much wickedness. When will your Kingdom come? Forgive the Governor's hatred of you. I pray that one day he will come to know and acknowledge your love. I pray too for Saul, Abigail, Simeon and your other followers. I truly believe that my darling daughter is with you, as I hope to be soon. I love you, Lord Jesus. Do not forget me."

Soon after, worn out by grief, physical and mental suffering, death came to Joseph. It was a blessed release.

News of Abigail and Simeon's arrest, along with some of their friends, soon spread amongst the remaining converts. They were worried about Joseph and Alitza too. Nothing had been heard from them for days. Jonathan had told them about their mysterious disappearance and the state of their house, but everyone was afraid to ask too many questions and put themselves in danger as well.

Jonathan was anxious for the safety of his wife Calisto. He gently placed his hands on her shoulders and looking deep into her eyes, he said "We must leave Damascus." As she made to protest, Jonathan's voice became firmer. "If you want to live, we have to leave."

"But what about Saul? We can't abandon him."

"Don't worry about Saul. I have spoken with Ananias and some other coverts. It has been decided. He will leave Damascus tonight."

"But how, Jonathan? How will you get him safely out of the city? You know that everywhere is being watched."

"Be calm, Calisto, everything is planned. I promise you he will be gone soon, and so will we."

# CHAPTER TWELVE

Jonathan, Calisto and Saul made their way cautiously along the dark street. Jonathan hoped that Mordecai, his friend and fellow convert, would not let them down. Mordecai had lived in Damascus all his life. He had been converted to the new religion by Ananias and strongly believed in the Lord Jesus. He had visited Jonathan's house and heard Saul speak and had been swept away by Saul's words and zeal. He had told Jonathan how amazed he was that someone like Saul, who had been an instrument of terror to the converts, had suddenly begun to praise the Lord he had once condemned. Something had surely happened on Saul's journey to Damascus to bring such a drastic change in him.

Mordecai was a respected wine merchant whose shop backed on to the wall that surrounded Damascus. Because of his trade, he owned many baskets, including some that could carry large supplies of wine. When Jonathan had approached him and asked if he could use one of the larger baskets, Mordecai was curious. What could he possibly want with such an item?

All had become clear when Jonathan had explained to him the basket's purpose. At first Mordecai was hesitant, but he finally agreed to help when Jonathan told him it was imperative for the safety of all of them to get Saul out of Damascus.

"Even out of the city, Saul will still be in danger," said Jonathan. "On foot he will not cover many miles before the guards catch up with him."

Mordecai hesitated, his mind considering a solution. He suddenly smiled and said, "A caravan arrived from Nabatea a few days ago. The leader has been my trading friend for years, and I know that for the right price, he will carry out my instructions. I'll send one of my men to him with a bag of money and ask him to carry out my request."

So Mordecai sent one of his men to the oasis where the caravan was sited. He had given the man a sum of money which he knew the caravan leader would not refuse, with the instruction to take Saul all the way to their destination in Nabatea. The leader was satisfied with the amount and agreed, but issued a warning: "The caravan must leave tomorrow morning. Make sure the person in question is here before then."

When told of this, Mordecai frowned; that would leave him very little time to prepare. He turned to his man and said "Go to Jonathan and tell him we must get Saul away tonight."

The man hurried to Jonathan and told him what the caravan leader had said. Jonathan gathered together Calisto and Saul and told them the disturbing news.

As Jonathan, Calisto and Saul were approaching Mordecai's shop, Jonathan signalled to the others to stop. He had spotted a faint glimmer in the distance. Torchlight! And it was advancing towards them. "Quick," he hissed, "a patrol!" The three of them ran down a nearby alley, away from the oncoming guards. The men held their breath, sweating in fear. Calisto thought she might faint with terror. Jonathan, sensing her panic, held her closely to him. If they should get caught with Saul, the punishment meted out would be dreadful. The patrol passed by without seeing them, and Jonathan let out a sigh. He raised his eyes heavenward and whispered "Thank you, Lord."

Soon they saw Mordecai's shop. After looking around to make sure the way was clear, they hurried towards it and knocked on the sturdy door, which was cautiously opened. They went inside to find Mordecai and two other men, who they knew were also followers of Jesus, waiting for them. In the middle of the room stood a large basket. Saul held his breath as a third man stepped out from a shadowy corner of the room. The man lowered his hood and Saul breathed a sigh of relief; it was Ananias.

"Were you followed?" Ananias asked anxiously. He was relieved when Saul shook his head and said "No."

Ananias put his hand on Saul's shoulder. "I wanted to see you, Saul, before you leave Damascus," he said gravely. He saw Saul's worried look and smiled. "I know you are afraid, but you have come this far and will go on to do great things, I am sure of it. Trust in the Lord, He will take care of you." Ananias and Saul embraced.

Mordecai pointed to the basket and said to the gathering, "If we are discovered and the guards should ask, I have already thought of a plan for what to say to them. I think it will be a perfect cover for our little adventure." He looked at Saul. "Saul, you will easily fit into that." Ananias stood back as Mordecai gestured to Saul to get into the basket. Making his final farewells, Saul quickly climbed into it. Once he was inside the basket, Jonathan fixed a cover over the top of it, carefully securing it.

One of the men went to the front of the shop, looking to see if there was any activity outside. He came back into the room and told Mordecai all was clear.

Jonathan spoke quietly to Calisto. "Stay in the house, my love."

"Be careful, Jonathan," came her worried reply.

Ananias came and stood by her side. "I will stay with her, Jonathan."

Jonathan thanked Ananias. Then he, Mordecai and the other two men lifted the basket and carefully carried it out and placed it with other baskets already waiting on the ground in front of the wall, guarded by another of Mordecai's trusty workers.

Saul's basket was the first to be readied for lowering over the wall. The four men pulled ropes through the woven handles at each of the four corners of the basket and holding the ropes tightly, they picked the basket up and carefully lowered it over the wall to where a cart and three men were waiting. The basket slowly descended to the ground and the trio lifted it onto the cart.

Mordecai knew how long the two guards patrolling the wall usually took to complete a circuit. Now he could see them in the distance walking in opposite directions. Good – if they hurried, Saul would be away before the guards returned.

He failed to see someone else approaching from a different direction. He froze as he felt a hand on his shoulder and heard a gruff voice say, "You're working late tonight, Mordecai."

Mordecai quickly suppressed his fear and said in a calm voice "I didn't expect to see you at this time of night, Captain Azif. You're out late aren't you?"

"Yes. Too late as far as I'm concerned!" He pointed to more guards, who were making their way towards them. "I've been ordered by the Governor to carry out extra patrols," he growled, obviously annoyed at having to do extra duties. "The Governor's spitting nails about this Saul of Tarsus. We've been told to keep our eyes open and if we spot him we have to arrest him and take him straight to the Governor." He saw Jonathan, stared at him suspiciously and said "You deal in cloth, not wine. What are you doing here?"

Jonathan tried hard to keep his voice from trembling. He swallowed, then spoke evenly. "This order has to be delivered quickly. Mordecai needed extra manpower, so he asked for my help."

Azif seemed content with that answer. He looked at the baskets arrayed on the ground. "Anything special going on?"

For a moment Mordecai felt a cold stab of fear, but he remembered his plan and regained his confidence. "It's a special delivery ordered by King Aretas," he said in a calm voice. "The King sent a message with the caravan that arrived the other day. The King is holding a feast for some important people and wanted my best wine delivered to him as soon as possible. As he and the Governor are both my patrons, I could hardly refuse." He was thinking on his feet. "The last time I sent His Majesty a consignment I made the mistake of waiting for the city gates to open. There were so many people coming in and going out of the city it took an age to get the cart out. The King refused to pay me as the delivery was late. I vowed I would not make that mistake again. So, my carter is going to deliver this particular order directly to the caravan waiting at the oasis nearby, before it leaves later this morning."

The Captain nodded, but then he looked over the wall

and saw the cart below and the three men waiting with it. Looking back at Mordecai, he suddenly said in a menacing voice, "Open the cover, I want to see what's inside. We can't be too careful these days, there are too many troublemakers about."

Mordecai gestured to one of his helpers to take the cover off. He stood motionless as Captain Azif peered inside and poked about with his sword. Mordecai protested. "Please, be careful, I don't want the contents damaged."

Azif stopped poking around. "It's as you say Mordecai, nothing but wine," he said. "But to be on the safe side, let's take a look at that one too." He pointed to where a second basket stood, already covered. He went over to it and repeated his actions, then did the same with a third one. Satisfied, he said to one of his guards, "It seems there's nothing to worry about here. This one's full of wine jars too." He turned to Mordecai. "Sorry for the delay, but orders are orders." Then to his guards, "We'd better start patrolling again, we don't want to get into any trouble with the Governor." They stood ready to march off.

All four men watched Azif and his guards march away to resume their patrol in another part of the city. They waited a while, then, satisfied that the guards were too far away to see their actions, Mordecai and Jonathan looked over the wall and watched the cart with its precious cargo pull away and the men who had helped load Saul onto the cart disappear into the shadows. Relieved, they carried the baskets containing the wine back into the house.

The carter caught up with the waiting caravan at the oasis. The carter, helped by one of the caravan drovers, opened the cover of Saul's basket. Saul joyfully breathed in the cool air as the two men helped him out of the basket. They took him to the caravan leader, whose name was Abdullah.

Abdullah smiled at Saul, showing large white teeth, then said jovially, "Welcome, my friend. When Mordecai's man came to see me with his proposition, he told me that you are wanted by the Governor of Damascus." His smile widened as Saul nodded. "Any enemy of the Governor is a friend of mine. That arrogant man has always treated me as no more than a humble slave, ignoring my importance, so I am very happy to take you to Nabatea. This is my revenge on him."

Abdullah looked at Saul's turban and said "Hmm... too small. You will need a larger head covering." He ordered the drover to bring a more suitable headscarf to him. The drover returned with a large piece of material. "Take this." Abdullah held out the head covering to Saul and demonstrated how to wrap it around his head and neck as protection from the fierce sun, adding "Pull the bottom of the material across the lower part of your face to hide your features." Then he added, "Have you ever ridden a camel before?" He was not surprised when Saul shook his head. "I thought not. Well now is your chance to learn. I have a spare camel just for you." He grinned at the look of horror on Saul's face as he and the drover led him to the chosen camel.

The drover issued a command to the camel and the animal sank down onto its belly. He then showed Saul how to climb onto the camel's back. Saul was unnerved by the animal's size and the way it turned its head and stared haughtily at him. He had never been so close to one before and, at first, he kept his distance. Spurred on by the drover's laughter and feeling embarrassed by it, he clumsily mounted the camel's back. With a tap of his stick on the camel's flanks, the drover commanded the camel to stand. As its large, wide feet splayed out on the sand, Saul lurched to the side. Fearing he might fall to the ground, he desperately clung to the saddle. At another command from the laughing drover, the camel stood still and Saul settled into his saddle.

Highly amused, Abdullah spoke to the drover. "You will travel close behind our guest, make sure he doesn't fall off." He then looked at Saul and said "My drover is a good, experienced man, he will take care of you and will ask no questions." He knew his caravan drovers and guards would not ask questions as to who this stranger might be for fear of losing their jobs.

Hearing Abdullah's command to make ready for their journey home, the carter said "Mordecai has one last request."

Abdullah raised an eyebrow. "What is it?"

"He asks if you will take the basket with you. You see, Mordecai is worried that bringing one empty basket back into Damascus might arouse the suspicion of the gate guards."

"That is not a problem," Abdullah replied. "I will find a use for it."

The carter lowered it to the ground. A drover was summoned by Abdullah, who ordered it to be fixed to one of the camels. As his order was being carried out, Abdullah turned to the carter and said "Tell Mordecai I thank him for his generous payment and I will see him the next time I come to Damascus." Making sure all was ready, Abdullah climbed onto his camel then gave the order for the caravan to begin its journey.

Pleased that the job he'd been given had so far been trouble free, the carter climbed up onto the cart and made his way back to Damascus to tell Mordecai that his daring venture had been carried out successfully.

Relieved to be safely back in their own home, Jonathan and Calisto were too nervous and excited to sleep. When Jonathan had told Calisto his plan, he had seen fear and anxiety in her eyes, but after he had stressed the danger of what might happen if they remained in Damascus, she nodded in understanding.

As early morning light appeared in the sky, Jonathan and Calisto left their house for the last time and went to their shop. They loaded their cart with all the good quality cloth they possessed, hiding it beneath the cart's loose boards, then placed on top of the boards a basket of food and wine. This, he hoped, would help them to begin a new life, with new trading possibilities elsewhere. Jonathan locked up their shop. He didn't care who might take over the empty place as he had no intention of ever returning to Damascus.

He had concealed some money in his tunic and, smiling at Calisto, he helped her on to the cart, then climbed up beside her. He urged the mule on and the animal pulled the cart down the empty street. They were amongst the first to go through the morning's newly-opened northern city gates. They had decided that if the guards on duty at the gate should ask where they were going, they would say they were going to visit Calisto's sick mother, who lived in a village north of the city. The basket of food and wine was for her. He hoped Captain Azif would not be on duty. Fortunately he wasn't, and the guards on the gates let them through without asking any questions.

Once on the open road, Jonathan took Calisto's hand and said, "We got out safely. Now we will begin our journey to Antioch."

"Antioch is so far away," Calisto said anxiously.

Jonathan sensed her fear and squeezed her hand. "We must put our trust in the Lord," he said.

She looked at him, saying in a small voice "I hope Saul is safe."

"I'm sure he is," he said, trying to sound reassuring, and then more confidently, "He has already suffered so much and come through it. I know the Lord will not desert him now, and who knows, perhaps one day we will see him again."

The mule plodded on slowly, and at last they left the city and all of its bad memories behind.

Saul said a silent prayer of thanks as the caravan travelled along the highway. At first the camel's movement made him feel as though he was on a ship being tossed about in the middle of a stormy sea, but as he gradually adjusted to the camel's rhythm, the sickness passed. He was relieved at that, yet still anxiety pulsed through him: he had no idea what awaited him in Nabatea. He only knew he had to put his trust in his Lord.

A few days later, the Governor of Damascus ordered Azif and the other troops who had been guarding the city into his audience chamber. His face was grim as he said: "Has there been any sign of Saul of Tarsus?"

Azif looked sheepish. "No, Governor, sir. We don't know where he is. We have watched the gates by day and night, he has not passed us. We've searched most of the households in the city, to no avail."

"He has escaped you, hasn't he?" The Governor leaned forward in his chair.

Azif could not look at him. "I don't know how, sir. As I said, we have kept watch day and night."

The Governor's face grew red with anger. He said menacingly, "I will give you and the guards who patrol with you until tomorrow morning. If you have not brought him to me by then, you will be executed. Do I make myself clear?"

Azif was so terrified that he could not speak. Instead he saluted the Governor, gestured to his men to follow him and together they marched out of the audience chamber, halting abruptly when the Governor bellowed "Send that useless Elias to me. Now!"

The Governor rose out of his seat and walked around a nervous Elias, looking him up and down disdainfully.

"It seems you have failed me and your masters in Jerusalem by not capturing Saul of Tarsus," he said. Elias had begun to protest, but he was quickly silenced. "I have had enough of you and your irritating religious fanatics! You will return to Jerusalem and tell the High Priests that Saul has managed to slip through your fingers. I will let them deal with you. Leave this city now. And take those other agents and Temple Guard morons with you. Now get out of my sight, before I change my mind and have you all killed!"

The next morning, as Elias, Jacob, the Temple Guards and the other agents of the High Priests began their journey back to Jerusalem, Azif, Captain of the Damascus Guard, was taken to the market square and publicly executed.

# CHAPTER THIRTEEN

It had been a long, tedious meeting of the Sanhedrin and Caiaphas and Annas were not in the best of moods. The sun was high in the sky when they left the Council Chamber and returned to Caiaphas' house. As they sat speaking of the morning's debates and arguments, a servant came to tell them that the Captain of the Temple Guard wished an audience with them.

"Ah," said Caiaphas expectantly, "perhaps he has brought Saul back with him. Send him in." The servant bowed and left the room. Shortly after, he returned with the Captain. Caiaphas and Annas sat staring at the Captain. Flanked by two other guards, he stood head bowed before them.

"Well, where is Saul of Tarsus?"

"I don't know, Lord Caiaphas."

Caiaphas leaned forward in his chair "You don't know?"

"I questioned those of my men who had accompanied Elias to Damascus to find Saul. They believed Elias' story about Saul's sudden blindness..." He hesitated.

Caiaphas picked up on this. "There's more, isn't there?"

The Captain could not look at the High Priests as he answered with undisguised anxiety, "Elias and Jacob are waiting outside my Lords, if you will permit, I think it's best the story comes from them."

"Very well," Caiaphas agreed, "bring Jacob in first, we will hear what he has to say."

The Captain escorted Jacob into the room. Jacob stood before the High Priests, wondering nervously what their reaction would be to his story. Prompted by Caiaphas, he said, "My lords, as arranged, Saul was taken to the lodging house in Straight Street where he stayed in his room, not leaving it because he was blind and ill. We went out into the city every day searching for converts, returning at night. Saul was still where we had left him on his sleeping mat." He swallowed, fearing the reprisal he knew would come. "Until the evening of the third day. When we returned to the lodging house, Saul had gone."

"Gone? Gone where?" Annas asked incredulously.

"We don't know, my lord." Jacob could not look at him.

Caiaphas and Annas exchanged glances and Annas leaned forward. "What are you doing here? Surely you should be in Damascus doing the job you were sent to do. And where are the converts you promised to bring back in chains?"

Jacob thought his treatment was unfair. None of this was his fault. Elias, as leader of the agents, should take responsibility for this failure. "My Lord High Priests, Elias is waiting outside. He is the best man to explain the circumstances to you."

"Bring Elias in," came Caiaphas' curt reply.

Elias was ushered in. He stood, head bowed, before his masters. When asked the same question, Elias, seeking to distance himself from Jacob's story, raised his head and said "Of course my Lord, when all of this took place I was here with you. Had I been there this might not have happened. I..."

Caiaphas' voice was sharp. "No excuses, Elias! You are just as culpable."

Suitably chastised, Elias humbled his tone and said "My Lords, none of us knew where Saul had gone, but several days ago, Jacob brought some irate members of one of the Damascus synagogue's congregation to me. They told me that Saul, his sight somehow fully restored, had visited their synagogue. At first they were happy to see him – after all, they said, he is a student Pharisee and in your service, they thought it right that he should have access to worship. Then Saul rose to speak, and these synagogue spokesmen became most upset about his tone when he began to speak about Jesus of Nazareth, not to condemn Him and His followers, but to praise Him and state that he had now become one of the blasphemer's followers and would no longer persecute others who felt the same way."

Caiaphas was incandescent with rage. "What?" he roared.

Elias continued, "The other agents and I hurried back to the synagogue to arrest Saul, but when we got there, others from the congregation said that Saul, and another man with him, had run off down an alleyway. My lords," his voice took on a whining note, "there are many interconnecting alleyways in the city. Some of the congregation, the agents and I began to follow them, but we lost them in the maze of streets. I don't know where they went."

Elias could feel the anger emanating from the two High Priests sitting before him, but he had to tell them the whole story. "A few days after that, my lords, he caused uproar in a different synagogue. This time we were ready for him and took hold of him, but the Damascus Guards intervened and he got away from us."

"And you didn't think to follow Saul, discover where he was staying?" Annas said sarcastically.

Elias held out his hands in supplication. "My Lord Annas, there was nothing we could do. We couldn't argue with the Damascus authorities and by the time they had moved on, it was too late." He took a deep breath, knowing the rest of his statement would make his superiors even more angry "But we did arrest some converts who we were sure knew of him and his whereabouts."

Caiaphas was growing ever more exasperated by the man cringing before him. "Why are they not here with you?"

Elias was scared now. "We had to hand them over to the Governor of Damascus."

He blanched as he saw the look of fury on the High Priest's face and blustered, "We had no choice, Lord Caiaphas. Begging your pardon my lord, he said that you had no jurisdiction in Damascus, that it is he who is solely in charge there – and he forced us to work for him."

"Did he indeed?" Annas said through tight lips.

Elias nodded and Caiaphas spat out "The audacity of the man!"

"And is he now holding Saul too?" asked Annas.

"No, my lord. Of that we are sure. It seems Saul has disappeared altogether."

"Don't be ridiculous!" Annas was shouting now. "A man can't just vanish off the face of the earth. He must be somewhere."

"Lord Annas, we have searched all of the synagogues and the city from top to bottom. He's nowhere to be found. It's as if he has been spirited away. We can't understand how he's escaped us. He must have had help from sympathisers. We and the Governor's guards had all of the city gates covered; he could not have passed through them without us seeing him."

"Fools!" Caiaphas smashed his fist down onto the arm of his chair." Snarling, he turned to the Captain of the Temple Guard. "Captain, at first light tomorrow, you will go with your men to Damascus. I don't care what this arrogant Governor says, you will send me reports on everything that happens there. Somebody must know where Saul is. You yourself will see to the arrest of any followers of the new sect." "He pointed to Elias and Jacob. "And you will go with them."

Elias panicked and blurted out "But, my lord, the Governor of Damascus had us all forcibly thrown out of the city. It would be dangerous for any of us to return there. If we do, he threatened to kill us and your guards."

Annas' face was grim "We do not want to cause a diplomatic incident, Caiaphas. The Governor of Damascus is, after all, King Aretas' spokesman."

Caiaphas huffed "It sickens me to admit that you are right, Annas. The Governor is well known for being a hard man to reason with. It might be more politic to let him deal with this problem himself. I don't care what he does with the converts, as long as they are stopped from spreading their poison." Caiaphas turned to look at Elias and Jacob and concentrated on pouring out his venom on them. "You are traitors!" he said in a harsh voice. "You are dismissed from our service."

Mortified, Elias and Jacob hung their heads. This dismissal would bring shame on them and their families.

Caiaphas continued, "You and your families are henceforth banned from the Temple and its precincts forever. You will leave Jerusalem today, never to return, on pain of death." Then to the Captain of the Guard he said "Get them out of here, and make sure they are escorted off the premises."

"Yes, my lord High Priest." The Captain bowed his head in deference, relieved not to have to go to Damascus with his targeted men. He ushered the two disgraced men outside and told his guards to make sure Elias, Jacob and their families left Jerusalem.

Annas sat deep in thought for a long moment, then turned to Caiaphas, saying, "If what these witnesses say is true, then none of it makes any sense. Saul was perfectly well when he left here. How can he have suddenly succumbed to madness and have gone blind, only to have his sight miraculously restored and then be free to go about the city?"

Caiaphas forced himself to reply in a calm voice. "And now, after so vehemently denouncing the followers of the Nazarene, which we ourselves witnessed, it appears he has become a convert himself." He raised his hands in frustration "What is going on here?"

Annas sat shaking his head, speechless with frustration.

Caiaphas, however, voiced his disgust. "I just don't understand how Saul managed to get past our agents, our guards and the Governor's guards, and escape from Damascus," he brought his clenched fist down on the arm of his chair again. "As for those agents, it is clear to me that if you want something done properly, you have to do it yourself. We must choose new men more carefully this time, to replace those useless individuals."

Simon the beggar and his granddaughter joined the

throng of pilgrims entering Jerusalem. It was only a few days until the beginning of the Passover Festival. There would be rich pickings for him and the girl amongst the unsuspecting visitors, and when ben-Ezra returned he would get the money the bandit chief had promised him for telling him where Al-Maisan lived.

It was good to be back in the city. These past weeks they had been holed up on the edge of a small town a few miles north of Jerusalem. They had found a place of shelter amongst the outcasts and dispossessed who had retreated there, some, like him, to escape from the authorities. These outcasts had created their own rough shelters on the outskirts of the town and lived by begging and the generosity of those townspeople who had taken pity on them. Simon and his granddaughter had been allowed to join them and eat their share of the food generously given by the townspeople, but Simon had mostly preferred to keep himself and the girl separate from the main group.

As the days had passed by, he had begun to relax. No one, it seemed, had followed them from Jerusalem. He had been too afraid to show his face in the town in case someone recognized him, so he had sent the girl out to beg for money, but had forbidden her to steal from anyone for fear of capture. As long as they kept a low profile, he knew they would be safe there. There had been no news filtering through about the capture of ben-Ezra by the Romans, so he guessed the bandit chief was still safely hidden in his winter hideout.

Simon and the girl made their way to his hovel. He looked up and down the dirty passageway he shared with many other beggars and undesirables. Satisfied he was not being followed, he ushered the girl into his own hut. With one last look up and down the passageway, he followed her inside and pulled the ragged curtain across the doorway behind him. Looking around, he saw that it was just as he had left it. No one had touched his few meagre possessions. He smiled, then sat down on his rickety stool and, with his granddaughter listening attentively, began to make plans.

Rebecca had a painful swollen nose and deep bruising around her eyes, but she had tried hard to give the impression that her fight with ben-Ezra at the rock pool had not seriously damaged their relationship. After that first night when they had slept apart, they had moved back into their alcove together and continued their lovemaking. He had not looked at Farrah again, but Rebecca did not forget, and she would exact her revenge. Over the past few days a plan had begun to form in her mind. She knew it would be dangerous, but she didn't care. She would wait, and when the time was right...

She smiled. That time was fast approaching.

Francus, a young Roman cavalryman, lay back on the cot. Breathing heavily, his lithe body covered in perspiration, he grinned and said, "That was the best yet, Sarah." He propped himself up on one elbow and looked into the face of the naked woman who lay at his side. "I would do anything for you, Sarah. I love you so much."

Sarah looked up at him and smiling in satisfaction, she gently placed her fingertips over his lips, softly purring "Hush now. It was good for me too." Yes, she thought, it was good to lie with a clean-smelling, smooth-bodied, virile young man who was far superior to her usual unkempt clients. He did not know it, but he had also proved to be very useful. The handsome young Roman recruit was younger than Sarah, but tried hard to appear older and worldly. He was so hopelessly infatuated with her that he had convinced himself that she was his woman and that she loved him in return, a situation she had nurtured, slowly gaining his trust. During careless 'pillow talk' he had often given her snippets of information concerning garrison business which she had passed on to ben-Ezra.

"You said you are due back on duty by midday," she said "You'd better return to the garrison – I don't want you getting into trouble." She got up from the cot and began to dress herself.

He dressed too, fixing his leather belt around his narrow waist and sighing. "I wanted to make the most of my precious time with you, I won't be seeing you for a while."

Was this the information she had been waiting for? She pretended to be disappointed and she asked innocently "Why is that?"

"All leave has been cancelled until after the Passover. Pilgrims have already begun to arrive." He puffed out his chest. "We soldiers have to make sure there's no trouble in the city. Pilate's due back here in five days' time, and he'll want the city nice and peaceful when he arrives."

Excitement coursed through her. She clung to him, murmuring "I will miss you so much. The time will pass slowly until I can be with you again." She gave him a lingering kiss.

When they had parted he looked at her with dewy eyes. "I can't wait to see you again, my love."

"I will be waiting," she purred. One last kiss and he was gone.

Waiting until she knew Francus had left the area, she sprang into action. She pulled a shawl across her head and shoulders and hurried into the city to tell Joel the longed-for news.

Abraham found ben-Ezra sharpening his dagger. "Joel's messenger is here."

Ben-Ezra quickly replaced the dagger in his belt, saying "Good. Bring him to me." Abraham did so then left the pair together, knowing his chief would let him know what Joel's message was in his own good time.

A wide grin spread across ben-Ezra's face as he heard the news. So in five days' time the Governor would be returning to Jerusalem, ready for the Passover festival. He did a quick mental calculation: it would take one day from Caesarea to reach the fort in Antipatris, where Pilate and his entourage, plus the legionaries from Jerusalem would stay overnight, then it would take a further day's journey from there to Jerusalem; what he had in mind would take place on the road leading to Jerusalem. The area he was interested in would be perfect; it gave him enough time to be in place and prepare. He nodded, satisfied, but knew he had to set everything up quickly.

"Are Joel's people ready?" he asked the messenger. When the man replied that his instructions had been carried out and Joel's people were indeed ready and waiting for the command, ben-Ezra nodded. "Good. Tell Joel that Pilate should supposedly be returning to Jerusalem in five days' time," he said, curling his lip in contempt. "Now, return to Jerusalem and tell Joel to pave the way for my triumphant entry into the city. He knows what he has to do." The two men clasped arms in comradeship.

On his way back to Jerusalem the messenger remembered all the stories he had grown up with, especially the story of the time when the Roman General Pompey had ridden into Judaea with his army and destruction, defeat and misery had been inflicted upon the Jews. He smiled to himself. It was time for vengeance.

After Joel's messenger had gone, ben-Ezra called his second-in-command and Rebecca to him. Rebecca listened impassively as ben-Ezra informed her and Abraham of his plan. She saw the fanatical light shining in ben-Ezra's eyes, a light that had grown stronger over the past few days. As he spoke, she was imprinting everything he said onto her brain. She could not believe what she was hearing. The original plans he had made were foolhardy and dangerous, but this... had he lost his mind? Had Al-Maisan bewitched him into madness? Whatever the reason, she wanted no part of it. She knew it would end in catastrophe. Her plan would have to be carried out sooner than expected.

"Do you understand, Abraham?" Ben-Ezra asked a bemused-looking Abraham. The second-in-command's mind was in a whirl, but knowing, for his own sake, it was best to agree with his chief, Abraham nodded. Ben-Ezra smiled and said "Good. Now go and get my armour from the store, sort out the weapons, make sure they are clean and sharp, then send Reuben and Isaac to me."

Reuben and Isaac stood before their chief and listened to his plan. Ben-Ezra pointed to Isaac and said "Isaac, you will ride to Jericho now and tell Josiah to mobilise his men. He has contact with the Zealots, so he will organize them. You will stay with Josiah, travel with him and his men and meet us at the appointed place in three days' time." Isaac kept his gaze steady as he saluted ben-Ezra, then went off to prepare to ride to Jericho.

Ben-Ezra turned to Reuben. "You will ride to Zeke. Tell him I want the cart covered and filled with the weapons he's purchased with my money, and our horses, brought back here by tomorrow. You will stay in Beth Bassi and make sure that wily old bastard hands over the weapons and returns every one of the horses to me and doesn't keep the best back for himself, then you will return here with his men and the goods."

Reuben saluted ben-Ezra and walked off towards the rocky outcrop where the remaining horses were penned. Rebecca touched ben-Ezra's arm and staring up at him, she asked in a concerned voice, "Does that mean we will soon be leaving this place?"

Ben-Ezra looked down at her and replied "Yes, my love, soon we will be away from here."

"You spoke to Abraham of my brother; where does he fit into all this?"

He gave her a consoling smile, saying "Don't worry your pretty head about Josiah. He knows what he has to do and where he has to be."

"Since when did you take up the Zealots' cause?" she asked cautiously.

"The only thing I share with the Zealots is the desire to be rid of our hated conquerors, but for my plan to be successful I need their help." He ruffled her hair, which hung loosely down her back.

Abraham returned with the helmet, breastplate and short Roman sword. Ben-Ezra took them from him and stroked the plume of the helmet, which had once belonged to a tribune. He said triumphantly, "With these trophies I will lead my army." He put down the helmet and picked up the sword, carefully feeling the sharpness of the blade with the tip of his finger. Without looking at Abraham, he said, "What about the other weapons and shields for the men?"

"Don't worry, chief," Abraham replied, "the weapons and the men are ready and waiting for your orders."

"Good." Ben-Ezra turned back to Rebecca. "Rebecca, get the women together, I need to speak to them."

Rebecca smiled to herself, then walked towards the women grouped around the fire, saying "The chief wants to speak to you." The women got up and went to their master, eager to hear what he had to say.

Before he left for Jericho, Isaac found Anna in their cavern alcove, nursing their baby. He knelt down beside her and said softly. "Anna, soon we will be leaving this place and things are going to get very dangerous. I don't want you involved, I fear for your safety and that of our child. You must leave here."

Anna looked up at him and said in a shocked voice, "Leave? But my place is with you, Isaac."

He shook his head "Not this time. I may not survive this, and I don't want you and our son to die with me. Go north to your brother's house, start a new life there, give our son hope for the future."

"Isaac!" tears flowed down her cheeks. "I can't live without you."

He took her hand. "You can and you must. Please, for my sake."

Anna nodded. "When all of this is over, will you come and find me?"

"I promise." Isaac kissed her forehead, saying softly, "Never forget, Anna, I love you." He gently stroked the baby's head, then handed Anna a small bag of coins. "Take this." He smiled as she took the bag from him, then with one last kiss, he turned away and prepared to ride to Jericho.

Wiping the tears from her eyes, Anna looked at her son, so small, so precious. Whatever Isaac was afraid of, she knew that what he had said had to be taken seriously. Without further thought, she took up her shawl and wrapped the baby in it. As the rest of the women stood listening to ben-Ezra's commands, Anna, unnoticed by the others, quietly left the cave with her son safely strapped to her breast. She knew it would be safer to follow the back roads and hill passes away from any Roman patrols to reach her brother and his family.

Later that day, Anna's absence was noticed by some of the women. They murmured amongst themselves. "Perhaps she has followed Isaac," Rachel offered. The women shrugged. Who cared anyway? If she wanted to endanger herself and her baby by braving the rough terrain and wild animals that roamed there, what was it to them?

The next morning, Reuben rode to Beth Bassi. Rebecca fought to contain her excitement. Her desire for vengeance was about to be satisfied.

That night Rebecca passionately kissed ben-Ezra, then, looking deep into his eyes, she smiled and said "Do you realize, Eleazar, that it's a year since you successfully killed that Roman patrol at the Ascent of Blood? Why don't we have a celebration in honour of that? After all, we have enough wine and food left; if we are to leave here soon we don't want to waste it." Rebecca looked wide-eyed at ben-Ezra. "Perhaps it will ease the tension a little."

A slow smile spread across ben-Ezra's face. "Why not? We can combine it with a pre-victory celebration and a farewell to this place. If all goes to plan we won't be returning here again."

The idea was met with enthusiasm by the rest of the gang. The women set to work organizing the food whilst the men carried in the remaining large amphorae of wine and water.

The members of the gang ate well and drank copiously, becoming gradually more drunken and bawdy. When Rebecca saw that ben-Ezra was sufficiently filled with wine, she leaned over him and whispered in his ear. He gave her a drunken leer, then got up and pulled her to her feet. He made his way to their alcove, pulling Rebecca behind him. Other members of the gang began to pair off too and disappear into the recesses of the cave.

Farrah and Ruth had been allowed to share the food and watered wine. They knew the time was coming when they would be leaving their prison and beginning their journey to further degradation for Farrah and slavery for Ruth. Left on their own, they clung to each other, afraid of what the coming days might bring. Eventually they fell into restless sleep, filled with tormenting dreams.

Rebecca used all the tricks of her profession on ben-Ezra until he fell back onto the dirty pallet, exhausted. "Enough, you witch, you've drained me," he said with a contented sigh. "Let me sleep now." He was soon snoring noisily.

Making sure he was fast asleep, Rebecca got up and went into the main area of the cave. All was quiet apart from sighs and snores coming from the recesses. She picked up the last small amphora of wine and shook it. Good – there was still some wine left in it. She took an earthenware flagon and poured the wine into it. Outside the main area, she lifted down a torch from its sconce and by its light, made her way to where Benjamin, the youngest member of the gang, was keeping watch close to the cave's entrance.

He was momentarily startled when he saw her face, eerily lit from the flickering torch light, and asked in a worried voice, "Rebecca? Is everything all right?"

She returned his smile and held out the flagon. "There's nothing wrong Benjamin, it just didn't seem fair that you should miss out on our celebration, so I've brought you some wine." His face lit up as she passed the flagon to him. He drank deeply from it. "I hope you enjoy it." Rebecca smiled again. Leaving the flagon with him, she turned and walked back into the cave. She had purposely left the wine unwatered to make it very strong, hoping it would have the desired effect on the young man. On her way back to the main cave she picked up a large stone and hid it in the folds of her skirt.

Replacing the torch in the sconce, she returned to the alcove. She knelt down beside ben-Ezra. He stirred and turned over towards her. Afraid he would wake up, she lifted the stone ready to bring it down hard on his head. He mumbled some incoherent words, then with a grunt and a loud snore, he rolled over, turning away from her, still fast asleep. She breathed a sigh of relief. She did not want to be responsible for his death; she had other plans for him.

A little later, making sure all was quiet, she stole out of the alcove again. She took hold of the torch and retraced her steps back down to Benjamin. Just before she reached the entrance, she put the torch down on the ground, then moved towards him. She came to an abrupt halt. He was still standing alert, not collapsed through drunkenness as she had hoped. His capacity for holding his wine was greater than she had expected.

Totally unaware of her presence, he casually took another swig from the flagon. As he did so, she crept forward and smashed the stone onto the back of his skull. The flagon fell from his hand and shattered on the stony ground, the remainder of the wine spreading like a pool of blood around his feet. She hit him again and again, turning his skull into a bloody pulp. His knees buckled and he sank to the ground. She checked him; he was dead.

She quickly made her way to where the horses were tethered. With Isaac and Reuben using two out of the three horses, hers was the only one left. She approached her horse slowly, not wishing to alarm the animal. Stroking the young mare's head, she whispered softly to her, calming her, then reaching down, she tore off strips from her skirt and, carefully lifting each hoof in turn, wrapped the material around them so they would make no sound on the stony ground. The bridle, saddle and blanket were lying on the ground nearby. She quickly put the bridle over the mare's head, then threw the blanket across its back, followed by the saddle, securing it underneath the horse's belly. All the time her heart pounded at the prospect of being discovered.

She led the horse from the pen. Reaching the outside of the cave, she looked back, making sure she had not been followed. Agitated, she held her breath, but no one appeared in the mouth of the cave. She led the mare away from the cave and down the rocky pathway onto a small plateau. Just a few more steps and she would be free.

She shivered in the chill air as she glimpsed the first glimmer of dawn appear in the east. She would have to hurry. Removing the material from the horse's hooves, she put them into the waistband of her skirt so they would not be found by ben-Ezra, then she carefully guided the animal down the treacherous slope towards flatter ground. Once safely down, she mounted up.

A bolt of fear shot through her as she heard the unearthly howl of jackals; howls that were swiftly answered by a loud roar. The terrifying sounds came from close by. Too close. The frightened horse reared up. It took several seconds for her to bring the horse back under her control. She could not return to the cave now, but she was determined to put her plan into action. There were now only four days to go before Pilate was due to return to the city. She had to hurry. Terrified she would be torn apart by the desert beasts, she kicked the horse's flanks with her feet, urging the animal onwards. The horse needed no second bidding and raced away from the danger.

After riding for several miles she saw Beth Bassi sprawled out before her. She skirted around it for fear of running into Reuben and Zeke's men returning to the cave with ben-Ezra's weapons and horses, and rode on towards Bethlehem.

Just outside Bethlehem, she suddenly pulled up her horse. A cloud of dust was rising in the distance. Horsemen! She looked around, trying to find rocks to hide behind, but there was no hiding place in that part of the bleak terrain. Frantic now, her eyes strained to see who the horsemen were.

As the riders drew closer still, she breathed a sigh of relief. Romans! She smiled. They would suit her purpose beautifully. Spurring her horse on, she rode towards the cavalry patrol.

Julius brought his horse to an abrupt halt, his men following suit behind him. He shaded his eyes against the fast-rising sun to get a better view of the solitary rider speeding towards the patrol. His patrol was performing its usual early morning search of the area; he hadn't expected to see anyone in this part of the wilderness at this hour. Especially not a wild-haired young woman.

Rebecca saw the Roman officer grow tense as she reined in her horse and stopped a short distance from him. She raised her hands to show she was not carrying any weapons and said in a clipped voice: "Take me to your Commander in Jerusalem!"

Julius looked at her warily. What could this woman possibly want with Quintus Maximus? "Who are you? What do you want with the Commander?" He demanded in an authoritative voice.

Rebecca looked at him defiantly. "I am Rebecca. I am – was – ben-Ezra's woman."

Julius was stunned. Thinking it was a trap, he looked out across the wilderness, any moment expecting to see ben-Ezra's men riding towards them ready to kill them; but the wilderness was empty, and there was nowhere for the gang to hide.

Rebecca's voice rose insistently. "If you want to capture ben-Ezra and his men you will take me to your Commander. Now!"

Julius frowned. Was she leading them into a trap? On the other hand, if she did have knowledge of the brigand's whereabouts, she might also know something about the missing Princess Farrah. He came to a decision. He would have to take a chance. "Move into the centre of my men," he said sternly. "We will escort you to the fortress Antonia."

Rebecca breathed a huge sigh of relief as she manoeuvered her mount into the middle of the cavalrymen. She felt safe with them surrounding her.

Julius gave the order and the patrol turned around and rode back to Jerusalem.

# CHAPTER FOURTEEN

Flanked by Julius, Antonius and Sextus, Quintus sat staring at the strange woman standing defiantly before him. He quickly summed her up: her clothes were gaudy and grubby, although her face, grimy with dirt and dust, held a kind of coarse beauty and properly tended, her wild, red hair could be tamed and fashioned into a blaze of red silken curls. He guessed she was a woman of the streets. He leaned forward and said, "What is your name?"

Rebecca stared back at him "Rebecca."

"What do you know about ben-Ezra?" His voice was wary.

"He is a complete madman. He thinks he is the saviour of Israel!" she replied, pulling a face.

Quintus shook his head. Not another crazy messiah.

"I can tell you where ben-Ezra and his gang are hiding," Rebecca went on.

Quintus was filled with suspicion. "Why would you betray him?"

Rebecca tossed back her windswept hair. "Because I was once his woman, but now I hate him. I don't want any part in his latest plan, it's a plan conceived by a madman! Besides, I want revenge."

Quintus wondered why she had left ben-Ezra and his gang. Why she wanted revenge. Could he trust her?

"Why should I trust a whore like you?" he asked, looking at her disdainfully.

Rebecca bristled at the insult, "If you value the life of your Governor you will listen to me."

At the mention of the Governor the Commander sat up and said quickly, "What about Governor Pilate?"

Rebecca smiled slyly. "Ah. I have your attention now."

"Don't play games with me," Quintus said angrily. "Tell me what you know."

Aware of the Roman Commander's hostile glare, she complied, answering "Ben-Ezra plans to ambush him on the route between Antipatris and Jerusalem."

Quintus narrowed his eyes "And just how does he intend to do this? The Governor will be guarded by a strong escort. Ben-Ezra surely can't hope to defeat so many men."

Rebecca moved forward and looked him squarely in the face "He won't be alone. There will be many others joining him."

"Who?"

She shrugged. "All I know is, Zealots are coming down

from Galilee to join with ben-Ezra. I don't know how many."

"Since when did ben-Ezra care about the Zealots' cause?" Quintus asked through tight lips.

"He doesn't. Eleazar ben-Ezra cares only for himself. He will use them for his own ends, then discard them, as he does to everyone who is no longer of use to him." Rebecca's voice held a bitter tone, not lost on the listening Romans. "Because you have so far failed to find him he has delusions that he is invincible. It is his dream to overthrow you Romans and rule Judaea."

Quintus turned sharply as he heard a stifled laugh come from Antonius and gave him a stern stare.

Rebecca ignored the interruption. "Then there is my brother, Josiah..."

"What about him?"

"He too is joining forces with ben-Ezra and the Zealots."

Quintus was astounded. "You would betray your own brother?"

Rebecca curled her lip. "I owe him nothing. It is his fault that I am brought so low."

Quintus leaned forward "How many men does your brother have?"

"Many. His own, along with those businessmen in Jericho he has dealings with, who will be sending their own men to swell his ranks." She sneered. "I know they would all be glad to see the back of their oppressors. There are also mercenaries in Jericho who will do anything for the right reward; and my brother is rich. He will pay them well if they join him." She flicked her tangled hair back from her face. "Then there is a horse dealer in Beth Bassi known as Zeke."

Quintus turned to Julius. "Is he the Zeke we trade with?"

Julius nodded. "Yes, sir. He's our main horse trader."

"Zeke is not his real name," said Rebecca. "He is Japheth bar Saraf, the brother of Abraham, ben-Ezra's second in command. He takes care of ben-Ezra's horses when he's in hiding and sells the goods ben-Ezra has stolen to buy weapons for him. From what I know about him he has never fought alongside ben-Ezra."

"His association with the bandit chief is enough to condemn him," Quintus snarled.

"Ben-Ezra has people in Jerusalem too. Simon, a beggar who lives in Beggar's Alley, who acts as a lookout in and around the city, and Sarah, a prostitute, who runs ben-Ezra's brothel a couple of streets away from there. I will tell you something you obviously don't know." She gave a wicked grin. "Sarah gains information from one of your young recruits, one who doesn't realise his careless pillow talk gives her important information which she then passes on to her master."

Quintus was shocked. One of his own men? "What's his name?"

Rebecca shrugged. "I don't know his name. I only know Sarah has laughed about his obsessive adoration of her and that he told her he is a new cavalry recruit to this garrison."

Julius blanched. He knew exactly who the new recruit was.

Quintus looked directly at him. "How many new cavalry recruits have joined us recently?"

Without hesitation Julius replied, "Only one, sir. A young man called Francus. Sir, if it is him I will make him regret what he has done."

Quintus waved his hand irritably. "Not yet. If we are to fight ben-Ezra and his people, I will need all the men I can get. Make sure this Francus is in the front line of the cavalry squadron when we face our enemies. If he survives, he will be dealt with after we have taken care of ben-Ezra and his rebels." He turned back to Rebecca. "Is there anything else you can tell us? If there is, you must tell me now." He grew angry when Rebecca hesitated and shouted, "Tell me now!"

She took a deep breath. "There is Joel. Joel is his main eyes and ears in the city. All I know is, ben-Ezra told him to attack this fortress. Joel has rebels hidden in the city who have sworn to kill you all."

"Do you know the names of these rebels?" the Commander asked in a clipped voice.

Rebecca shook her head "No. That information is only between ben-Ezra and Joel.

"When is the attack due to take place?"

"On Pilate – within three days. As for the attack on the city, sometime before that. I don't know exactly when."

The Commander uttered a curse under his breath.

So little time to prepare. Hiding his frustration, he said "Where is ben-Ezra now?"

"In a cave in the Judaean wilderness," came Rebecca's quick reply.

Quintus frowned. "That area has been covered many times. How could we have missed him?"

Rebecca smirked "There are roads known and built by you Romans – and there are tracks and caves known only to us Jews."

"And Joel?"

"He has many different addresses. I don't know any of them."

The Commander's voice held a warning note. "If you are lying to me…"

Rebecca shrugged. "I am not told everything. There are some things ben-Ezra keeps close to his chest."

"What are ben-Ezra's plans after the ambush, assuming he survives?"

"He said when he has gained victory over the Governor and those guarding him, he will ride into the city as a conqueror, with the foreign woman at his side. She curled her lip.

Quintus sat bolt upright, "Foreign woman? What's her name?"

"I heard him call her Al-Maisan."

Quintus roared "Body of Juno, she is alive!" He was shocked to the core by this news, but his hopes soared.

Antonius stepped forward. "Commander, if this woman can lead us to ben-Ezra now, we can rescue the Princess and capture him before his plans come to fruition."

Quintus turned on him. "Think, Prefect! If we storm the cave we could endanger Princess Farrah's life. Besides, we need to capture them all." He got up and walked over to where a detailed map of Judaea and Samaria was laid out on another desk, then beckoned Rebecca forward. "Show me where the ambush is to take place."

Rebecca studied the map, then seeing a place name she recognized, she pointed to it.

"Here, at the Beth-Horon Pass," she said.

"You're sure?" Quintus asked tersely.

Rebecca nodded. "That is the name ben-Ezra said. He intends to amass his men in those surrounding hills and from there attack the unsuspecting Governor and his escort with every weapon he possesses."

The Commander called Antonius, Sextus and Julius to the map. He prodded his finger at the place on the map. "Here, approximately four leagues north west of Jerusalem at the Beth-Horon Pass. That's where the attack will take place."

Sextus was worried. "With respect sir, we can't let Governor Pilate ride into a trap."

Quintus shook his head irritably. "Of course not." He looked at Rebecca and said sternly "How will I distinguish ben-Ezra from his men?"

"He will be wearing Roman body armour and a plumed

tribune's helmet, stolen from one of the Roman officers he killed at the Ascent of Blood, and no doubt, in his vanity, he will be at the head of his small army. His own men will also be using armour and weapons taken from that and other massacres too. As for the rest..." She shrugged.

Quintus grimaced, then called for one of the sentries stationed outside the door. The sentry entered, saluted and waited for his orders. "Take this woman to the dungeon."

Rebecca protested loudly. "Is this the way you treat someone who has helped you?"

Quintus roared, "Be silent woman! It is for your own protection." As the legionary took hold of Rebecca's arm, he said, "See no harm comes to her. When you have delivered her, send the Sheikh to me." He watched as the sentry saluted, then led a screaming and kicking Rebecca away. He saw the questioning look on the others' faces and said "Don't worry. If she has lied to us she will suffer the consequences."

Within a short time, Sheikh Ibrahim came into the office. "You sent for me, Commander?"

Quintus pointed to a stool and Ibrahim sat down.

"I have been given information that ben-Ezra intends to lead an attack on the Governor. There is also news of your niece." He paused at the look of consternation on the Sheikh's face, then continued, "The informer says she is still alive." He saw the older man relax. "We are going into battle with ben-Ezra and hopefully we will rescue her, but you must be made aware of the great danger she is in."

Ibrahim looked earnestly at the Commander. "I have a request." Quintus guessed what was coming. "You know my men are highly skilled in warfare, I ask that they be part of the battle operation."

The Commander nodded. "I agree. I have need of good men, especially those skilled in tracking."

"One more request, if you please. I want to go with your troops, with Drubaal at my side. He has recovered from his injuries."

Quintus sighed. He knew how much the Sheikh's niece meant to him, so he reluctantly agreed – but under his own terms. He sat deep in thought for a long moment then suddenly sat upright and called for a second sentry. "Bring Centurions Fabius and Batitus here and Tribune Commodus."

A short time later Centurion Fabius of the Second Century of the Third Cohort and Centurion Batitus of the First Century of the Second Cohort, along with Tribune Commodus, joined the rest of the officers in Quintus' office. Having been briefed on the situation, they stood waiting for Quintus to come up with a plan. Quintus knew he had to handle this carefully; one mistake and all their lives would be at risk. He sat deep in thought for a long moment, the others growing increasingly concerned at his silence. Then he cleared his throat and said, "Gentlemen, give me ideas. We must work out a strategy for how to deal with both of these dangerous situations."

Sextus and Commodus came up with suggestions, but none pleased Quintus. They were closeted in Quintus' office for over two hours before a feasible plan was finally put forward. They pored over the map as Quintus pointed out various positions. When the officers could see the plan was workable, much to Quintus' relief, they readily agreed to carry it out.

Quintus returned to his seat and took a wax tablet and stylus from the desk drawer. He quickly wrote information and instructions on it with the stylus, then pushed the identification markings of his signet ring down hard into the wax to make it official. When the wax had dried, he covered the tablet with a fresh unwaxed one and bound them together. Turning sharply, he handed the bundle to Julius, saying, "Pick your most trusted cavalry officer and tell him to ride to the fortress at Antipatris and give this tablet to Prefect Aelius. Impress upon him that he must place it in the Prefect's hands himself, and no one else, however senior they may be. The tablet gives Prefect Aelius all the information he needs along with my recommendations. Tell your chosen man to stay at the fortress until the Jerusalem Cavalry arrives, when he will rejoin them. You and your squadron will accompany Chief Centurion Sextus, Centurion Fabius and their legionaries to Antipatris. Decurion Julius, you know what is required from your squadron. Go now and give them my orders, but not to Francus – the less he knows about our plans the better."

Julius saluted, then quickly left the room. Otto was his chosen man. Once given the bundle and his instructions, Otto saddled his horse and began the journey to Antipatris.

Quintus looked directly at Sextus and Fabius and said, "Make sure your men and their weapons are prepared, their funeral money is up to date and they are put in the picture about the coming battle. You march in two days. Gentlemen, you are dismissed." He turned to the rest of the waiting officers. "Stay here, we must discuss further the back-up plan to defeat ben-Ezra and ensure we are ready to deal with the coming trouble in the city."

The Commander turned to Batitus. "Centurion Batitus, you will stay here in the Antonia until I give you the order to march." Then to Antonius, "Your cavalry will ride with Batitus' troops and with you, Sheikh Ibrahim." He turned to the grateful Sheikh and said, "Put your guards in the picture, go and see Drubaal and tell him the plan." Ibrahim went straight to Drubaal and his guards to tell them what they had to do.

Quintus then turned to Commodus and outlined what the man Joel intended to do and how he wanted it dealt with, adding "I will send a message to the High Priests informing them of our forthcoming action. I don't want any of the Temple authorities getting caught up in this. Go now all of you, and pray that the gods have helped us to make the right decisions."

Antonius bristled with anger as he mustered his North African Cavalry to tell them Quintus' orders. How dare the

Commander embarrass him in front of the other officers? He was far senior in rank to Julius, yet it was the younger man who had been given the honour of meeting and escorting Pilate from Antipatris, whilst he and his men had to ride as back-up as part of an inferior infantry force. He took this as a personal insult, one he would not forget.

Ben-Ezra woke up in a daze. He turned over expecting to see Rebecca lying next to him, but the bedding was empty and cold. He got up and lurched into the main cave. She wasn't there either. He questioned a few of the women who were already busily preparing the morning food, but they told him they had not seen her since the night before. He was puzzled. Where was she? He searched the cavern, finally arriving at the entrance to discover, with a shock, Benjamin's battered body. Who had done this?

He made his way to the horse shelter; it was empty. Realisation hit him. Rebecca! She had killed Benjamin, then escaped, taking the last remaining horse with her. Without a horse, he could not hope to track her down. Where had she gone?

A sudden thought came to him: she must still be angry with him about Al-Maisan, even though their lovemaking the previous night had been more passionate than ever before. Perhaps in her anger she had ridden back to Jericho? And do what? He quickly dismissed that thought. Even if she did go to her brother, would Josiah care? He had never worried about her before – after all, what loving brother would place his own sister into prostitution? No, Josiah cared more about making money and killing Romans. There was no doubt in his mind that Josiah and his men would join him at the meeting place. His eyes scanned the surrounding wilderness. Where was Reuben with the horses? And where was Rebecca?

It was another hour before Reuben, along with some of Zeke's men, returned with the horses and a cartload of weapons. Ben-Ezra checked the weapons over and nodded in satisfaction. Zeke had done well. He rallied his people and told them to prepare to leave the cave sanctuary. Some of Zeke's men returned to the horse-dealer while the rest stayed with the brigand chief, eager to have the chance to destroy the hated enemy.

Farrah and Ruth had their hands tied behind their backs and were bundled into the covered wagon which had once held Farrah's treasured possessions. Rachel and the other women joined them. Rachel kept a close eye on the captives. She was tempted to push Ruth out of the vehicle in a remote area so that she would either die of thirst or be devoured by the roaming desert beasts, but ben-Ezra had made it plain that neither woman should be harmed, a directive she dared not break.

When the gang were mounted up and ready, they rode away from their hiding place and took the road to Beth-Horon.

# CHAPTER FIFTEEN

Otto stood straight-backed before a grim-faced Prefect Aelius. Aelius quickly scanned the wax tablet, then raised his eyebrows in surprise as he read Quintus Maximus' instruction: 'No catapults.' He stroked his chin as he read on. So, ben-Ezra was holding a very important hostage and catapult barrages must not be used because of the danger to them. Besides, Quintus had added, it would take too long to get them to their destination and time was short. Well, if that was what was wanted, that was what he would do.

Having been dismissed, Otto made his way to the fortress cavalry block to meet the men of the Antipatris Cavalry. They welcomed him, but Otto was anxious to rejoin Julius and his own unit, men he knew he could trust, men who would watch his back in the fight to defeat Rome's most dangerous enemies.

The next day, when Pilate and his entourage reached Antipatris, Prefect Aelius and his senior officers presented themselves to the Governor with the news of ben-Ezra's forthcoming attack. Aelius nervously offered an opinion to Pilate, saying that perhaps he should travel to Jerusalem by a different route. The Prefect blanched at the response; Pilate turned on him and said firmly "No! I will return to Jerusalem along my usual route. I may be many things, but I am not a coward."

The Prefect stepped forward and spoke in a calm voice.

"Governor Pilate, sir. No one here doubts your bravery, but surely in this case... may I recommend that perhaps someone else takes your place and you could stay here until this enemy force is defeated? I really think..."

He did not finish his sentence. Pilate slammed his fist down on the desk in front of him and cast a steely eye over the garrison officers standing before him. "Let me make this clear to you all; ben-Ezra will undoubtedly know my face. If he sees somebody else he may not attack, and I want him and those who are with him brought to justice. I will brook no argument. I *will* ride back to Jerusalem via Beth-Horon. My decision is final!"

Taken aback by Pilate's furious reaction, Prefect Aelius took a step back, then said quietly, "In his communiqué, Commander Quintus Maximus also says that there are two women being held hostage by ben-Ezra and one is apparently a Princess Farrah. Do you know of such a person, Governor Pilate?"

"By the gods! She lives!" Pilate shouted, feeling relief flood over him. He controlled the excitement in his voice as he answered the Prefect's question. "Yes, I know her. The Princess is one of my most trusted agents."

Flavius, standing close to Pilate, had jumped as Pilate's fist connected with the desk. Until that moment he had not really listened to the argument going on around him. All his brain now registered was that his beloved Farrah was alive. After all these months of uncertainty, there was a chance now, however slender, that he would see her again. His heart raced. He tried hard to concentrate as Pilate called for the Cavalry officer in charge of the escort from Caesarea telling him to order his men to return to Caesarea and put the garrison there on full alert, then he turned to the Prefect spelling out the procedure for the next day's journey. Aelius acted immediately on Quintus Maximus' and Pilate's recommendations and issued clipped commands to his senior officers, ordering that troops be made ready to back-up Sextus' and Fabius' legionaries as well as Pilate's entourage. There was a flurry of activity as the Tribunes, Centurions and Decurions returned to their men, repeating the orders the Prefect had given them.

Flavius frowned, wondering if it was to be a journey to happiness, or to death.

In the hills overlooking the Beth-Horon Pass, ben-Ezra and Josiah met and clasped arms in uneasy comradeship. Ben-Ezra said, "Did you have any problems getting here?"

Josiah smiled, showing white teeth. "We ran into one of Herod's patrols just outside Jericho, but we dealt with them." Followed by ben-Ezra, he walked over to a cart covered in sacking. "Look." He lifted the sacking to reveal a number of Herodian swords and spears nestled within a large cache of assorted Roman weapons.

The bandit chief looked at them. "Good. Any survivors?"

Josiah grimaced at the audacity of ben-Ezra's question and said sharply, "What do you think?"

Ben-Ezra saw the small number of men Josiah had brought with him from Jericho, plus the carts filled with provisions, and said sharply, "Where are the others and the Zealots you promised me?"

Josiah frowned. "Don't fret, my friend, they will be here by nightfall. A large group travelling together across country would have looked too conspicuous. The rest of my men will come from different directions, but they will meet with us here." He looked around, puzzled. "Where is my sister?"

An icy finger slid down ben-Ezra's spine. "I thought she would be with you?"

Josiah shrugged. "I haven't seen her in months. Why isn't she here?"

"A good question. Truthfully, I have no idea where she is." Ben-Ezra decided he would not tell Josiah about their argument.

Josiah shrugged. "Perhaps she was afraid of the coming battle and has gone to our sister in Galilee. In any case, we can't spend valuable time worrying about her, we have plans to make." He placed his arm across ben-Ezra's shoulder as the two men made their way to a small rock. Josiah raised his eyebrows as a stifled groan came from behind the rock. He walked around it and saw a trembling Farrah and a tearful Ruth sitting on the stony ground, their hands tied behind their backs, being watched over by Rachel. He gave the prisoners a lingering look, then turned to ben-Ezra. "Who are they?"

Ben-Ezra tried hard to keep a steady voice. He could see Josiah was very interested, too interested, in the two women. "They are MY captives. I captured them when I was last in the Jerusalem area."

"Why did you capture them? Are they important?"

Ben-Ezra thought it was not the time to tell Josiah the whole truth. "They are pretty, and they'll bring me a lot of money in the slave market."

Josiah looked at Ruth. She was dirty and obviously heavily pregnant, but underneath the grime she was indeed pretty. The other captive stunned him. Despite the privations she must have endured, her beauty and proud bearing shone out. Josiah began to guess at the reason for his sister's defection: it must have something to do with the beautiful woman staring back at him. The loss of Rebecca as the star of his Jericho brothel had cost him a great deal of money, but these two would help rebuild his fortune. Although she was thin and wan, with proper nourishment and a great deal of pampering, the woman staring at him with large doe eyes would have her full beauty restored and become his new star. He turned his gaze away, not wishing to allow ben-Ezra to read his thoughts. "Come," he said matter-of-factly, "let us make our plans for tomorrow."

"I prefer to wait until the Zealots and the rest of your men arrive. I have a special task in mind for the Zealots and you know what your men have to do."

The two men settled down on the rock. Ben-Ezra continued, "Meanwhile I have sent lookouts to strategic places along the route between Antipatris and here. As soon as the Romans are spotted, signals will be sent to us, the most important one being as Pilate approaches. That way we will know their every move. I don't want anyone to be seen in these hills until I give the order to attack. I hope that's clear."

Josiah looked at him. "Why did you choose Beth-Horon for the battle?"

"Because it is a fitting place," said ben-Ezra. He saw the inquisitive look on Josiah's face. "Remember the history of our people, the battle fought here between Joshua and the five kings of Canaan, heralding Joshua's great victory for Israel. Then Judas Maccabees. His army was so much smaller than that of the Syrian commander, Seron, yet by clever strategy he slaughtered hundreds of the enemy down there." He pointed to the valley below them. "If those heroes of Israel could achieve such great victories, why can't we?"

"Yes, but the forces we will face are far superior to any

that have come before. How will we defeat the Roman fighting machine?"

"By using the same strategy as Joshua and Judas. We will harry them, pick them off a few at a time, until they are gradually worn down. Now do you understand?"

Josiah nodded in satisfaction. "It seems, my friend that you have thought out a good plan. When we hit the Romans they won't stand a chance."

"Especially as they are not expecting an attack – or the one on the garrison in Jerusalem." He saw the surprise on Josiah's face. "Even as we speak, my man Joel is preparing his men. They will storm the Antonia first thing tomorrow morning and kill all the Romans there. When that is done, he will send a messenger to me proclaiming that the way is clear for me to enter Jerusalem as a conqueror. My friend, I am on the verge of a great victory. I will claim back our homeland from the enemy."

Josiah grew uneasy. He had been told none of this in the original plan. He forced a grin and slapped ben-Ezra across the back, saying "But tell me, what made you think that it was your place to become the sole leader of a group of rebels? You know the punishment if you, and the rest of us, fail and are caught."

"For years I have wrought havoc upon the Roman forces, yet still they have been unable to capture me," replied ben-Ezra. "It is my destiny to free our land from the invaders. I know now I am the chosen one our people have been waiting for."

The answer staggered Josiah. Had this man, this common bandit chief, gone mad? Was he acting out in his twisted mind the role of the Messiah? How dare he compare himself to those great heroic figures of Joshua and Judas? Unable to find the words and keeping a blank expression, Josiah nodded, made his excuses and said goodnight, leaving ben-Ezra sitting on the rock, staring up at the sky and the steadily-building clouds.

On his way back to the encampment, Josiah came to a decision. If – no, when – they beat the Romans and Pilate was dead, he would kill ben-Ezra, make himself the new leader of the rebels, take over the businesses ben-Ezra ran and keep these captives for himself. He had far more men at his disposal than the deluded bandit chief. He knew his associates back in Jericho would follow him. He smiled to himself. Yes, it would be easy.


Ruth turned a tear-streaked face towards Farrah. "I'm so afraid, my lady. What's to become of us?"

Farrah shifted uncomfortably. "I always thought ben-Ezra was unstable, but after hearing him just now I know he is a complete madman. If he and the stranger with him win the battle, we must find a way to kill ourselves. Neither man will show us any mercy. If the Romans win, and I have prayed to every god I know that they will, then we have a chance of freedom. Hold on to that last fact and pray as you have never prayed before."

Ruth felt guilt flood through her. She had turned her

back on God and his Son, the Lord Jesus. How could she pray to them now? What if they had turned their backs on her? With that thought, she leaned back, trying desperately to relieve the pain gnawing at her distended belly, and the pain in her heart.

Farrah hugged her knees and bowed her head disconsolately, hoping desperately that ben-Ezra would be defeated.

Later that evening, the rest of Josiah's men began to arrive; they had women with them so that they would look like family groups, in order to stop any suspicion as they journeyed to Beth-Horon. They came from different directions and assembled before their leader. Not long after, the Zealots arrived. Ben-Ezra was pleased by their numbers. He was now the leader of a small army. When everyone was assembled, he faced them and issued a stern warning: "Leave the captive women alone. There will be no drunkenness. If I catch anyone near the captives or drunk, I will kill them myself."

As the first shadows of night appeared, he posted lookouts along the perimeter of the hillside to watch the Pass below, and more to watch over the horses. He forbade the lighting of fires. He doubted the Romans would travel during the hours of darkness, but his nerves made him anxious; he knew the enemy was capable of anything. He, Josiah and Moshe, the leader of the Zealots, sat together making their plans. The rest of the men were busy checking swords and spears making sure they were sharp and in good order. Bows were strung, arrows, slings, lead pellets and stones made ready. Being excited but nervous by the coming battle, no one wanted to sleep. Their one aim was to kill the extortionate Governor and destroy his hated Roman minions.

They were so immersed in their plans and camaraderie that they did not see the two Nabatean scouts lying flat on their stomachs, watching from the peak of the wooded hillside opposite. The scouts had been there for a long time, having tracked the hooves and footprints of the first horses and felons to have arrived in that area. Dressed in local clothing, the scouts had appeared to be just two more travellers on the road. The scouts had dismounted and tied their horses to an olive tree and then, well out of sight of the would-be assassins, they had quickly and quietly scrambled up the hill. From their vantage point they had seen ben-Ezra talking with some of his men, then watched as a man whom they took to be Josiah with his first force stop at the foot of the hill encampment, then begin to climb steadily until they disappeared over the crest. Later they saw the rest of his men begin to arrive. The Zealots had mainly come down from the north, so they could only guess their numbers. They would overestimate them to be sure.

They now knew the approximate number of ben-Ezra's small army and the position of his stronghold. Satisfied that the would-be assassins were too engrossed to notice them, they quietly made their way back down and retrieved their horses. They walked them in the shadows for a short distance, fearing neither wild beasts nor capture, then they mounted up and galloped back to the Jerusalem garrison.

# CHAPTER SIXTEEN

The columns of legionaries marched along the dusty road leading to the hills of Beth-Horon. The Gallic squadron of cavalry, led by Julius, made up the vanguard which was set equally either side of the First Century of the Second Cohort of auxiliaries, together with a detachment of Syrian archers, led by their standard bearer who, with great pride, carried the Century's standard, the flag bearer, who carried a red cloth flag on a horizontal bar fixed to a lance, and a Cornicen carrying a horn, marching alongside them. The auxiliary unit was led by Centurion Fabius. Following close behind came the First Century of the Third Cohort standard bearer, flag bearer and Cornicen, followed by Centurion Sextus and the First Century legionaries marching briskly and alert, ready for action.

The early morning spring sunshine was gaining in

strength, but Sextus seemed not to notice the steadily growing heat as he marched straight-backed with a determined expression on his face. The Nabatean scouts had done a good job, and they now knew exactly where ben-Ezra and his army of cut-throats and thieves were hiding.

His Optio, Drusus, fell into step beside him.

"What is it?" Sextus growled.

"Centurion, I just saw a flash of light come from the hilltop over there."

Sextus followed the Optio's eye direction and a thin smile spread across his face "So, the cunning bastard has posted lookouts, telling him our position. No matter, he doesn't know what our plans are. Did any of the men see it?"

"I think a couple did," came the Optio's reply.

"Right. I hope Centurion Fabius saw it too. He will have to keep his men in line, or else deal with them. If any of our own men did see it and falter, they will feel the weight of my vine stick across their backs. Now fall back into place, Drusus, we mustn't let the lookouts know you've spotted them."

"No Centurion." Optio Drusus quickly returned to his rightful place at the side of the leading century.

Up in the hills, the watching hot-headed Zealots wanted to kill the legionaries then and there, but ben-Ezra calmed them down and told them to be patient and wait for the bigger prize.

The Jerusalem troops reached Antipatris, where

they were fed and watered. Soon after, the Governor, Aelius, Sextus and Fabius, along with Centurion Primus, Centurion of the Antipatris First Century, and Julius were closeted in Aelius' office going over Quintus Maximus' plan to decide if it was worth merit. All were in agreement that it was.

After the briefing Julius was on his way to see Otto when he met Flavius, who was checking that Saturn was being groomed properly in the fortress pens.

Flavius smiled at the young Decurion. "How are you, Julius?"

Julius returned his smile. "I am well, sir. Excuse me, sir, did you see my family in Caesarea?"

"Yes, they are well. Your sister is getting married soon." He tried not to smile at the surprise on the young man's face. "To a member of Pilate's staff. In fact he is here with us now. When this is over, I will introduce you to your prospective brother-in-law."

Julius grinned "Thank you, Tribune." Julius turned away, then turned back again. "Tribune, sir. What do you think will happen at Beth-Horon?"

Flavius grew serious. "I think given the terrain it will be a hard battle. We must hope that Quintus Maximus' plan works out." He saw a look of concern cross Julius' face and placed his hand on his shoulder. "Don't worry, just remember your training, then you can't fail."

Julius managed a grim smile. "Yes, Tribune. Thank you, sir. I will heed your advice." As he walked away, Flavius' eyes followed him. He was a decent young man. Flavius prayed the gods would protect him, for Cornelius' sake.

Julius found Otto and told him the battle plan. Otto nodded. "It's a good plan, but it won't be an easy victory. I hope the gods will favour us."

Julius tried hard to push his own doubts away. "Of course they will." He slapped Otto on the back and the pair went off to find some refreshment.

The sun had been up for an hour. Joel had waited all night, watching for any further activity coming from the Antonia. The previous day he had been filled with nervous energy and excitement as he had seen two centuries of legionaries and their cavalry escort leave. That meant all was going to plan. He had not expected to see this morning a further century of men, this time with a group of foreigners on horseback and another cavalry escort, leave the Antonia just after dawn. Where were they going? Was it to join with the other Romans against ben-Ezra? Or was it a routine patrol? If they were to swell the numbers against ben-Ezra it was too late to warn his chief, but on the other hand, with more legionaries on the road, there would be fewer inside the fortress making their surprise attack more successful. His men were ready, awaiting his signal, but he would wait until he was sure the legionaries were too far away to help their comrades in the fortress.

How he hated these foreign conquerors. He had never known a time before their cruel dictatorship. How many

Jews had he seen crucified on trumped-up charges? How many women in the Judaean villages had been raped and abused? He still trembled with hatred when he remembered the cruel abuse and deaths of his family and the people in his own village, including the family of his friend ben-Ezra. When ben-Ezra had set about forming a gang to seek revenge on the Romans, he had at first been wary of joining them, but as the atrocities carried out on the Jews by their conquerors had escalated, he had changed his mind and had readily agreed to be the eyes and ears of the bandit chief in Jerusalem, reporting on the Antonia garrison movements and activities. Now here he was, elevated to the position of leader of the Jerusalem insurrection against the hated Romans. When ben-Ezra destroyed Pilate and he had brought down the Fortress Antonia, he knew there would be much rejoicing amongst his people. Then they would continue until the whole of Judaea was free.

Joel waited for what seemed like an eternity. Finally, sure that the troops were far enough away, he blew on a small ram's horn and shouted at the top of his voice "Now!" At that signal the rebels poured out of their houses and shops and ran out from dark alleys, pulling hidden axes, swords, spears and bows with sharp arrows from out of their coats and from baskets hidden under shop counters by merchants, sympathetic to their cause. The two-pronged attack had begun.

With Joel leading, they ran through the streets and up the hill towards the Temple Mount and fortress; in their feverish haste, they pushed aside anyone who got in their way. Men shouted and cursed at them, women screamed and bewildered children, clinging to their mother's skirts, cried in fear, wondering what was happening around them. When the innocent bystanders and pilgrims realised what was about to happen, they turned and ran back into the city. At the top of the hill the wooden latticed fence of a house swung open and eight burly men pulling ropes fixed to a wooden frame set on sturdy wheels poured out into the street and joined the mob. Within the frame was a battering ram made from a tree-trunk, its tip encased in iron, to batter down the gate leading to the fortress, and a hidden cache of assorted weapons.

Some of the frenzied mob who had reached the Temple area's Western Wall charged through the open gate of the Temple Courtyard of the Gentiles, intent on taking revenge on the merchants who dealt with changing money into Temple currency and the sellers of sacrificial animals, all of whom had relentlessly cheated them for many years. The mob came to a street with a row of small shops which housed the money-changers, small animal merchants and souvenir sellers.

As the mob rampaged down the street, some of the merchants fled into their houses. The money-changers shouted as their stalls, laden with shekels ready to change foreign monies into Temple currency, were tipped up, scattering the coins everywhere; the sacrificial animal sellers wailed as the cages holding small animals for sacrifice hit the ground and burst open, sending the frightened animals inside them running to and fro in a mad dash for freedom; the souvenir merchants shook their fists as the mob rushed by overturning their stalls, shattering many expensive Temple trinkets into fragments.

A few men stopped briefly to pick up the shekels and hide them in their pockets, an opportunity too good to miss. One money-changer, horrified that his money was being stolen, knelt down trying desperately to collect the shekels left on the ground. So intent was he in his task that he did not see one of the rebels come up behind him. The money-changer screamed as the man lifted his dagger high, then brought it down hard between the merchant's shoulder blades, shouting "That's for all the times you have cheated me, you filthy pig!" He watched as the man fell forward onto the ground, sprawled amongst his shekels, then turned away to catch up with some of the mob as they thundered on to their goal: the west cloisters and the access to the aerial bridges that led to another entrance to the Antonia fortress.

Many of the insurgents were still running through the Temple courtyard trying desperately to catch up with them as the spearhead of rebels reached the bridges. Suddenly, to their shock, the upper fortress gates opened and legionaries marched out to meet them. In the mayhem that followed, the desperate mob began to turn and run back across the bridges. In the ensuing panic, some fell to their deaths. The remnants of the mob ran down the west access passageway to the Temple courtyard below, into the path of the waiting legionaries of Tribune Commodus, who had emerged from the fortress' north cloisters' access leading to that side of the Temple area.

Commodus shouted the order "Phalanx!" and the legionaries quickly manoeuvered into formation. They began to move forward, their short swords and javelins ready to kill those before and around them without mercy. Those rebels that had escaped death by Roman javelins felt the terrible thrust of the legionaries' swords slicing into their bellies. The phalanx ploughed on until the Temple courtyard was awash with blood and gore.

Outside the Temple complex, the rest of the mob, led by Joel, made their way up the stairs leading to the Tedi gate, the entrance to the Antonia. The battering ram was hauled up the stairs by the burly men, who heaved the tree-trunk back and forth until it first splintered, then smashed through the wooden gates of the fortress. The front-runners of the mob surged through into the fortress courtyard. Discarding the battering ram, the men retrieved their weapons from the frame and followed them.

Amazed that there was no sign of any Roman legionaries coming out to tackle them, the mob grew suspicious, and some began to look around bemused. A man screamed as an arrow thudded into his chest. As he fell dead, some of those who stood nearby looked up, horrified to see Roman archers appearing on top of one of the towers looming over the courtyard. In a very short time, many of the rebels were killed or wounded by the relentless shower of arrows raining down on them.

In the far corner of the courtyard, a camouflaged screen was pushed onto the ground from behind, revealing grim-faced legionaries standing beside two small, bolt-firing catapults, ready loaded with lead-tipped bolts. The first bolt was let loose and a rebel frontrunner was cut down, the bolt piercing his body, its momentum hurling him backwards. As the catapult was being readied to fire a new bolt, a bolt from the second catapult was fired into the mob, quickly followed by another from the first. This was continuously repeated, until the rebels' bodies lay in heaps before their terrified compatriots.

Joel was in despair as he saw the carnage taking place all around him. How had the Romans known they were going to attack? Who had betrayed them? He knew the uprising was doomed and turned to follow the rest of those running back towards the Tedi Gate, wondering if he managed to escape the Romans' retribution, how he could flee from Jerusalem and Judaea. He could not face ben-Ezra after his abject failure.

As the other rebels neared the gate, they came to an abrupt halt. Columns of legionaries were surrounding it. With the Roman arrows and catapults still firing their missiles at them from behind, and the legionaries standing waiting before them, they could move neither backwards nor forwards. The missiles stopped as the legionaries began to march towards them in dense, unbreakable ranks. Joel ran to and fro frantically seeking a way of escape until he felt a terrible agony as a Roman javelin lodged deep into his spine. He cried out, sank to his knees and fell face forward onto the blood-soaked ground.

Ignoring the pleas of the wounded and dying, the legionaries relentlessly moved onwards, marching over the fallen rebels and finishing them off with their swords. The slaughter in both the Temple area and that of the fortress courtyard continued until there was not one rebel left alive.

When the battle was over, Commodus gave orders that the dead from the Temple area and the fortress should be loaded onto carts and taken outside the city to be burnt, and that the gates of the fortress should quickly be replaced.

When the High Priests were informed that the battle was over, they stood on the top of the steps overlooking the Temple courtyard, shaking their heads and wailing in despair and anger. So much blood had been shed in this Holy place. They sent for people to wash away the blood and gore. As this grisly task was being done, the Priests covered their heads and, their upper bodies rocking backwards and forwards, intoned prayers for the cleansing of the great sin that had been performed there and asked God's forgiveness for the desecration of His Holy Temple.

# CHAPTER SEVENTEEN

The legionaries returning to Jerusalem from Antipatris marched in their columns, the Syrian archers and unproven soldiers of the auxiliary unit of Centurion Fabius leading the way. Sextus, following on a short way behind, led the First Century of veteran, battle-hardened troops, with Pilate and his entourage, including Flavius and Marcus, in their midst. Julius' cavalry rode as vanguard. Some way behind them marched Aelius' troops, led by Centurion Primus. Their orders were to act as back-up to Sextus.

The road leading to Beth-Horon narrowed. Tension amongst the troops increased as the auxiliary unit and Sextus' Century entered the Pass. The heat was stifling. Flavius was sweating in anticipation of the coming battle. Would this be his one and only chance to be reunited with Farrah, or did death await them both?

Saturn felt his tension and tossed his head. Flavius spoke calmly to the horse, which resumed a steady trot.

Deeper along the Pass, without warning, Zealot slingers appeared on the hill crest. Their deadly accurate stones and lead pellets rained down on the helmets, bodies and legs of the soldiers marching at the front line of the auxiliary unit. This was followed by a shower of arrows from Josiah's archers. Centurion Fabius shouted an order which was relayed by the horn of the Cornicen and the furious flag waving of the signifier, giving the order to the auxiliaries to turn and face their enemy in the hills above. Their mail armour glinting in the sunshine, the infantry closed into battle order, their oval shields protecting their bodies, their swords and javelins ready for close combat. The Syrian archers, protected by the infantry shields, moved forward, nocked their arrows, aimed high and let them loose. Some fell too low onto the side of the hill, but most found their targets.

Flavius longed to be in the midst of the battle, to have a chance of killing ben-Ezra, but Pilate had ordered him to stay close to him. He shaded his eyes, anxiously looking above to the hill where the slingers were in action. He saw a slinger home in on Pilate and raised his shield just in time for it to take the brunt of the lead pellet aimed at Pilate's head. A stone hit the point of the shoulder of a cavalry officer's horse nearby. The horse whinnied pitifully and reared up, sending its rider sliding backwards onto the hard ground. Terrified, the horse bolted. The officer staggered to his feet, shocked and bruised, but otherwise unhurt. He quickly ran behind the other cavalry horses, whose riders struggled to keep their horses calm, preventing them from following after the bolted horse. Pilate and his staff officers immediately retreated behind the lines, out of range of the deadly missiles.

Although he did not care for Marcus, Flavius wanted him to stay safe for Julia's sake, so he ordered him to stay in the inner circle. Julius and his squadron joined them, forming a tight circle around the Governor and his officers to make sure they could not be surprised from any angle.

The slingshots and arrows rained down on the infantry, and Sextus cursed. Ben-Ezra was indeed cunning; he had moved some of his men onto a different part of the hills overlooking the Pass. Sextus ordered the Cornicen to blow the orders for his Century to turn towards the hill, for the legionaries to step into the gaps and form a phalanx, a rectangular block of soldiers. He shouted: "Shields up!" The troops immediately linked their rectangular shields together top, bottom, front and sides to form a *testudo* (tortoise). The dazzling sunshine reflected off the shields' bronze bosses and bindings creating a burst of light around them. They looked like fiery demon warriors spewed up from the depths of Hades.

The auxiliaries were taking the brunt of the action. As Centurion Fabius turned to his Cornicen to relay an order, an arrow found its mark between the man's helmet and armour, piercing his throat. He died instantly. Several other auxiliaries fell wounded and dying under the onslaught.

Sextus ordered his troops to stay in testudo formation. The attacks suddenly stopped and the slingers and archers moved back behind the hill. Sextus was about to give the order to re-form into battle lines when, having obviously re-armed, the attacking force reappeared on the hill and the onslaught began again. Sextus swore out loud as he saw ben-Ezra appear on the top of the hill, dressed as Rebecca had described in Roman helmet, breastplate and grieves. Another man stood close by, dressed in a plain grey, leather-belted tunic, signalling to the slingers to prepare. Sextus guessed this was the Zealot leader. Further along stood a tall, well-built man who was shouting orders to the archers and spearmen. Was this Rebecca's brother, Josiah?

The usually unflappable Sextus now felt panic overwhelming him as he saw horsemen riding down the side of the hill, followed by men carrying spears and swords, with women armed with knives and small axes running behind them. The horsemen were manoeuvering ready to attack them from behind; the spear and swordsmen, together with the women, began to attack from the front, while the bombardment continued from above. Sextus ordered the legionaries to form a square. The unit turned as one to face the attackers coming at them from all sides. They could not lift their shields over their heads this time as their bodies would be left open to the spears and swords, knives and axes coming towards them, so several of the legionaries fell under the barrage of stones and lead pellets raining down on them.

A rebel, wielding his sword, closed in on Sextus. Before the rebel could strike, Sextus angled his shield and rammed it down the shins of the attacker, ripping the flesh off the bone. As the man toppled forward gasping in shock and agony, Sextus brought his shield up sharply, smashing the boss into the rebel's face, shattering his nose and cheekbones. Sextus' sword flashed out from behind his shield and he delivered a killing stab to the man's heart. The man fell to the ground, blood pumping out from his wounds.

Sextus quickly re-focused on the enemy. He was afraid they were slowly gaining ground on his men. He saw another rebel running towards him and drove his sword out through the shield wall and into the man's midriff, twisting it before withdrawing it again. Disembowelled, the man fell on top of the bloody corpse lying at Sextus' feet.

Some of the rebel horsemen were closing in on Pilate and the cavalry. Flavius, Marcus and Julius' cavalrymen drew their swords and moved in closer to protect the Governor, creating an impenetrable wall around him. Flavius lashed out again and again with his sword at rebels who got too close.

Sextus shouted to the Cornicen and flag-bearer to give the signal for Batitus and Aelius' men to join them. There was no answering horn or flag. Where were Batitus' and

Aelius' men? Sextus knew that without backup they were doomed. Terrible thoughts crossed his mind: had the rebels in Jerusalem defeated those left at the Antonia? Had ben-Ezra's men cut off the back-up forces before they could reach him? He hurriedly dismissed these thoughts and through gritted teeth he growled "Jupiter's thunderbolts! Where in Hades are the reinforcements?" He ordered the Cornicen and flag-bearer to repeat their actions, hoping that this time somebody would answer the desperate call to arms.

From his vantage point above, ben-Ezra smiled. It was all going to plan. Soon Pilate and the Romans would be dead. Victory would be his. He envisaged himself riding in triumph through the streets of Jerusalem and being honoured by the grateful citizens.

Centurion Batitus and his Century had left Jerusalem before dawn and were nearing the Beth-Horon Pass. Travelling with them, surrounded by his bodyguard, was the Sheikh. By his side rode Drubaal, who had begged his master to let him ride with him although he was still in pain from his injuries. Sheikh Ibrahim, knowing the guilt the Carthaginian felt about his failure to stop the capture of his niece, had readily agreed. Antonius and his North African Cavalry squadron rode closely behind.

Batitus' orders were to keep his men back in formation on the edge of the Pass and block and kill any rebel who tried to make their way back to Jerusalem, unless Sextus had desperate need of them.

As they drew closer to the Pass, Batitus heard the loud braying of the First's horn. Sextus was in trouble. He turned to his ranks of legionaries and shouted "The first four lines of the Century follow me." To his Optio he ordered, "Stay here with the rest of the Century to guard the Sheikh and the Pass." Led by Batitus, forty legionaries, half of the force, ran towards Sextus and his troops, eager and ready to join the battle.

At the same moment Centurion Primus' legionaries also heard the second horn and saw the flag waving frantically. On Primus' orders they began to close in on the rebels from the opposite direction. When Sextus saw the reinforcements appear he smiled, muttering grimly, "About time! Thank you gods." Seeing Batitus, he knew that the Antonia was safe and the rebels in Jerusalem had been defeated. Now was the time to end Eleazar ben-Ezra's ambitions once and for all.

Sextus screamed out, "Arrowhead formations!"

The infantry manoeuvered quickly into the shapes of arrowheads and surged forward. The pincer movement between his men and those of Batitus, Fabius and Primus quickly hemmed in the rebels and their slaughter began.

Horrified at this turn of events, ben-Ezra immediately ordered his remaining slingers and bowmen to concentrate on this new onslaught. A barrage of slingshot and arrows showered down on the Romans. Some of Fabius' and Batitus' men fell, but the rest, undaunted, closed in on the rebels, driving them towards Sextus' Century. The attackers, now getting the worst of the battle, began to scramble back up the hill but were cut down by the Syrian archers and the Second Centuries' javelins. Isaac took a javelin in the back. He screamed, then fell dying with Anna's name on his lips. An arrow pierced Reuben's skull, killing him immediately.

During the mayhem, Antonius and his squadron had stayed back to protect the Sheikh and his guards until ordered to join in the battle; when the Sheikh, his patience running out, turned to Drubaal and his Nabatean guards and said "Let us join the battle!" Antonius took this to mean himself and his men too; after all, Quintus Maximus had ordered him to stay with the Sheikh, although he had no intention of doing so. There was glory to be had this day and he would make sure he was covered in it.

He shouted at his cavalrymen "Come on, let's finish the bastards!" Immediately his men raced forward, eager to reach the killing fields. The protesting Optio watched as Antonius and his men galloped in the opposite direction to the Sheikh, Drubaal and the Nabatean guards. There was nothing he could do except follow Batitus' orders and stay with the rest of the Century guarding the exit of the Pass. He just hoped and prayed that nothing would happen to the powerful emissary of the Nabatean King, for he knew the blame would fall on him and not on the detested Prefect Alae Antonius.

Knowing the battle had turned in their favour, Sextus yelled at the top of his voice: "No pity! No mercy!" Protected by their shields, the Romans hurled their javelins, the iron heads wreaking havoc amongst the rebels; the screams of dying men, women and horses reverberated around the hills. The units pushed forward, tramping over blood and gore. Flavius and Marcus were amongst those ordered to stay guarding Pilate as the bulk of the cavalry was let loose, the Sheikh, his Nabatean guards and Drubaal riding with them.

Batitus' Optio was glad that he had obeyed his orders and made sure he and his men had maintained their position. Some of the rebels who had survived the javelins, arrows and lethal short swords of the legionaries were now trying to escape back to Jerusalem along the edge of the Pass, but he and his men were ready for them, blocking their escape route and quickly cutting them down.

Francus, in the front row of the Gallic cavalry, screamed as a rebel spear hit him in the thigh. He fell sideways off his horse and frightened by the battle, one of Josiah's horses, now riderless and running amok, came galloping towards him. It reared up and trampled him to death. Julius saw it. He was sorry, but felt that Francus' quick death was a mercy; it was better than the punishment for a traitor.

During the ensuing slaughter, Antonius saw Drubaal and rode up behind him. This was the perfect time for him to take his revenge on the man who had insulted and humiliated him. Antonius lifted his sword and was about to bring it down on the back of Drubaal's head when it was deflected by the shield of a furious Julius who, with Otto at his side, had seen Antonius' intention and galloped over to stop him.

Alerted by the clang of sword on shield, Drubaal turned and quickly summed up the situation. Let Roman deal with Roman. He smiled at Julius, then rode on to deal with another of ben-Ezra's men.

Antonius turned on Julius, hatred etched on his face. He would have struck him, but Otto was watching him intently. Otto lifted his sword menacingly and Antonius, snarling, rode away to take out his anger and frustration on a Zealot who was trying to grab his horse's reins. Antonius lopped off the man's arm.

Watching too was Sextus, who had seen the Prefect's action before hurriedly turning aside to defend himself from the sword of a rebel. Unaware that Sextus had seen the attempt on Drubaal's life, Julius quickly turned to Otto with a questioning look. Otto nodded in agreement. If they survived the battle, they knew what they had to do. They turned their horses and rejoined the Gallic squadron who had taken on ben-Ezra's horsemen.

Satisfied that the enemy ground force had been put out of action, the remainder of the three infantry centuries began clambering up the hill, their thick leather studded sandals slipping on the blood-soaked, rugged surface. Josiah and Moshe were quickly taken and tightly bound, ready to be taken back to the Antonia to be put to the question and ultimately executed. The slingers and bowmen surrounding them were killed where they stood.

Drubaal, who had ridden to the top of the hill, now began to search for his mistress. He saw Abraham bar-

Saraf standing in front of a large rock, his drawn sword stained with blood. Drubaal recognised the man who had so gravely injured him. He disliked fighting from horseback, so he dismounted. A legionary was homing in on the bandit. Drubaal pushed the legionary out of the way, growling "He is mine!"

Seeing the fierce look on Drubaal's face, the legionary turned his attention to a rebel creeping up behind the Carthaginian, drawing his dagger and driving it into the rebel's unprotected midriff. The rebel dropped the weapon and fell to the ground, clutching his stomach.

Drubaal drew his curved sword and moved towards the bandit. Abraham stared at the Carthaginian. "I thought you were dead," he snarled.

Drubaal stood motionless for a brief moment, then, like an angry lion, he sprang forward aiming at Abraham's body. Abraham deflected Drubaal's blows again and again, all the time moving back to try to get away from his powerful adversary. Undeterred, Drubaal advanced on his quarry. Abraham swung wildly with his sword and a glancing blow caught Drubaal across his injured rib. Drubaal roared in anger and pain, but continued his advance. Ignoring the searing pain in his side, he suddenly spun on his heels and with all his strength, brought his sword down, slicing through Abraham's collar bone, sinew and muscle down to his breastbone. Mouth open in a silent scream, Abraham dropped his sword and fell to his knees. Drubaal heaved the sword out of Abraham's body and Abraham fell forward, his blood pumping out over the ground. Drubaal turned him over with his foot. Abraham bar-Saraf was dead. A long-overdue score had been settled.

Seeing that defeat was now inevitable, ben-Ezra dragged Farrah from her hiding place and lifted her roughly onto his horse, then mounted up behind her. He lashed the horse and galloped down the right-hand slope of the hill.

Drubaal searched around for his mistress. He heard a cry coming from behind the rock and went to investigate, to find Ruth cowering there with Rachel holding a knife to her throat. He moved forward slowly.

"Don't come any closer or I'll kill the slut," hissed Rachel.

Drubaal hesitated, seeing a legionary creep up behind her. Seeing Drubaal glance to one side, Rachel half-turned. That was Drubaal's chance. He sprang forward, tore the knife from her hand and knocked her sideways onto the ground. He stood guard over Ruth while the legionary tied Rachel's hands behind her back, dragged her to her feet and frog-marched her down the hill at sword point. It would be the Governor's decision as to whether she lived to become a slave or was put to death.

Drubaal saw the relief on Ruth's face as she recognised him. "Where is your mistress?" he asked urgently.

"Ben-Ezra has taken her," replied Ruth. Drubaal realized that his fight with Abraham had given the bandit chief time to make his escape, taking his mistress with him. He must let the Sheikh know, but his terrified horse had ridden off. How would he get Ruth safely down the hill? He would have to carry her, and that would take time on this rough ground.

As she stood up, he saw her swollen belly. He grimaced; she was with child. He pulled himself up. No matter, he had to get her to safety.

Julius rode up and saw Drubaal carefully lifting Ruth up into his arms. Seeing his predicament, Julius said "I will take her to the Sheikh."

"You must tell him that ben-Ezra has taken the Princess," Drubaal said, as Julius lifted Ruth onto his horse. The sooner his master and the Romans knew about his mistress, the quicker they could follow ben-Ezra and, with the gods' help, save her. Holding Ruth steady, Julius rode back down to the Sheikh, with Drubaal striding down the hill behind them.

Flavius let out a cry as he saw a horse gallop down the hillside. On it was ben-Ezra, with a woman seated precariously in front of him. Was that Farrah? He gave an anguished look at Pilate who, guessing Flavius' intention, nodded his approval. Pilate signalled to Marcus to go with him. With Flavius leading the way, the two horsemen gave chase.

Flavius was desperate. If only he could get closer to ben-Ezra, but the rebel chief was driving his horse on faster and faster. Flavius urged Saturn on and his hooves thundered over the ground as Saturn gradually caught up with the felon. At last Flavius was close enough to hurl his javelin at ben-Ezra's horse. The iron tip ripped into the horse's rump and it whinnied pitifully as its hindquarters collapsed, throwing ben-Ezra and Farrah off onto the hard ground.

Flavius quickly dismounted and approached ben-Ezra. Seeing that he had been knocked unconscious, Flavius took his sword, and using all his strength, he threw it as far as he could. Heart pumping, he ran to Farrah, who lay on the ground dazed and trembling with fear. Satisfying himself that she had only a bruised arm and was otherwise not badly injured, he carefully helped her to her feet. Overcome with emotion, he whispered "I thought I'd never see you again." He held her close. "I love you so much."

Farrah pulled away from him, and with tears streaming down her face said "No, you cannot love me. I am unclean." She turned her face away from him. "You should have left me to die."

Puzzled, Flavius tenderly turned her face back to him and studied it. He winced as he saw the purple shadows beneath her terror-filled eyes, her thin face and that once beautiful ruby-red mouth, now colourless and twisted in fear. What brutalities and indignities had she suffered at the hands of the monster sprawled out before them? Her eyes mirrored her deep shame and hopelessness, and he realised what ben-Ezra had done to her. Love and pity washed over him. He stroked her hair, no longer like spun silk, now filthy and matted, and kissed her forehead and her tear-wet eyes. "Nothing and no one will ever change my love for you," he murmured.

Ben-Ezra had regained consciousness, and looked round to realise that his prize was being taken from him, by the one he hated most in all the world. He might have possessed her body, but her heart and soul had always belonged to the man who now held her in his arms – the Roman. Ben-Ezra felt a wave of bitter jealousy sweep over him and scowled. He would not lose her to another man; she was his and his alone. If he could not have her, then no man would.

Just then Marcus rode up to see Flavius with the woman he guessed to be the fabled Princess Farrah, and the bandit chief lying on the ground nearby. As he dismounted, he saw a sudden movement from ben-Ezra and watched, horrified, as the bandit reached down into his boot and pulled out a knife. With no time to stop him, Marcus could only let out a warning cry. Too late. Before Flavius could move Farrah out of the way, ben-Ezra had thrown the deadly weapon. It hit Farrah between her shoulder blades and she slumped with a gasp into Flavius' arms.

Flavius held her to him for a long moment as the realisation of what had happened gradually set in, then he let out an anguished cry. "NO!" Gently laying her on the ground, he knelt beside her. She looked up at him, her face a mask of pain, her eyes already misting over with the shadow of approaching death. "Flavius... my love..." she whispered. She coughed deeply and blood appeared at the corners of her mouth, trickling down over her chin. Then her head lolled back in death.

Flavius lifted her upper body, the knife still protruding from her back, and held her to his chest, his tears falling unchecked. Grief and guilt overwhelmed him. This was his fault. He should have made sure the bandit chief was immobilised and weaponless, but he had been blinded by seeing Farrah again; now the love of his life lay dead in his arms.

Flavius pulled out the knife and laid Farrah back down, anger replacing grief. He strode over to where ben-Ezra sat. Marcus had already tied ben-Ezra's feet and hands, using the rope once attached to his javelin. "Move back, Marcus!" Flavius growled, his face a terrible portrait of anger.

Ben-Ezra looked up at him. Flavius ripped off the Roman helmet then aimed a vicious kick at the bandit's sneering face with his iron-shod sandal, shattering his nose and ripping out teeth; ben-Ezra groaned as his head snapped back with the impact. Flavius wanted so much to kill the murdering rapist, but, tempting as it was, he knew Quintus Maximus wanted ben-Ezra alive. He consoled himself with knowing that the Commander had planned a death for the brigand which would be more leisurely and infinitely more painful.

He returned to where Farrah lay. His face a mask of grief, he lifted her up and gently laid her across Saturn's back, then climbed up behind her. Holding her steady, he rode back to face Pilate and the Sheikh.

Ben-Ezra's face was covered in blood from his smashed

nose and torn gums. He cursed as he spat out blood and the remnants of broken teeth. Marcus yanked him up off the ground, then dragged him across to his horse, tying the rope securing his hands to his saddle. He removed the rope from ben-Ezra's feet and mounted up, leaving the bandit chief to stagger and stumble behind his horse.

Sheikh Ibrahim, already shocked by Ruth's appearance, wailed in grief as he saw the body of his beloved niece. He dismounted to help Flavius to lift her off Saturn's back. Drubaal, seeing the lifeless body of his mistress, let out a mournful cry. Flavius respectfully stood aside as together, Sheikh Ibrahim and Drubaal carefully laid her on the ground. Drubaal stood watching as Ibrahim knelt down beside her, took her cold hand and held it, all the while murmuring prayers. At his master's signal, Drubaal lifted his dead mistress and carefully laid her in one of the horse-drawn carts brought down from the hill.

Pilate rode over to Ibrahim and consoled him as best he could, then returned to a distraught Flavius. His voice was clipped as he said, "We will discuss this tragedy when we return to Jerusalem." Pilate shook his head, grimacing. This would have to be reported to the Emperor, who he knew would not be pleased that a newly-created Roman citizen, one who had done so much for Rome, had met such an unfortunate end. When they returned to Jerusalem, all he could do would be to learn the truth of what had happened, then send an emissary to King Aretas and wait for his and the Emperor's wrath to subside.

He turned his horse to face his men and spoke to the exhausted legionaries.

"Today you have saved us from a mortal enemy. I commend you for your bravery and salute you and those of your comrades who have died in Rome's cause." He looked around at the corpses littering the hills and the Pass. "The bodies of our brave and honourable legionaries must be collected. They must be stripped of all reusable equipment. As for the dead and dying rebels, kill any who have even the smallest amount of breath left in their bodies, then leave them all where they lie for the carrion crows and wild beasts to devour as a stark warning that this is what happens when a conquered people foolishly defy the power of Rome and her mighty, all-conquering army."

Pilate turned his horse away and ordered Flavius and the rest of his cavalry entourage to wait until his orders had been carried out.

Sextus, Primus and Batitus oversaw their men as they finished off the injured rebels, then collected the bodies of the dead Romans and stripped them of all reusable equipment, which would later be cleaned and shared out amongst the rest of the Centuries. This done, the armour and weapons were piled onto two carts, one to be returned to Jerusalem, the other to Antipatris. The carts ben-Ezra had used to store provisions and weapons were utilized to carry the wounded legionaries back to the fortress' hospitals. Antonius' cavalrymen were ordered to catch the rebels' horses, which were careering around in terror, and tie them by their reins into a line in order to return them to the garrison. Ben-Ezra remained secured to Marcus' saddle. Julius and Otto had secured Josiah and the Zealot leader, Moshe, to their saddles, ready to be dragged along the road to Jerusalem to face torture and certain death.

Once the rebels' horses were securely tied, Antonius reformed Julius' squadron with his own and the combined cavalry quickly surrounded Pilate and his entourage, the Sheikh and his guards. Drubaal begged the Sheikh to be the one to drive the cart carrying his mistress' body, and Ibrahim agreed. With a heavy heart, the Carthaginian climbed up onto the cart and took the reins. An equally heartbroken Ruth was helped up to sit beside him.

When all was ready, Drubaal flicked the reins and the horse moved off at a slow pace. Behind them came the cart bearing the retrieved weapons. On it, flanked by two legionaries, sat Rachel. With her hands and feet securely tied, she sat staring straight ahead. The cart carrying the wounded followed on close behind. A detail of legionaries was ordered to stay behind to forage for wood and build pyres, ready to place the legionaries' bodies on them to be cremated. The dead rebels would be left to the crows and the jackals, as Pilate had ordered.

The Antipatris troops, led by Primus, began their journey back to their fortress to give a report to Aelius. Sextus and Batitus reformed their men on their Century Standards. The standard bearers proudly held their standards aloft and the march back to Jerusalem began.

The Centurions too would have to give their report to a waiting Quintus Maximus.

As he rode along, Flavius thought his heart would break. In his tormented mind, he accepted full responsibility for Farrah's death. He touched the amulet Farrah had given him, remembering the magical time in the garden in Bethany when he had first kissed her and told her that he loved her. His own life had no meaning now. He didn't care what became of him; all he knew was that the woman he loved above all others had gone forever.

# CHAPTER EIGHTEEN

In the aftermath of the shocking events that had occurred at the Temple and the Fortress Antonia, the citizens of Jerusalem stared, stunned, as Pilate and the blood-stained remnants of the three Centuries and the cavalry entered through the city gate. The evening sun was now casting long shadows, but the streets were still packed with people. The jostling crowd jeered when they saw the three prisoners; some spat on the ground as the felons were dragged past behind the cavalry horses. Some women turned their faces away as they saw Rachel, her hands and feet tightly bound, cowering between two legionaries sitting on the second cart.

Flavius was anxious that trouble might break out, but nothing happened and Pilate was safely escorted to his residence at Herod's Palace, taking some of his staff officers with him, including Flavius and Marcus. The legionaries and cavalry, together with the Sheikh, Drubaal and the Nabatean Guard, returned to the Antonia; the remainder of Pilate's Staff Officers went with them in order to take their turn in guarding Pilate's residence. Back inside the fortress, ben-Ezra, Josiah, Moshe and Rachel were taken to the Antonia dungeon.

Rebecca retreated to the shadowy corner of her cell as the felons were dragged past, worried that they would see her, but they were wrapped up in their own misery and kept their eyes on the tiled floor. They were thrown into cells further down the dungeon. Rebecca smiled. So ben-Ezra's daring plan had not worked. The Romans would most certainly take their revenge out on him now, and soon she would be free.

Pilate sent a message ordering Quintus to go to the palace, bringing the Sheikh with him. Before Quintus left he ordered a fresh squadron of legionaries to go into the city to flush out Simon the beggar and Sarah the prostitute and place them in the Antonia dungeon ready for questioning. A cavalry unit was ordered to ride to Beth Bassi and arrest the horse trader Zeke, along with those of his men who had not gone to Beth Horon to fight with ben-Ezra; Zeke's horses were to be brought back to the garrison. Although bone-weary from the battle, Julius and his men volunteered, and with fresh horses, they were soon on their way.

Simon the beggar was panic-stricken when he heard

about Joel's failure and ben-Ezra's capture. In desperation, he and his granddaughter planned an escape from the city. They were about to leave Simon's hovel when the legionaries came. The wiry young girl made a dash for the doorway but was cut down by a legionary; the old man cried out as the child dropped to the floor, blood pouring from her wound. He was silenced by a blow to the chin. The legionaries hauled him back, semi-conscious, to the fortress, where he joined the other prisoners.

Sarah was told about Joel's death and ben-Ezra's capture by the fat merchant she was entertaining, but she wasn't worried. How could anyone know she was connected to the rebels? Totally unconcerned, she was slowly undressing ready to pleasure her customer when the legionaries burst into her room. The legionary in charge shouted to the terrified merchant, "Get out!" The merchant needed no second bidding. He heaved himself up, hurriedly dressed and ran away as fast as his short, fat legs could carry him. Sarah screamed as the soldiers roughly took hold of her. The one in charge threatened her with his sword, yelling "Get dressed!" Sarah quickly dressed, trembling as she realised someone must have given the Romans her name. She doubted it would be ben-Ezra. Surely Francus had not betrayed her?

Pilate stared at Flavius and Marcus and said grimly "What happened back there?"

Flavius relayed the events of Farrah's death. His story

was corroborated by Marcus. Flavius was grateful to the young officer for not telling Pilate about the obvious close connection he'd shared with Farrah and made a mental note to thank him for his discretion. Pilate's voice was harsh as he said "You were irresponsible, Tribune, you should have checked ben-Ezra had no concealed weapons." Flavius hung his head in shame.

Pilate was in a quandary. What was he to do? He knew the wrath of both King Aretas and the Emperor would fall not only on Flavius but on himself. He suppressed a shudder as his imagination conjured up the punishment both rulers would inflict upon him. He would have to make up an excuse to exonerate Flavius and, more importantly, himself, from blame. He sat deep in thought for a long moment then, looking at Flavius, he said, "However, in the heat of the moment, having disarmed ben-Ezra of his sword, I understand your sole intent was to make sure Princess Farrah was safe." He pointed to Marcus. "It's a pity young Marcus here was too far away to have any effect on the unfortunate outcome." Marcus looked down, red-faced. Pilate turned back to Flavius. "And there were no other witnesses to this?"

Flavius lifted his head and said "No, Governor Pilate."

Pilate sat up straight in his chair, relief flooding over him. He had thought of the perfect solution to the problem. After all, it was as near to the truth as was possible. He cleared his throat and said in a stern voice, "It is therefore my judgement that the Princess, who was being held prisoner by her captor, the felon Eleazar ben-Ezra, was killed by him during his capture as a vengeful act against Rome." Yes, he was sure that was the perfect way out of his predicament. He continued, "That is what I will tell King Aretas and the Emperor, assuring them both that ben-Ezra will pay dearly for this and for all of the other crimes he has committed." He looked at the two officers standing relieved before him and said, "Now, I suggest you visit the baths, put on fresh clothes and then resume your duties at the Antonia. That's all!" He waved them away, and Flavius and Marcus saluted and turned to leave.

As he dismissed the young officers, Quintus and Ibrahim arrived. The Commander stood at attention before the Governor.

"Stand easy, Commander," ordered Pilate. He pointed to a chair, inviting the distraught Ibrahim to sit down. His face was grim. "As far as the rebels are concerned, the battle has been won," he said. He cleared his throat. "However, as you know, the Princess unfortunately died." He picked up an official scroll from his desk and turned to the Sheikh, saying "It is such a pity that the Emperor has just bestowed the honour of Roman citizenship upon her and, of course, on you, Sheikh Ibrahim."

Flavius, who had not quite reached the door, heard that and froze. How cruel fate was. It cared nothing for love or happiness. He quickly pulled himself together and, with head hung low, he hurried out of the room without waiting to hear the rest of Pilate's speech. He made his way back to the fortress and his quarters, where his personal servant, Gebhard, was waiting to welcome him back to Jerusalem.

Ibrahim listened as Pilate said, "As a Roman citizen, one who worked tirelessly for myself and our Divine Emperor, Princess Farrah is entitled to a full military funeral. I would like…"

Ibrahim held up his hand and Pilate stopped. Ibrahim looked straight at him and said curtly, "Forgive me, Governor Pilate. I thank the Emperor for making my niece and myself citizens of Rome and it is very kind of you to offer the privilege of a full military funeral, but I want my niece laid to rest in Nabatea. We have our own burial rituals, but it will take some time to return there, and in this heat…" he left the sentence incomplete. "Those rituals, for now, must be laid aside. She must be cremated and her ashes put into a casket. I will take that casket home to Nabatea so that her remains can be buried with her parents, her brother and baby sister in their family tomb."

Pilate nodded. "As you wish."

Quintus looked at Ibrahim. "It will be an honour to carry out the cremation at the fortress," he said.

Ibrahim shook his head. "Thank you, Commander, but a small private funeral outside the city will suffice. Now if there is nothing else, Governor, I am weary and would like to rest."

"Of course, forgive me," Pilate said, concerned. He watched as Ibrahim and Quintus left the room to return to the Antonia, then he retired to his private quarters where his personal body slave removed his battle-stained armour and tunic. He went to his bathroom and soaked in his bath for a long time in an effort to bathe away the stench of blood and death.

He grimaced as he remembered the invitation that had been sent to him by Herod Antipas. Herod Antipas had just returned to Jerusalem for the Passover Festival from his fortress, Machaerus, built on the eastern side of the Dead Sea, and had invited him to a banquet that night. Pilate did not really want to go, but he knew diplomacy required it. He had no particular liking for the minor potentate and would enjoy telling him about the act of rebellion carried out by rebels from Jericho, part of his territory, and how the Romans had destroyed them. He would also add, with a note of menace in his tone, that perhaps, in the areas granted to him by Rome, he should keep an eye on his people and govern them more strictly. He would enjoy seeing the look of panic on that flabby face. Cheered up by that prospect, he got out of the bath and let the slave dry him, then massage perfumed oil into his body.

In the garrison hospital, one of the medical orderlies draped material over the posts surrounding Ruth's bed to give her some privacy from the prying eyes of wounded legionaries lying close by. He then brought her a bowl of water and cloths with which to wash and dry herself, followed by a clean robe. Ruth washed her body and her hair as best she could, then put on the robe. When she was ready, the orderly removed the bowl and cloths and the tattered, filthy robe she had worn in the caves was taken outside and burnt. He then brought her some soft food and watered wine. Ruth slowly sipped the wine. She had no appetite, but she nevertheless forced down the food, knowing she had to build up her strength. After she had finished her meal, exhaustion overcame her and she lay back on the bed.

When Drubaal enquired after her he was told she was weak, but with rest and good food she would slowly improve. The medical orderly added bluntly, "She can't stay here. Does she have any family or friends in the city?"

"We are her family, but ben-Ezra destroyed our home. For the present, we are living at the fortress." Drubaal shrugged. "As for friends... I don't know."

"Talk to her, find out. She will give birth soon. A garrison is not the place for that."

The orderly walked off and Drubaal approached Ruth's bed. She smiled weakly when she saw him. He broached the subject of friends very carefully and was relieved when the answer came back, "Yes I have some good friends in the city." His smile soon faded when she added "But I am ashamed of my condition. I don't want them to see me like this."

Drubaal would brook no argument. "Your condition is no fault of yours. I will explain everything to them. If, as you say, they are good friends, surely they will help you in your time of need."

Ruth was in turmoil. She hoped Mary would help her, but if so, how could she face John Mark?

"Early tomorrow it is Princess Farrah's funeral," said Drubaal. "Afterwards I will take you to them."

"The funeral is tomorrow? I must be there," said Ruth. She tried to raise herself up, but weakness overcame her and she sank back onto the bed.

Drubaal soothed her. "You must rest and try to regain your strength."

Ruth looked earnestly at Drubaal. "We shared so much together. How can I desert her now?"

Drubaal took her hand as her tears began to fall, shook his head and said, "It will not be pleasant. And in your condition..."

"Please ask our master's permission for me to be there," Ruth implored him.

Seeing her expectant face, Drubaal said, "I will ask him, but I do not know if he will allow it."

"Please beg him to give his permission, I must be there. I will be there. I will!"

Drubaal knew Ruth too well to doubt her determination to be present at the funeral of her beloved mistress, despite her delicate condition. "I promise I'll ask him," he said. He released her hand. "I have to go into the city now to find Menachem the perfume merchant and bring back some perfume for the funeral. He is one of our master's main customers, I know he will gladly do his bidding. Then I have to purchase a cedar wood box, for our mistress' ashes." He saw Ruth's expression and immediately regretted having been so blunt. "I'm sorry," he said. "Now I must hurry, as it will soon be dark. When I return and have given the purchases to our master, I will speak with the orderly and see what he says about you being well enough to attend the funeral, if our master agrees, of course."

"I don't care what the orderly says. If our master says I may go, then I am going to the funeral and that is that!"

Drubaal smiled as Ruth's small hands balled into fists of defiance. He nodded, then turned, left the hospital and went into the city.

Once his errands were complete, Drubaal went to Sheikh Ibrahim and gave him the vials of costly perfumes and the ornately carved cedar wood box. "I have left the amphora of wine with Quintus Maximus who will choose the legionaries to be in charge of it at the ceremony tomorrow," he said.

Ibrahim looked at the vials of perfume and the cedar wood box and nodded, satisfied. Drubaal, choosing his words carefully, said, "Master, there is another matter." The older man gestured for him to speak. "It is Ruth..." He saw the scowl appear on the Sheikh's face but continued. "Master, she asks your permission to let her be at the funeral to say goodbye to her beloved mistress."

Sheikh Ibrahim waived his hand dismissively "I don't care if she attends or not." He looked straight at Drubaal. "In truth, it would have been better if she had died instead of my Farrah."

Drubaal was shocked. Was this the same man who had rescued Ruth from the streets as a child and raised her up to be his niece's servant? Surely he must have cared for the girl once. The house they had in Bethany was gone and along with Jerusalem, it had held too many memories. What if the master decided to return to Nabatea with no position for Ruth? What would she do? Where would she go? And with a child? Surely she would be forced to return to the streets or starve. He had grown fond of the little Jewish girl and did not want to see her suffer. Perhaps there was still hope for her. He knew how much the Sheikh was hurting at the loss of his niece and put his outburst down to grief and shock. He hoped that, in time, he would relent and accept Ruth back into his service.

Wanting to make a diplomatic exit, Drubaal said "If there is anything else, master?" The Sheikh shook his head then turned away. Drubaal bowed and left the room.

# CHAPTER NINETEEN

Early the next morning, a sad procession wound its way up the hill above the city. The fragrance of olive groves growing on the opposite hillside carried on the slight breeze, perfuming the dewy air. Sheikh Ibrahim, surrounded by his Nabatean guards, rode straight-backed on his horse. Flavius rode alongside Quintus. Flavius had been surprised when Sheikh Ibrahim had asked him to join them for the funeral. He wondered why, as he had always thought that the Sheikh had never approved of his liaison with Farrah. And then there was his own carelessness, which, in his own mind, had caused his beloved's death. He was sure the older man felt that way too.

Ruth had told the medical orderly that she felt better rested and strong enough to go to her mistress' funeral; doubting it, but seeing how determined and upset the girl was, he reluctantly agreed, as long as she rode on the cart that carried her mistress' body. She sat next to a sombre Drubaal, who was driving the horses pulling the funeral cart. Drubaal had told her as kindly as he could that their master would not acknowledge her presence at the funeral and had advised her to stay quietly on the cart. He had wrapped the cedar wood box in a silken cloth and placed it securely in the cart. The vials of perfume were in a leather bag slung across his shoulder.

As Ruth was unable to prepare her mistress' body for the funeral, Quintus had paid for a woman from the city to look after this. The woman had eased out the tangles in Farrah's hair until it was smooth, then washed the long tresses and brushed them until they shone. Then she had respectfully washed Farrah's body and anointed her with costly oils and spices. She had dressed her in a simple white robe held at the waist by a thin white cord, then placed a small bouquet of colourful wild flowers in her hands, finally fixing a white bloom into her raven hair. Even in death, Farrah's beauty was breathtaking.

As this was not to be a Roman funeral, there would be no musicians, wailing women or men carrying wax masks leading the procession. Ibrahim had told Quintus that he would carry out the correct Nabatean funeral rites once back in his own land.

Quintus had sent troops in advance to build the pyre ready to receive Farrah's body and to act as a guard of honour during the ceremony. Two other chosen legionaries took charge of the large amphora containing fine wine ready for the culmination of the ceremony. The Roman guard of honour was joined by the Nabatean guards.

Farrah's body was lifted off the cart and placed in Drubaal's arms. The guard of honour flanked Drubaal and his precious burden until they reached the funeral pyre. Farrah's body was carefully laid on top of the pyre by Drubaal and one of the Nabatean guards, and the honour guard formed a semi-circle around the pyre and stood silent, waiting.

The Romans stood to attention as one of the Nabatean guards handed Ibrahim a flaming torch. He thrust it into the pyre. The dry wood soon caught fire and the flames began to lick around Farrah's body. Through his tears, the Sheikh intoned prayers to the Nabatean gods:

"Dushares, great god of the sun, accept the body of my beloved niece into your almighty kingdom. Divine goddess, Allat, whose incomparable beauty is supreme, I humbly ask you to take care of my Farrah and let her earthly beauty dwell in the shadow of your radiant form forever. Manawat, decider of our destiny and fate, the Divine Being who rules over us all, you have decided the fate of my Farrah. Let her after-life destiny be yours." His voice broke with emotion. Drubaal went to his side and handed him the vials of perfume. Ibrahim threw the perfume onto the flames. There was a brief crackle as the cold liquid met the dry heat. The smell of sandalwood and myrrh filled their nostrils.

The flames raged, gradually consuming the once voluptuous body. Flavius closed his eyes, unable to bear the sight. He tried desperately to focus on the remembrance of the beautiful dancing girl he had seen in that grimy tavern. Was it only a few months ago? He had loved her from that first moment and knew that later, she had shared that love in return. For so many nights he had dreamed of finding her again, of holding her in his arms, covering her face and body with kisses and caresses. Now that dream would never come true. At that moment he decided he would never love another the way he had loved Farrah. He bit his lip, trying hard to stem his tears.

After what seemed an eternity to Ibrahim and Flavius, the pyre's flames gradually died down. The legionaries in charge of the amphora of wine picked it up, stepped forward and poured the wine over the embers to cool them. Later, when the legionaries were satisfied that the remains of the fire had sufficiently cooled, Farrah's ashes were gathered and placed in the cedar wood box. The clasp of the box was fastened and the box was handed to Ibrahim who, still intoning quiet prayers, lovingly held it to his chest. Reluctant to let the box go, Drubaal gently reminded him that they had to return to Jerusalem. Ibrahim handed the precious reliquary to Drubaal, who re-wrapped it and placed it safely on the cart.

The funeral rites finished, Ibrahim and his Nabatean guards mounted their horses. Quintus, Flavius and all but three of the legionaries, who had been ordered to stay behind and clear the remains of the pyre and embers, got into formation ready to return to the Antonia. Drubaal climbed up onto the cart and sat beside Ruth, gently touching the weeping girl's hand to offer solace to her. She looked up at him and gave him a wan smile in return. He manoeuvered the cart and horses into the gap between the leading Romans and the Sheikh and his Nabatean guards. When all was ready, the sad procession made its way back down to Jerusalem.

On the journey back, Drubaal cast a glance at a silent Ruth who sat slumped by his side. He saw her pale, pinched face and knew something was wrong. If he guessed right, he would very soon be taking Ruth to her friends.

Flavius left Saturn in the capable hands of Zeno, the fortress' equine expert, then entered his quarters, where Gebhard awaited him. Gebhard offered his master refreshment. Flavius ignored the food but took the jug of wine and filled his glass to the brim. He drank it down in one gulp, then turned to his slave and said gruffly, "Leave me, Gebhard."

Realising how distressed his master was, Gebhard bowed and left the room. Flavius threw himself down onto his bed, his pent-up pain overwhelming him, and wept bitterly.

# CHAPTER TWENTY

All the way back to the Antonia, Ruth had fought the urge to cry out as pains had begun to course through her frail body. As soon as they had reached the fortress, she had followed Drubaal's advice and stayed on the cart. She had watched as Drubaal had handed the cedar wood box containing her mistress' ashes to the Sheikh and had heard him tell the older man what was happening. She still felt disturbed by her master's cold comment: "I really don't care. Take her where you will, as long as it's away from here." Tears had stung her eyes as Drubaal had quickly climbed back onto the cart. What was to become of her if she no longer had a home with the Sheikh?

Agony shot through her again, and she knew she must worry about her future later. All she wanted now was to rid herself of this pain and the unwanted, unborn child causing it. Through gritted teeth, she directed the Carthaginian to Mary's house.

Frightened by the loud, incessant knocking on her door, a stab of fear shot through Mary; had the authorities come to arrest her? Then she heard an anguished voice, a voice she recognised, pleading, "Mary, please let us in." Mary quickly opened the door and saw a huge foreign stranger standing there supporting Ruth. Mary was stunned by how ill Ruth looked but, praise be, she was alive! She looked closer and saw Ruth's swollen belly and the blood staining her robe. Without a word, she went into action, helping Drubaal to get Ruth inside and onto her bed.

Horrified, she turned to Drubaal. "How long has she been like this?"

"Not long," came the reply. "Surely she can't be giving birth, it's too early?"

Mary set about bathing Ruth's face with a cloth dipped in a bowl of cool water, trying to ease the girl's suffering. "How many months has it been since you first knew you were with child, Ruth?" she said. She leaned forward to hear Ruth whisper, "I don't know." Her head spinning, Ruth tried to remember when Abraham had first forced himself on her, but that was just the first of many abuses she had suffered at his hands, so she could not be sure.

Drubaal intervened. "You and the Princess were captured almost seven months ago," he prompted gently.

Ruth grimaced. "I think I knew for sure about five months ago, so I must have been with child for six months."

Mary frowned. It was worse for the mother when a child was eager to enter the world before its due time, dangerous for both mother and child. She spoke gently to Ruth, trying hard to soothe her as she lay groaning on the bed.

Drubaal stood there, not knowing how to help Ruth. He screwed up his eyes as he heard Ruth suddenly scream, then went to her side and took her hand. "I will stay with you my friend," he said. He saw the look Mary gave him. "No. I am not the father. When this is over I will explain everything to you."

Mary nodded, then went to the water jar and poured out a cup of water. She helped Ruth to sit up and placed the cup to her lips, urging her to drink. She was pleased that Ruth was able to sip a little of the water, but frowned when Ruth, unable to support herself, fell back onto the bed, groaning in pain.

As time passed and there was still no sign of the child entering the world, Drubaal became more and more concerned. Ruth had become so weak that her screams had turned to groans. He could see the pallor of her face and the dampness on her forehead and knew she had succumbed to a fever. If only there was something he could do to help.

The evening was drawing in when John Mark came home. He was happy; it had been a good day and more people had been converted. His happiness faded when he heard groaning. Panicking, he called out "Mother? Are you all right?" Not seeing his mother in the living area, he rushed to her bedroom. He stared at the figure writhing in agony on his mother's bed, not believing his eyes, then he cried out, "Ruth?"

Mary was wiping the perspiration off Ruth's forehead when she heard her son's voice. She looked up at him and said quietly, "I know you have many questions, son, but they will have to be answered later. For now we must concentrate on helping Ruth through this ordeal."

John Mark looked from Ruth to the foreigner holding her hand, then at the bloodstained bedspread. He put his hands over his ears as Ruth clutched her stomach and suddenly let out moan after moan of agony; it seemed to him to go on for an eternity. What had happened to the girl he loved? Where had she been all these months? Why was she in this predicament?

Mary shooed the men out of the room, then examined Ruth. She kept her voice steady as she said, "The baby is coming. Stay strong Ruth, it won't be long now."

A short time later, Mary helped to deliver Ruth of a tiny scrap of humanity. Leaning towards an exhausted Ruth, she smiled and said, "You have a daughter." After attending to the umbilical cord and wiping the baby clean, Mary quickly wrapped the child in a warm shawl and placed her in her mother's arms.

Ruth was so weak that she could barely hold her tiny daughter and was glad when Mary took the baby away. She had no feelings towards the child; her only thought was that it was the shameful result of her terrible treatment by a vile criminal.

Outside, John Mark and Drubaal grew anxious when Ruth's groaning stopped; had she survived her ordeal? Drubaal smiled when he heard the mewling of the newborn and heard Mary talking to Ruth. At Mary's call both men entered the bedroom.

"Ruth has a daughter." Mary showed them the baby, whose tiny face peeped out from the folds of the shawl. She saw the confused look on John Mark's face and the relieved look on the foreigner's, then said sternly, "Leave us now, please. I must attend to the new mother."

The men left the room and Mary turned her attention on Ruth. Concern flooded through her as she saw her lying there, her face chalk-white, her sunken eyes filled with fever. She had lost a lot of blood before the birth, and now fresh blood was spreading across the bedspread. Mary spoke to her, but received no answer. She put her ear to Ruth's mouth; the girl's breathing was shallow and fading fast. Mary called John Mark back into the room. "Where's Peter?"

John Mark stood there, staring at Ruth. His mother repeated the question, rousing him from the shock of what he had just witnessed. He spoke falteringly. "Peter's preaching at the Pool of Siloam."

Mary frowned and said "Fetch him here. Tell him it's a matter of life and death. Go quickly, son." She watched as John Mark hurried out of the room, closing the front door behind him with a bang. She turned to Drubaal, who had realised something was wrong and had entered the room to see for himself. "I'm sorry, we are losing her," she said. She wiped the tears from her eyes. "Only Peter can save her now."

Drubaal was stunned by Mary's words. Ruth was dying! Who was this Peter she spoke of, and how could he save his young friend?

Peter was speaking to a group of men who had come to bathe in the pool. He was in the middle of telling them about the resurrection of Jesus when he saw John Mark hurrying towards him. Something was wrong. He excused himself from the group and went to meet the young man. He was astonished when, in an excited jumble of words, John Mark told him that Ruth was alive, at their house, had just given birth, and was now dying. Peter did not hesitate; there would be time for questions later. He simply said, "We must hurry back."

Her face wet with tears, Mary cradled the baby in her arms. Relief flooded over her as her son rushed into the house, followed by Peter. She looked earnestly at Peter and said, "I have been praying for Ruth, but I think the birth was too much for her. I know only you can save her."

Peter shook his head. "I am only the instrument the Lord uses to work His miracles, Mary. You know that." He saw a contrite Mary nod, then said "Now, where is Ruth?"

Peter followed Mary into the bedroom and saw the still form of Ruth lying on the bed with Drubaal holding her cold, lifeless hands in his own. He gently asked Drubaal to step away from the bed, then, placing one hand on Ruth's head and raising the other, he looked heavenward and prayed softly for a moment, then said in a loud voice "In the name of Jesus of Nazareth, rise up."

Drubaal was utterly confused. What was the man saying? How could the dead rise again? But then he suddenly felt a change in the atmosphere. Someone else had entered the room. He looked around to see who it was, but there was no one there. A profound sense of peace filled the room. Was it his imagination, or could he detect the fragrant scent of flowers? Where had that come from?

Then, after what seemed an eternity but in reality was only seconds, he saw a slight movement on the bed. He watched, amazed, as Ruth slowly opened her eyes and looked up into Peter's smiling face.

Peter nodded and offered a quiet prayer of thanks, then turned to Mary and said, "If you will wash Ruth and replace her garments and the stained bedclothes, our guest, John Mark and I will wait in the other room." Mary kissed his hand in gratitude, and Peter spoke to Drubaal. "Come, my friend. Ruth will sleep for a while, but she will make a full recovery." He saw the concerned look on Drubaal's face. "I promise you she will recover. Come, we must let Mary get on with her work, we will speak outside." He let John Mark lead the way, a still bemused Drubaal following on with Peter behind him.

When they entered the main room of the house, Peter pointed to the wooden bench placed before the communal dining table. "Please, sit down." A wondering and confused

Drubaal sank down onto the bench. He stared at Peter, still not understanding how a man could bring someone back from the dead. Was it a trick? If it was, it was a very clever one. He had seen Ruth pass on from this world. If it wasn't a trick, then what was it? He was determined to find out the truth.

Aware that the stranger was staring at him, obviously confused by what he had witnessed, Peter said "But where are my manners? You have not been offered refreshment. As Mary is busy, I will remedy that." He went to the shelf holding the wine and water jugs and cups, placed them on the table and began to pour out the liquid into three of the cups.

Drubaal spoke instantly. "Could my cup be well watered, please? My master will not be pleased if I return to him smelling of wine."

Peter carried on pouring the wine, mixed it with water from the jar and placed it in front of Drubaal. "You said master. Are you a slave?" he said.

Drubaal smiled. "There are no slaves in my master's household. My name is Drubaal, I am originally from Carthage and I have the honour of being bodyguard to Sheikh Ibrahim bin Yusuf Al-Khareem, a very important man in his native Nabatea. Ruth is the personal servant of the Sheikh's niece. Our mistress was killed in the battle between the Romans and the rebels." He looked down, hiding his emotion at the memory of his mistress. Was it only a few hours ago that they had attended her funeral pyre?

Peter frowned. He had heard about the rebels' annihilation at the fortress and the Temple and had witnessed the return of Pilate and his forces, leading the three prisoners into Jerusalem. Seeing the anguish on Drubaal's face, he sat down beside John Mark on the opposite bench and asked quietly, "Can you tell us how Ruth came to be in this position?"

Drubaal stared at him. "I can only tell you what I know," he said. He told them that when his master had been called back to Nabatea to serve King Aretas, the women had been left behind with another servant, Boraz, and himself. He spoke falteringly of the attack, of the brutal deaths of Boraz and the Roman guards, his own injuries and the women being taken captive. Then he stopped and shook his head. "Ruth must tell you the rest. I wasn't there. I can only imagine the horrors she and my mistress suffered."

Peter was so shocked by Drubaal's terrible story that he did not know what to say. He turned as Mary came out of her bedroom, with a worried expression on her face and still holding the baby, and asked "How is she?"

"She is sleeping now. As for the baby..." Mary shook her head. "Her breathing is shallow, she has not cried for milk and she is limp in my arms. I think she is dying."

Peter immediately got to his feet. "Let me see her." He looked at the tiny face and put his ear to the rosebud mouth. Mary was right, her breathing was shallow. He knew it would not be long before the baby lost what little strength she had. "Give her to me," he said. Mary carefully placed the baby into Peter's arms. He lifted his eyes heavenward and again quietly intoned a prayer.

Drubaal sniffed. There was that unseen presence and the fragrant smell of flowers again – and that sense of peace filling the room. Bemused, he heard a weak mewling come from the baby, which gradually increased in strength. Satisfied, Peter gave a prayer of thanks, then handed the baby back to a relieved Mary.

Mary's relief was replaced by a look of concern. "What will become of the child? Ruth is not interested in her. I pray that when she has regained her strength, a mother's love will come to her."

Peter spoke solemnly. "I will pray for her and for the child. By what our friend here has told us," he looked briefly at Drubaal "it seems Ruth has suffered a terrible ordeal. We must help her to recover from it."

Mary nodded. "In the meantime, the baby needs milk. I will speak to our neighbour, Elizabeth. She has recently given birth to her third child. I'm sure she will agree to act as temporary wet-nurse for Ruth's little one." Content that all would now be well with the baby, she asked John Mark to put a blanket into one of the drawers of a wooden chest that stood in the corner of the room. The drawer would act as a cradle until one could be found. After this was done, Mary carefully placed the baby in the open drawer and hurried out to see Elizabeth, whose house was situated just a few doors away.

Peter invited Drubaal to stay to share the evening meal

with them, but he shook his head, saying "Thank you, but I must return to my master now and tell him about Ruth and the baby." He did not add that the Sheikh could not care less about them. He stood up, filling the room with his huge frame. As he reached the door, he turned and looked intently at Peter. "If it is possible, I should like to return here sometime. I am intrigued by the way you brought Ruth back from the dead and saved the life of the baby. I would know what clever magician's trick you used."

Peter smiled. "It was no trick, my friend. Please do come back here and I will be more than happy to explain everything to you. You returned our Ruth to us, so you will always be welcome here."

Drubaal opened the door and went out into the street. As he climbed onboard the cart he pondered on what he had just witnessed. He wondered what he would say to the Sheikh. Should he tell him this fantastic story?

He flicked the reins and the cart moved off, slowly making its way back to the fortress.

# CHAPTER TWENTY-ONE

Adolfo was making his way back to Pilate's residence. As he walked down an alleyway, he suddenly felt a tap on his shoulder. He turned and saw a cloaked man looming over him.

"Where have you been?" said Adolfo. "I've been waiting for days to see you." His voice was clipped.

"Mind your own business!" The man said menacingly, pulling out a sealed scroll from the folds of his cloak. "Take this. You know what you have to do."

Adolfo took the scroll from the hooded man and put it into his bag.

The man spoke. "This is the final scroll. I will be leaving soon." The man could see the relief on Adolfo's face. With a warning note in his voice, he added "This is the most important scroll of them all. When are the next dispatches going to Rome?"

"In two days."

"Good. Make sure it's included with the other dispatches." The man placed a hand on Adolfo's shoulder. "You have done well. Our master will be very pleased."

Adolfo smiled. "When will I receive my reward?"

"Soon." Without another word, the man turned and walked away, leaving an angry Adolfo staring after him. How soon? He was relieved that it was over and he had not been caught, but he had grown tired of running errands for the man without seeing any sign of his due reward. Yet again, what he wanted had been promised but not delivered. Adolfo just wanted the privileges he deserved.

After visiting the garrison hospital, where the wounded were being tended by the medical orderlies, Quintus returned to his office. He sat down heavily. Winning the battles at the fortress and at the Beth-Horon Pass had been a great success, but he had lost some good men and there were those in the hospital whose injuries meant they would never soldier again, something that always made him sad. Although there was a legionary savings scheme, some of them were too young to have accumulated enough money to replace their regular army pay. What would happen to those crippled for life by the loss of an arm or leg, or a skeletal injury?

His thoughts were disturbed by a knock on his door. He sighed. Why couldn't he be left alone even for a few minutes? "Enter," he said wearily.

Julius and Otto entered the room. He looked at the pair and failing to hide the annoyance in his voice, said "Well, what is it?"

Julius saluted, "Commander, sir. We need to speak to you on a matter of some importance."

"Can't it wait?" Quintus asked irritably.

"I'm afraid not, sir," Julius said grimly.

Quintus let out another sigh. "Look, it's been a trying morning. What is so important that it cannot wait awhile?" He saw the concerned look pass between the two cavalry officers and said grudgingly, "Very well. You'd better tell me what it is."

As Julius reported the incident concerning Antonius and Drubaal, the Commander felt anger well up inside him. "You have proof of this?" he barked. Julius and Otto answered in unison, "Yes, sir." Quintus called for the guard standing outside his door. The guard entered and awaited his instructions. "Fetch Prefect Alae Antonius to me." The guard saluted and hurried off to find Antonius. Soon the Prefect was standing in front of the Commander, with Julius and Otto standing to the side.

Quintus stared at Antonius. "A serious charge has been brought against you. The charge states that you tried to murder the Sheikh's bodyguard, Drubaal. Do you deny this charge?"

Antonius stood grim faced before Quintus. "The charge is untrue, sir," he said. Without taking his eyes off the Commander, he added "I was too busy trying to stay alive to worry about taking revenge on a common slave."

Julius stood his ground. "We both saw it, sir." He turned to Otto, who nodded in agreement.

Antonius sneered at them, then spoke directly to Quintus. "They are lying, sir." He saw the questioning look on the Commander's face and pointed at Julius. "This junior officer has given me nothing but trouble since I first arrived here – it is common knowledge he does not respect me. Whose word do you believe, sir? This troublesome Decurion's, or the word of a Prefect Alae, specially commissioned by the Governor to join you here in Jerusalem?"

Quintus looked sternly at Antonius. "That's enough, Prefect! In any case, what were you doing on the battlefield? I gave you explicit orders to stay with the Sheikh and the back-up force."

"That is correct, Commander, but it was the Sheikh who wished to join the battle and he gave me permission to follow him with my men."

Quintus had a hard time keeping his patience. "Did he now? Well, we shall see about that." Antonius stared him out as Quintus continued, "You left Batitus' Optio with half a Century to guard the end of the Pass leading to the Jerusalem road. Thankfully, the Optio refused to order his men to follow you into the battle, so he was later able to cut down the rebel stragglers who tried to escape." His tone was sharp as he cut off Antonius' excuses. "You may wish to deny it, but I can soon check the facts with the Sheikh and the Optio." He turned to the waiting guard. "Go to the

Sheikh and Drubaal and say I respectfully request they come here as a matter of urgency. And bring Batitus' Optio back with you too."

Drubaal had just arrived back at the fortress to find the lonely figure of the Sheikh sitting in his quarters, staring mournfully out of the small window overlooking the parade ground. He was wondering how to tell his master the news about Ruth when the guard knocked on the door.

Upon hearing the Commander's request, Sheikh Ibrahim, with Drubaal close behind him, followed the guard back to Quintus' office. Ibrahim sat down in the chair provided for him. When all the witnesses were assembled, Quintus turned to Ibrahim and began his questioning.

"Sheikh Ibrahim, did you give Prefect Alae Antonius the order to follow you onto the battlefield?"

Ibrahim looked first at a sweating Antonius, then at Quintus, and said in a firm voice, "No, Commander, I did not! It was the Prefect Alae's own decision to take his men into battle."

Quintus looked sternly at the Optio standing at attention before him. "Optio, did you hear Sheikh Ibrahim order the Prefect Alae to follow him onto the battlefield?"

"No, Commander," came the quick reply. "The way I heard it, the Sheikh was ordering only his own men to enter the battle and nobody else."

"Did you see the Prefect Alae and his men follow Sheikh Ibrahim into battle in order to protect him on the battlefield?"

The Optio stood tall and said confidently, "No, Commander, I saw the Prefect Alae and his cavalrymen ride off in the opposite direction to the Sheikh. After that I lost sight of them." He turned his face away as he caught Antonius' murderous glance.

Quintus fought back the urge to give the order for Antonius to be killed there and then. Taking a deep breath, he said "There is no doubt in my mind, Prefect Alae Antonius, that it was your decision, and yours alone, to lead your men into battle, thus disobeying my direct order. I therefore..." He was interrupted by the arrival of Sextus. "Sextus, what do you want?"

Sextus saluted. "Sir. I have just been told that the Decurion and his junior officer are reporting the incident concerning the Prefect Alae and the slave, Drubaal."

"Yes, what of it? Do you have any further information to add to the accusation?"

Sextus pulled himself up to his full height "Yes sir. I too witnessed the incident. Decurion Julius and Cavalryman Otto are telling the truth."

Antonius spun round to face Sextus. "You are all lying. All three of you are involved in a plot to blacken my name."

Quintus stood up and said angrily, "If there is one man in this fortress I would trust with my life it is Centurion Sextus."

Quintus sat down again, turned to Drubaal and asked him to give his side of the story.

Drubaal narrowed his eyes and looked straight at the

defiant Antonius. Then he faced Quintus Maximus and said in a calm voice, "Commander, during the battle I became aware of a presence behind me. I half turned expecting to see one of the rebels trying to kill me from behind. Instead I saw Prefect Antonius with his sword raised above my head. If it hadn't been for Decurion Julius, who deflected the blow from me with his shield, I would not be standing before you now."

"Thank you, Drubaal. You may stand down." Quintus stared at Prefect Antonius, unable to find adequate words to express his anger. Instead he called the guard, who stepped forward smartly saluting, and snarled "Call out the guard and bring them here."

Soon, six bull-necked legionaries marched into the room. Quintus growled "Take the Prefect Alae to his quarters and place him under guard until I send for him. Make sure he stays there!"

The legionaries saluted and surrounded Antonius. Two of them took hold of the now panicking Prefect, while the other four flanked them and all marched quickly out of the room.

Sextus could see how angry the Commander was, but ventured: "Excuse me, sir. What will you do with him?"

Ibrahim leaned forward and asked sternly, "Yes, Commander, what will you do with him? I demand he be punished for the attempted murder of my bodyguard."

Quintus took a deep breath and regained control. "Firstly, Sheikh Ibrahim, I must report this to Governor

Pilate. It is up to him to give or reserve punishment."
He hurriedly wrote a message to Pilate outlining the
accusations against Antonius. He handed the sealed wax
tablet to Sextus and said, "Give this to one of your men to
deliver to the Governor."

Sextus saluted, then hurried out of the office. Quintus
turned to Julius and Otto and said grimly, "Thank you for
informing me of the situation. I've no doubt the Governor
will call upon you to act as witnesses, but for now, just
return to your duties."

Julius and Otto saluted, then returned to the cavalry
block. They did not have long to wait. Orders came from
Pilate to have Antonius and the witnesses brought to him
for questioning. Quintus and the Sheikh were to go with
them.

Pilate sat gripping the arms of his official cross-legged
chair, placed on the raised dais in the audience hall of
his Jerusalem residence, waiting impatiently for them to
arrive. Scribonius, the Chief Scribe, sat at a small table
nearby, with quill, ink and parchment laid out before him
ready to record the hearing. When all were assembled,
Pilate opened the proceedings. He sat bolt upright, wearing
a stern look on his face, as he listened to the accusations
brought against Antonius: disobedience of a direct order,
gross dereliction of duty and the attempted murder of the
Sheikh's personal bodyguard. When the witnesses had
given their evidence, he stared hard at Antonius, who was
flanked by the six guards from the Antonia. "You have

heard the charges brought against you, Prefect Alae. What have you to say in your defence?"

Antonius looked arrogantly at Pilate. "They are lying, Governor. They have conspired against me."

Pilate stared at him. "Why would they do that?"

"Decurion Julius..." he pointed to Julius, who stood at attention opposite. "Decurion Julius has never liked me, even though I trained him and taught him all there was to know about the cavalry. This is how he repays me. As for the Sheikh's slave, he seeks revenge."

Pilate bristled. "Why should the Decurion's junior officer and Chief Centurion Sextus collaborate in that so-called lie? What's in it for them? And why should the Sheikh's trusted bodyguard want revenge on you? Explain!"

"I told you Governor, they all hate me and want to be rid of me. Even after I helped to bring ben-Ezra and the rebels to justice. As for the Carthaginian slave, he seeks vengeance after I had him punished." Pilate's eyebrows lifted at that last statement. He would find out later what that punishment had been for and why.

Flavius, who stood behind Pilate, drew himself up, disgusted by what he was hearing. Quintus, standing beside him, laid a hand on his arm and shook his head in warning, but Flavius decided he could no longer wait to speak about the brutal treatment Antonius had inflicted on Julius. He stepped from behind Pilate's chair and stood before the Governor. He saluted.

"Governor, sir. May I speak?"

Pilate gave a curt nod of his head. "Sir, the accusations are true. I myself witnessed the brutal treatment the Prefect Alae inflicted on the Decurion. In fact I warned the Prefect Alae that I would report him if I saw it happen again."

Pilate frowned. "And yet I received no such report from you."

Flavius continued, "I went to Caesarea with you, sir, so I was not at the Antonia to witness any further violence carried out by the accused, but before I left Jerusalem, I told the Decurion that if he was assaulted again by Prefect Alae Antonius, he was to go to Chief Centurion Sextus with the times, dates and description of any offences committed against him."

Pilate looked at Sextus and said "Can you produce these communications, Chief Centurion?"

"No sir," came Sextus' embarrassed reply.

Pilate turned to Julius "Did you write down any communications concerning your treatment at the hands of the Prefect Alae and give them to the Chief Centurion?"

Julius stood straight. "No sir."

Pilate shook his head. "If the Prefect Alae's treatment of you was as Tribune Silvanus has said, then why didn't you report him?"

Julius swallowed. "Because I was afraid to, sir. I knew that if the Prefect Alae found out he would make my life even worse."

Antonius smiled to himself. He could see the Governor

was becoming annoyed. The smile disappeared when Sextus stepped forward.

"Governor, sir. The Decurion did not come to me, but plenty of others did. The Commander instructed me to keep watch on the Prefect Alae and tell him of any misdemeanors carried out by him."

"Is that so, Commander?"

Quintus stepped forward "Yes sir. Over the last few weeks, I have received many reports about the Prefect Alae's conduct. I asked Chief Centurion Sextus to keep an eye on him. It appears the Prefect Alae carried out his violent acts when no one in authority was around, so evidence against him could not be gained. Until now." He hesitated briefly, allowing his words to sink in, then continued "Sir. If you will allow Chief Centurion Sextus to confirm the accusations against Prefect Antonius?"

Pilate spoke irritably. "Let us hear them."

Sextus looked directly at Pilate and said "Sir, what the commander says is true. Many legionaries came to me personally to report the Prefect Alae's violent behaviour towards them. I did keep watch but he was too clever – until Beth-Horon, where he overreached himself." Sextus drew himself up to his full height. "I too saw the attempt on Drubaal's life, it was in the middle of the battle at Beth-Horon when he thought no one was watching. If it had not been for Decurion Julius' fast action in deflecting the sword with his shield, the Sheikh's bodyguard would have been killed." He saw Pilate's expression change and ploughed on. "Sir. I know for a fact that he particularly dislikes both Decurion Julius and the Sheikh's bodyguard; he even demanded that Drubaal be crucified after he had stood up to him for his treatment of the Decurion. Fortunately, the Commander refused."

Pilate sat stony faced as he saw the Commander nod in agreement with Sextus' testimony. Horrified thoughts ran through his mind at the repercussions that would follow if a powerful ally's personal servant had met such an end. He looked directly at Antonius and said through tight lips, "What is your answer to these allegations?"

Fearful now, Antonius knew there was too much evidence against him, but he continued to try to bluff his way out of his predicament. "Sir, I repeat, I am not guilty of these spurious allegations. Surely the correct discipline must be maintained at all times. I found the Decurion to be insubordinate."

Sextus could not stop a snort of disgust escaping at this. Antonius noticed it and sneered "You see, Governor Pilate how I am held in contempt by these people?" Pilate sniffed loudly. "Sir, Drubaal assaulted me in front of some legionaries," Antonius went on. "I could not let that go unpunished, and after all, the Carthaginian is only a slave of no importance. I thought an example should be made to deter other slaves from rebelling. Has the Governor forgotten the old story of the renegade slave Spartacus?"

At that, Sheikh Ibrahim rose from his seat, a murderous look on his face. He sat down again as Pilate raised his hand and shouted, "Enough! I have heard all I need to." He stepped down from the dais and faced Antonius. "You are an absolute disgrace!" He turned to Sextus. "This man is to be taken to the dungeon immediately. He will not be tortured, ill-treated or questioned further. Is that clear?" He turned back to Antonius. "I will consider your punishment and send for you again when I have reached my decision."

Sextus gave a full military salute, then ordered the waiting legionary escort to take Antonius away. Pilate dismissed everyone else and left the hall with Scribonius, clutching the testimonies of Antonius and the witnesses, who were scurrying behind him.

After spending the rest of the day and most of the night thinking about how to suitably punish Antonius, Pilate came up with a plan. The following morning he summoned Sheikh Ibrahim, Quintus, and all the other witnesses back to the audience hall. He stood grim-faced before them and said to the waiting legionaries who flanked him, "Bring Antonius to me." The legionaries saluted and did as ordered. Soon, a quivering Antonius stood before the assembled gathering.

Pilate's tone was imperious as he gave his verdict. "Prefect Alae Antonius. This is my judgment: I find you guilty of all charges against you. I will not order your immediate execution, it is too quick a punishment for you. However, from this moment on you are stripped of your rank and demoted to legionary status. Two days from now, you will be taken to Joppa under armed guard; there you will board the appointed military ship sailing to Libya, where you will become part of the guard protecting the Libyan salt mines. This will be for an indefinite period. The Legate in Syria will be informed of my decision."

Antonius, knowing this punishment was worse than a quick death, let out a whine. "It was at your request Governor Pilate that I came here from Syria."

"A request I now regret," Pilate said sharply.

"But you asked me to tighten up the discipline in the Jerusalem garrison. I was only doing my duty as I saw fit..."

Pilate tried hard to control his mounting anger. "Silence!" He gestured to the waiting guards. "Take this man back to the Antonia and place him in the dungeon until his ship is ready to sail."

As the guards took hold of Antonius, he panicked and blurted out "You should be taking out your anger on your scribe, Adolfo, too."

At that Pilate became alert. "Wait." He signalled the guards to stop where they were. "What do you mean?"

A look of sheer malice crossed Antonius' face. "How do you think Calpurnius Aquila knows about the Princess and your continuous lax conduct? Yes, I have been spying for him. I recruited Adolfo to become part of Aquila's network of spies. For some time now, he's been hiding my reports amongst your dispatches to Rome."

Flavius started at the name Calpurnius Aquila; he had heard it before. Two years ago, he had attended a private reception in Rome with his father, where Aquila had also been a guest. Afterwards, his father had warned him to stay away from Aquila, saying he was a dangerous accomplice of Sejanus. Flavius wondered how he had survived Sejanus. More importantly, he now realised that Aquila was the thin-faced man who had appeared at Pilate's Saturnalia party. Why had he been in Caesarea?

Pilate paled. So that was how Aquila knew all about Princess Farrah's abduction. Pilate raised his hand ready to strike Antonius, but thought better of it. Instead he said bitterly, "Why did you turn traitor?"

"Why?" Antonius sneered. "How do you think I became a Prefect Alae? It was my reward for services rendered. I earned more money from Aquila than the Legion could ever pay me."

Pilate barked, "Fetch the scribe Adolfo to me now!"

The guards soon returned with a trembling Adolfo. The scribe had not had time to conceal the scroll with the other documents going to Rome, so the guards had easily found it hidden in his desk. Adolfo shuddered as the scroll was handed to Pilate.

Pilate quickly read it. It spoke of his failure to save the Princess, the attack on the fortress and the near annihilation of the troops at Beth-Horon. Shocked by the contents, Pilate angrily threw the scroll on the floor and vented his fury on Adolfo. "You ungrateful... How many other scrolls have found their way to Aquila? How long has this been going on?"

"For months, Lord Pilate. I didn't want to do it but he made me." He pointed to Antonius. "He promised me wealth and power…" He flinched as Antonius shot him an evil glance.

Pilate put his face close to Adolfo and said angrily "This confirms your guilt. You have sealed your own fate."

Adolfo spoke calmly and confidently, "You can't touch me. Antonius promised that Aquila would protect me. I have his assurance."

Pilate laughed cruelly "If you believe that, you are even more of a fool than I took you for. Get him out of here." He spoke quietly to two of the guards. "Get rid of him. Do it quietly, then dump the body away from here. I don't want this made public." The guards took hold of the squirming scribe and took him away.

Taking a deep breath to control himself, Pilate moved closer to Antonius and hissed "I should have you killed right now."

"Then do it. A quick death would be preferable to years spent sweating under the Libyan sun, if I don't die of some disease before then."

"And deprive myself of the satisfaction that you will die a slow death, either by deprivation, or by the guards there who will relish the chance to take revenge on a demoted Prefect Alae? Especially when they find out they have a murdering traitor in their midst, which, I promise you, will be made known to them, have no doubt about that." He turned away and shouted at the guards holding Antonius, "Get him out of my sight. Now!"

Antonius snarled and struggled as the guards dragged him out of the room and took him back to the fortress dungeons.

Sheikh Ibrahim looked at Pilate. "In my country he would have been executed on the spot, as you could have ordered."

"I fully sympathise with you, Sheikh Ibrahim, but with all due respect, we are not in your country but in Roman territory, and there are certain protocols I must adhere to. I'm sorry, but that is the way it is."

He turned to Quintus. "I want an escort of your cavalry to take Antonius' North African Cavalry as far as Galilee, where they will be handed over to the garrison there. Their cavalry will then escort them all the way to the Legate in Syria. Scribonius will supply you with my written instructions for the Legate in due course. As for ben-Ezra and the others, I want them executed tomorrow. As far as the women are concerned, I give you my full authority to do with them as you will."

With that, Pilate left the room, followed by a shocked Scribonius, who had been frantically taking down the witness statements and the results of the hearing. Out in the corridor Pilate snapped at his secretary, "I trust you didn't record Adolfo's part in this in the report?" The secretary shook his head. "Good. Make sure that report to the Legate about Antonius is scribed at once." He grimaced. "I'm sure it won't be too long before Aquila finds out about this whole sorry mess." He did not add that it would be something else the Emperor's chief spy would gloatingly blame him for. As the secretary bowed and turned to leave, Pilate barked, "And make sure you keep an eye on your staff in future!" Pilate entered his private apartments, banging the door behind him. Scribonius hurried back to his office, away from the growing wrath of the Governor.

In the fortress grounds, Adolfo, who had for so long dreamed of rising to the top of his profession, was brutally cut down by the legionaries' razor-sharp daggers. Under cover of darkness, his body would be taken from the fortress and dumped in an alley the other side of the city. The Jews would simply think that Adolfo had been murdered by a brigand.

Sheikh Ibrahim and Drubaal returned to the Sheikh's quarters. The Commander, Julius, Otto and Sextus stayed in the audience chamber. They were stunned by the confessions of Antonius and the scribe. Sextus whistled through his teeth, "The traitorous bastards!"

Quintus was satisfied with the outcome. To think he had been unwittingly harbouring a cold-blooded murderer and spy amongst his men. He knew the judgment must have been difficult for Pilate, but at the time of Antonius' arrival, he had taken it as a personal insult that Pilate had thought he could not handle the situation. Fortunately his quick reaction to the information Rebecca had given him, plus the bravery, discipline and strength of his Antonia troops, had shown Pilate that he, and they, had handled it very well.

He let out a sigh of relief. "Well, Antonius is finished now. Not many survive too long guarding the salt mines. Besides, Pilate's right, legionaries don't much care for demoted, traitorous bullies. They have their own way of dealing with them."

Flavius joined them in time to hear the last few words of Quintus' statement. He smiled. "I'm sure they have, Commander." He turned to Julius. "Well done for standing your ground. Pilate has delivered a good judgment." He smiled at Sextus. "Thank you, Chief Centurion, you conducted yourself bravely and admirably."

Sextus nodded. "Thank you, Tribune. I was determined that scum was not going to get away with it. He's got what he deserved, it's been a long time coming."

The Antonia officers returned to the fortress, leaving Flavius standing alone. He had put on a brave face during the hearing, but inside he was still in turmoil at the memory of Farrah's death. He would never see his love again. How could he bear it? But he knew that he must. He had shown no emotion in front of the Governor, who he knew would most certainly disapprove of his close relationship with Farrah. When Pilate had said the Emperor had bestowed Roman citizenship on Farrah, he had almost crumbled. Surely as a princess with such citizenship, his family might have allowed their marriage. Now it was too late.

With these thoughts running through his mind, he made his way back to his quarters to await Pilate's further instructions.

In the Sheikh's apartments Drubaal struggled to find a way of telling his master about Ruth and the baby. He decided it would be best if he just came out with the story.

The Sheikh sat stony-faced as Drubaal told him the extraordinary news. Without looking at Drubaal, he held up his hand to interrupt him, saying "I have told you, I really don't care about them, or about being made a citizen of the Country that helped to destroy my Farrah. Now leave me in peace. I must make plans to return to Nabatea to take my niece's ashes home."

Drubaal knew it was futile to continue with his miraculous story. He bowed and left the room.

# CHAPTER TWENTY-TWO

Quintus smiled thinly when he saw the tortured figures of Josiah and Moshe the Zealot leader chained up in the Antonia dungeons. Slumped on the blood-soaked ground nearby with his hands tied around a wooden post lay the badly-beaten figure of Zeke, who had been captured and brought to the Antonia the night before. The horses he had had for sale had been rounded up and brought into the fortress. The trained eyes of the cavalry officers soon picked out those that had been clumsily re-branded, not fully covering the easily recognizable markings of various Roman Legions on their rumps. These had obviously been taken, over a time period of several months, from dead and dying Roman cavalry officers, without doubt killed by ben-Ezra and his gang. The few men working for Zeke who had not gone to Beth-Horon with ben-Ezra had been killed on the spot trying to defend their master.

Not far from Zeke lay Simon the beggar, whose old, emaciated body had succumbed to the torture inflicted on him. Quintus turned to Sextus who was in charge of the prisoners' interrogation. "Have they said anything yet?"

"The Zealot leader doesn't have much to tell us, sir; in any case, his followers all died at Beth-Horon. He's just a stupid outsider who chose to join with ben-Ezra on some kind of hopeless mission for so-called freedom. Zeke has admitted that he never fought with the gang, only looked after ben-Ezra's horses and provided him with weapons. However, Josiah seems to be much more important."

Quintus looked at the battered and blooded Josiah, whose back was lacerated through whipping. "In what way?"

"Well, sir, we've managed to get a bit of information out of him that ties up with what the woman Rebecca said. It seems he's a powerful man in Jericho, in charge of brothels and murderous gangs."

On hearing his sister's name, Josiah lifted his blood-stained face. Sextus put his face close to Josiah's and said sarcastically, "Of course, you don't know... it was your sister Rebecca who alerted us to the plot to overthrow the fortress and assassinate the Governor at Beth-Horon." He laughed as Josiah groaned, then said harshly, "A fine brother you are! You should have taken better care of her, not force her to be a prostitute in one of your brothels."

Josiah spat on the ground, the bloody globule just missing Sextus' feet, an insult Sextus answered with a blow from his vine stick on Josiah's torn back. Josiah howled in pain.

Sextus turned back to Quintus. "This man here is responsible for the deaths of Herod's soldiers as well as ours. I recognised some of the Herodian weapons used in the battle, and he's admitted he co-operated willingly with ben-Ezra in the plan to attack us."

Quintus grimaced and said in an authoritative tone, "No more torture now. The Governor wants them alive; he's issued a death sentence on them all. Tomorrow morning they will be crucified. Now I want to see ben-Ezra. I ordered that he was not to be tortured. I hope that order has been obeyed, for I want him fully conscious at his execution. He will find out his punishment when it's his turn to die at the Place of the Skull."

It was early the next morning. Although Flavius wanted ben-Ezra and the others to suffer badly for their crimes, he was always sickened by watching violent executions and hoped he could cope with what was to come. He had been commanded by Pilate to lead the detail of soldiers, including Sextus, to the Place of the Skull to carry them out. He would have preferred to have been in charge of the garrison legionaries as they returned Herod's weapons, found at Beth-Horon, to Herod's Palace, where, by prior arrangement, Herod's Captain of the Guard, Malachi, was waiting to collect them.

As the weapons were being handed over to Malachi and his guards, three of the condemned criminals were having cross-beams tied to their torn and bloodied backs. Knowing the Jerusalem streets would be packed with pilgrims who had arrived for Passover, Quintus had ordered his legionaries to line the streets between the fortress and the place of execution, in case of a last-minute rescue attempt by sympathizers of ben-Ezra or the Zealots.

Through blood loss and exhaustion the condemned men, who had been stripped down to their loincloths, struggled to keep their feet as they staggered along the streets. When they faltered, whips were lashed across their lower backs and thighs by the prisoner escorts. The felons were met with jeers by most of the watching public, but a few men in the crowd stared stony-faced at the Roman guard. Rachel and Sarah, their hands tied by ropes, were pushed along the road by legionaries marching behind them. Rachel fell to the stony ground, but was roughly hauled to her feet by a legionary. She stumbled along, her knees bleeding from the impact.

Led in chains by Sextus, a swaggering Eleazar ben-Ezra was part of a separate procession following on behind. He was surrounded by those of the Chief Centurion's legionaries who had survived the battle of Beth-Horon. With the Commander's consent, Julius had chosen three other cavalry officers from his squadron to escort them. Each horseman had heavy, thick rope tied to his horses' sides, a fact noticed by some of the bystanders, who wondered what they were for.

Eventually the procession reached the Place of the Skull, or Golgotha as the Jews called it. On the crest of the barren hill where all the public could clearly see the executions, the crucifixion structure stood ready.

The women would be the first to die. Two legionaries stood by each of two deep pits that had been dug one on each side of the structure, with the coarse, stony earth taken from the pits piled up by their side. As Rachel and Sarah were stripped naked, a joker from the jeering onlookers said out loud, "That's not the first time I've seen Sarah without her clothes on." Some men standing next to him laughed, but were soon silenced when a legionary standing nearby turned and gave them a threatening look. The joker gasped in horror as the women were simultaneously thrown down into the black holes.

Rachel tried to climb out of the pit, but was brutally kicked back down by a legionary boot. The women cried out for mercy as the legionaries began to shovel the earth back into the pits. Their screams diminished as more and more earth was piled on top of them. When the pits were filled, the legionaries placed large stones on top of them so the women, in the remote chance they were still alive, could not escape from them.

As he watched the legionaries filling in the pits, Flavius thought of the well-known story of the Vestal Virgin, Marcia, who, a hundred or so years before, had been buried alive after being found guilty of taking a lover, something forbidden by the Vestals, the most sacred and powerful priestesses in Rome. Rachel and Sarah were no religious virgins, but it seemed a fitting punishment to him for all they had done.

Josiah was the first one chosen to be crucified. Flavius grimaced when Josiah, his arms already tied to the crossbeam for support, screamed as two legionaries drove iron nails into his wrists, nailing him to the wood, which was then hauled up and fixed onto one of the upright posts of the crucifixion structure. His feet were forcibly placed one over the other and secured to the post by huge nails. The other condemned men shuddered as they watched, knowing it would soon be their turn to face this unspeakable agony.

Moshe was the next to suffer the indignities and agony of the cross. He yelled obscenities at the soldiers as they drove in the nails. Zeke, who had collapsed whimpering, shook with fear as he was roughly thrown backwards onto the ground. As the nails pierced his flesh, his bowels gave way with shock. Tears poured down his ravaged face as he was fixed to his crossbeam, then in turn fixed to the upright post. For most of his life he had done all he could to avoid the punishment suffered by his father and uncle, but his luck had at last run out. Through his agonized moans he cursed ben-Ezra.

Ben-Ezra, who had been watching the punishment of his comrades, wondered why he had not been tortured or had a crossbeam tied on his back. If not crucifixion, then what was his death to be? His question was soon answered.

"Grab him! Hold him fast!"

At Sextus' command, two burly legionaries took hold of ben-Ezra and forced him to the ground. Sextus stepped forward. He ordered those horsemen carrying the ropes to fix them to their horses' saddles who, with their reins held by four legionaries, stood opposite ben- Ezra's prone body. Those carrying the rope ends began to tie the ropes around ben-Ezra's wrists and ankles. He struggled and lashed out with his feet, kicking a legionary in the face. Sextus brought his iron-shod boot down hard on ben-Ezra's shin, crushing it. He screamed with pain and trembled as he realised what was about to happen.

At a signal from Julius, the horsemen urged their horses forward. As the ropes tightened, for a brief moment, ben-Ezra was lifted off the ground, then, going in their four different directions, the horses picked up speed. Desperate, agonized wails came from ben-Ezra as his body was slowly torn apart. Some of the people who had followed the processions from the city fainted, while others covered their eyes and ears, trying to blot out the sight and sound of the terrible scene unfolding before them.

Flavius tried desperately to hold back the nausea that threatened to engulf him. He did not want to vomit and make himself look weak and foolish in front of Sextus and the legionaries. Although he had never hated a man as much as ben-Ezra, he nevertheless felt a wave of pity for him as he endured such unspeakable agony.

Finally, after what seemed an eternity to felon and watchers alike, came silence. Ben-Ezra's body lay in pieces on the blood-soaked ground.

A legionary cut off his head and stuck it on a pole;

others picked up the various body parts and nailed them to a post for all to see. Shocked and sickened, the crowd quickly melted away. Sextus spat on the ground and said loudly, "Perhaps after seeing how we deal with rebels and assassins, the mob will think twice about taking on the power of Rome."

Flavius ordered Sextus to leave a small guard at the site to make sure any sympathisers did not try to take down the bodies of the crucified prisoners from their crosses and take them away for burial. Then, glad it was over, he led Sextus and the rest of the legionaries back to the fortress. Flavius returned to his quarters and let Gebhard remove his armour and hand him clean clothes. He then made his way to the baths where, after giving a slave his sweat-soaked tunic to wash, he lay down on a marble slab ready to let a skilful slave scrape the sweat and dirt off his skin. That done, he went to the first bath and immersed himself into the warm water, vainly trying to blot out the horrors he had witnessed.

# CHAPTER TWENTY-THREE

Shortly after Flavius and the execution detail returned, Rebecca was set free. She was taken to Quintus' office, where he handed her a bag of coins, saying, "This is your reward for successfully betraying your former gang members. Take it and go as far away as you can travel, for if you are seen anywhere near Judaea or Jericho again, I swear that you will meet the same fate as the women we buried alive today."

Rebecca flinched at the thought of that hideous death. She would make sure she left the area as soon as she could. Pretending to be grateful, she took the money from Quintus and hurriedly left the fortress. Once outside, she looked inside the bag and smiled. There was more than enough money to get away from Judaea. She rapidly made plans in her head. After the Commander's threats, she knew she could never return to Jericho; although it was in Herod's territory, too many people would recognise her and for the right reward, would hand her over to the Romans. If she could reach the coast safely, maybe she could board a ship bound for Egypt. With her looks, perhaps she might even meet a new man who would take care of her. Not like her brother.

On her way from Jerusalem she would pass by the place of execution and see what had happened to him, and to ben-Ezra. She secreted the bag of money in the folds of her skirt, knowing how many thieves in the city would love the chance to steal her treasure. Well, they wouldn't get her money. Smiling to herself, she made her way to the Place of the Skull.

What she saw there made her retch and almost pass out with shock and disgust. Her brother was writhing in agony on the cross, bearing down onto his nailed feet and then pushing himself up, gulping air into his tortured lungs. He was covered in blood, sweat and dirt. Zeke and a man she didn't recognise but guessed must be the Zealot leader were nailed up either side of him. They too were suffering agonies. She cringed as Josiah looked down at her and recognised her, unpunished and free. His blistered lips formed into a snarl and his battered face was filled with hatred as he looked at her. He tried to speak, but no sound came out. He was too weak through shock and blood loss. Shame engulfed her. No matter how he had treated her in the past, he did not deserve this.

She tore her eyes away from him and looked for ben-Ezra. He had not been crucified, so what had the Romans done to him?

She turned around and gasped in shock to find herself looking at ben-Ezra's lifeless head, stuck on a pole. He was staring at her with horror etched into his sightless eyes and mouth gaping open in a silent scream. His limbs and other parts were nailed onto a post nearby. She put her fist to her mouth and bit down hard on her knuckles to stem her screams, then crumpled to the ground in a dead faint.

As she slowly regained consciousness she became aware of a stranger looking down at her. When her vision cleared she saw that he was a man aged around thirty with a neatly-trimmed beard and shoulder-length brown hair.

"You should not be here. This is no sight for you." His voice was deep and low and full of concern. "Come, let me take you away from this place."

She let him help her to her feet. Still feeling unsteady, she clung to his arm. When she was ready, still holding onto his arm, she allowed him to lead her away from the place of horror.

After a while, as they left the city, he told her that his name was Aaron and that he had come to Jerusalem with a group from Alexandria to celebrate the Passover Festival. As she took in his words, a glimmer of hope surged through her. He was a pilgrim, from Alexandria. If she could join the pilgrim band and gain passage with them when they returned home, she could change her identity, live there and start afresh.

She casually asked him if his wife and children had journeyed with him. When he told her he was a widower without children, her hopes soared.

"I too am widowed," she said softly. In her mind ben-Ezra had been almost as a husband to her and now that he was dead, well why not? She must make up a story in order to convince the stranger; it would also help to fix on something else and drive away the horrific images she had just witnessed. She began to think fast.

"My husband was a fisherman working on my father's boat," she told Aaron. "They were out fishing on Lake Galilee when a sudden storm blew up and the fishing boat capsized. He and my father both drowned." She hesitated for a moment, letting her words sink in, then continued "I still live there, but now I am all alone."

When he asked her name and where she was staying, she said coyly, "My name is Miriam." It was the first name that came into her head, a name that brought back memories of the woman she had never liked, the woman ben-Ezra had murdered in the caves, but a name she must now use if her plans were to be realised. She looked up at him and said, "I am also a pilgrim here for the Passover, but I seem to have lost my friends somewhere. If I can't find them I'll be on my own and the city is so busy – and very frightening. I've already got lost and wandered into that place of..." She lowered her head. She felt pressure from his hand on her arm and looked up at him through tear-wet eyes.

His dark eyes showed concern. "I won't rest knowing you are wandering around this dangerous city alone," he said. "Come and stay with me and my friends. We are camped outside the city. Perhaps tomorrow we can come back here and search for them."

She wiped away her tears and looked at him from beneath long eyelashes. "That is very kind of you, Aaron." She had to make up an excuse, knowing she could never return to the city, as she knew what awaited her if she was caught by the Romans in Jerusalem. She suppressed a shudder, then said, "But I don't think I can ever go back into the city, not after..."

There was a look of understanding on his face. "What about buying your offering for sacrifice at the Temple and paying your Temple dues?"

"I have already made my sacrifice at the Temple and paid the dues. I was coming from there when I was caught up in the crowds and got separated from my friends."

"Then, perhaps if you describe them to me, I can search alone and bring them to you."

She smiled at him. "Thank you," she said. He returned her smile, showing strong, white teeth. Her mind working overtime, she quickly put together made-up descriptions of the people she had supposedly travelled with. The Festival would begin tomorrow evening. She had a few hours before then to try and worm her way into his affections. By the appreciative way he looked at her, she knew that would not be too difficult.

When Aaron and Rebecca arrived at the camp, Aaron introduced her to his friends and explained her predicament to them. She was warmly welcomed and invited to join them in their small encampment, especially by Daniel, a man in his early forties, and Naomi, the wife of Solomon, Aaron's best friend.

Naomi's voice was warm when she beckoned Rebecca to sit with her and offered her some food and watered wine. Suddenly realising how hungry she was, Rebecca smiled and sat down by Naomi's side, gratefully taking the proffered refreshment. She spent a pleasant evening with her new friends. She felt a little guilty telling them lies about her non-existent friends, but if she wanted to stay with these people, she had to go on lying to make them accept her.

She needed to get rid of her old clothes and get some fresh garments to wear. She turned to Naomi and said sweetly, "After my awful experience I am terrified of returning to Jerusalem, so Aaron has offered to go into the city tomorrow to look for my friends. Is it possible that you could go with him? I need new clothes, these are old and dirty now. I have a little money." She produced a few coins out of the bag secreted in her skirt.

Naomi smiled at her. "Of course I'll go for you, Miriam, just tell me what you would like me to buy."

Rebecca smiled gratefully, then explained exactly what she wanted.

The next morning, Aaron and Naomi went into the city. When they returned, Aaron told Rebecca that he could find no sign of the people she had described. Naomi handed her the new clothes she had bought. "Here, Miriam. I hope you like these. I thought the colour would suit you."

Rebecca was overjoyed at Naomi's choice. There was a dark blue dress with a paler blue and gold striped panel down the front, together with a dark blue head covering, a pale blue and gold striped shawl and a woven drawstring bag. She was even more pleased when Naomi gave her some change from the money she had given her. She gave Naomi a kiss on the cheek in gratitude, then looked around. "I need somewhere to wash and change," she said. She readily accepted Naomi's offer of using the tent belonging to her and her husband, Solomon.

Once in the tent, she hastily discarded her old, filthy garments, washed herself and her hair and put on her new clothes, making sure she hid the rest of her coins inside her new bag. She came out of the tent and heard the appreciative comments of the group, especially from Aaron. Looking up at him, she saw admiration in his eyes. She smiled at him and asked, "Where can I put these old clothes?"

Aaron pointed to the fire where some of the other women would soon begin to cook the communal evening meal. "If you don't want them, I suggest you put them on the fire."

Rebecca did so and the clothes were quickly consumed in the flames. She heaved a sigh of relief. It was another part of her old life gone forever.

When it was time to go to sleep, Aaron led her to his tent. As he handed her his woven sleeping mat, Rebecca looked at him and said coyly "But where will you sleep?"

He smiled at her and said, "Don't worry about me, I will share with Daniel in his tent." He added softly, "I'll see you tomorrow, Miriam. Until then, I bid you good night."

Aaron's heart sang as he made his way to Daniel's tent. Miriam was so lovely, and the colours of her new garments enhanced her beautiful hair and her eyes. As he lay down on his spare mat, he couldn't get her image out of his mind. He wondered if she liked him too. Filled with hope, he drifted off to sleep.

He was awakened by fitful cries coming from his tent. Something was wrong with Miriam. He hurried out of Daniel's tent, trying not to wake him. It seemed he had been the only one to hear her cries. He heard someone cough from one of the other tents, but no one emerged from it. He entered his tent and saw Miriam thrashing around in her sleep. She was obviously having a nightmare. He gently laid a hand on her shoulder, withdrawing it quickly as she woke up with a start, tears streaming down her face.

Gradually recognizing him, she spoke haltingly. "It was horrible. In my dream I saw those terrible crosses... and that head on a pole..." She buried her face into his shoulder. "Please don't leave me, don't let me sleep. I don't want to dream again."

As he comforted her, she looked up at him and was met with a barely concealed look of longing. She looked away from him, not wanting to force the pace; she wanted to leave him wanting more from her. She knew she had him where she wanted him.

Although Aaron had known Miriam for just a short time, there was something about her that touched his soul. Not only was she beautiful, she obviously needed somebody to take care of her. Perhaps, if she would let him, it would be him. He held her in his arms for the rest of the night, comforting her, promising himself that when morning came, he would ask her if she would go with him when they returned to Alexandria.

The bodies of Josiah, Zeke and Moshe hung on their crosses all night. When the next day came, the Romans had to make sure the felons were dead and their bodies were removed and disposed of quickly, as Passover would begin at sunset. Zeke was already dead, but Josiah and Moshe were still alive, so the legionaries broke their legs to hurry the process of death. Once the procedure had been carried out, the rebels quickly gasped the rest of their lives away. The legionaries knew no one would be brave enough to bribe them to let them have the bodies for a proper burial, so the corpses, including the remnants of the dismembered ben-Ezra, were thrown onto the bonfire blazing at the foot of the hill.

Knowing his days were numbered, a silent, grim-faced Antonius was taken in chains by four legionaries to the port of Joppa, where he was manhandled onto a military ship bound for Libya. To make sure he didn't try to drown himself or escape by throwing himself overboard, the legionaries chained him to the ship's main mast, where he would stay until the ship reached its destination.

The senior legionary had in his bag Pilate's written instructions to give to the Libyan fortress commander. The instructions were that on arrival at the fortress, a message was to be sent to the officer in charge of the salt mines. Antonius was to be kept in the fortress dungeon until guards from the mines came to collect him. After that, the four legionaries were to return to Joppa.

Chained to the mast, Antonius knew the journey to Libya would be unpleasant. He would be wet, hungry and increasingly uncomfortable. The prospect made him feel hostile to his captors. How dare they treat him as a common criminal? Yet for all his bluster, worrying thoughts nagged at him: what horrors awaited him at the mines?

The Festival passed without incident, either because of fear of receiving the same punishment as those who had suffered so terribly on that hill of pain and death, or, because now the rebels had been killed, things had genuinely quietened down in the city, though for how long was anyone's guess.

As Flavius and Marcus were preparing for the return trip to Caesarea with Pilate, Rebecca, in her fresh clothes, with her new head covering hiding her distinctive hair colour and her shawl covering her lower face, was making her way to the coast with her new friends to pick up the ship that would transport them back to Alexandria. Aaron, smitten by longing and desire, had made it plain to her that he welcomed her company, with the hopeful promise of more. She acted as though his attentions were welcomed, but deep down, although he was good looking and kind, he was no more than her ticket to Alexandria. After a while she would leave him and make her own way in that new country. She had made a promise to herself that she would never be tied to one man again.

Anna and her baby, Asher, had reached her brother's home in the town of Archelais. He had not seen his sister for some time and did not know where she had been living, nevertheless, he and his family, at first, welcomed her and her child, glad that she had returned to them safe and well. When he asked where the baby's father was, Anna replied that he was working elsewhere but would be joining them soon.

Anna waited patiently for Isaac to come as he had promised. News began to reach the town about the slaughter of the rebels by the Romans at the Temple and fortress, and the annihilation of ben-Ezra's army at Beth-Horon, followed by the executions of ben-Ezra, the other leaders of the rebellion, and two women. She wept bitter tears knowing she would never see Isaac again. Anna's brother wondered why the news had upset her so, then realised that she must know the brigands involved. He bullied her into telling the truth and eventually she gave in and told him the whole story.

Her brother became worried. This meant that things had changed. What if the Romans' discovered that he was harbouring a member of those rebels in his house? Instantly reaching a decision he said harshly, "Take your baby and leave here. You are placing me and my family in danger. Get out!" Shocked, she picked up Asher and held him to her, pleading for sanctuary; but her brother did not care. He bundled her out of the door and into the street, closing the door firmly behind her.

Heartbroken, she wandered through the busy streets. She had paid her brother for her board and lodging with the money that Isaac had given her. There was nothing left. She was destitute. If the Romans captured her, she knew they would inflict a dreadful punishment on her. Despite her fears, her natural instinct was to protect Asher.

She came to a wealthy part of the town and seeing a well-kept house, she kissed Asher and with tears streaming down her face, she laid him at the foot of a palm tree close to the house. She desperately hoped that perhaps the house owners would take him as their own and give him a better start in life than she could ever offer him.

Without looking back, she walked away. Life meant nothing to her now. She had lost the man she loved and had abandoned her child. She had nowhere to go and no one to take care of her. She walked to the edge of the town and climbed up a tall hill. She looked down at the rocky valley a long way below. In the depths of her despair, with Isaac and Asher's names on her lips, she threw herself off the hill. Her body lay sprawled over the jagged rocks. She suffered a few moments of agony, then she sank into merciful oblivion.

# CHAPTER TWENTY-FOUR

Ruth was recovering slowly from her ordeal. With Mary's encouragement, she had begun to hold her baby, but she still refused to feed her and happily gave her over to Elizabeth, who acted as the baby's wet nurse.

John Mark sat stony-faced. The story Drubaal had told them about Ruth's kidnapping had shaken him to the core. When Ruth disappeared and he had searched fruitlessly for her, he had come to realise just how much she meant to him. His joy at finding her alive and in his mother's house had been cut brutally short by the realisation that she was giving birth to another man's child. Now he did not know what his feelings towards her were. At mealtimes, when Ruth had been well enough to join them around the table, he had turned away from her. Ruth had left the table, unshed tears glistening in her sad eyes, a sight not lost on Peter, who had sadly shaken his head.

Peter decided that tonight he would speak to John Mark about his behaviour. After dinner, while Mary was busy cleaning the pots, plates and utensils and Ruth had gone to bed, he looked at the young man, cleared his throat and said "John Mark, I have not been blind these past months to the growing affection between you and our sister Ruth, in fact it has pleased me greatly." He smiled and laid a hand on John Mark's arm "I understand the turmoil you are going through, but think of the horror Ruth has endured. I ask that you show her charity, for is she not still our Ruth?" He saw the angry look on the young man's face and ploughed on. "If ever she needed love and kindness, it is now. Our Lord showed His love and compassion for her and the child when He saved them from death. Can we show anything less?"

John Mark's face reddened in shame. He sat deep in thought for a long moment, then said quietly, "Yes, Peter, you are right. I have been selfish, thinking of my own feelings. I will speak to Ruth and say sorry to her for my behaviour towards her and her child."

Peter smiled and patted his arm. "Good. Besides, John Mark, who knows? The Lord may yet have a purpose for them."

John Mark left the table and stood outside his mother's bedroom door. He called out softly, "Ruth, Ruth. Please let me in." When there was no reply, he gingerly entered the room and saw Ruth lying on her side on the bed. He moved closer to her and heard her sobs. Shame overcame him and he went to her side.

Without looking at him, Ruth moved away. "Leave me alone. If you have come to torment me..." Her voice broke.

"No, Ruth, I have not come to torment you. Please listen to me. I am so sorry for the way I have treated you. I was wrong." He reached out and gently touched her arm.

She flinched and said tearfully, "I am ashamed to look at you. I am a sinner."

"You are not a sinner, Ruth," he said quietly "you were sinned against. You and your child are innocent victims. I want to take care of you – and the baby, if you will let me."

She turned back to him and saw the contrite expression on his face. Wiping away her tears with her sleeve, she let out a sigh of relief as he drew her into his arms and held her close.

Soon after, Ruth told Mary that she would try to feed the infant herself. Mary was overjoyed, but wondered why Ruth had suddenly changed. Then she saw the look of happiness on her son's face and nodded, satisfied.

With Mary's guidance, Ruth held the tiny scrap of humanity to her trembling breast and the eager mouth began to feed. Ruth suddenly felt a wave of love engulf her, and the bonding between mother and child began.

Sheikh Ibrahim, dressed in a woollen cloak hiding the richness of his clothes beneath, hovered outside Mary's house as Drubaal knocked on the door. After much persuasion from Drubaal, gently reminding him of how he had once taken pity on Ruth as a pauper child and had taken her into his household, he had grudgingly agreed to see Ruth and her child.

Mary's welcome to the Carthaginian was warm. She stepped back, startled, as Ibrahim appeared behind him and followed him into the small house. When Drubaal introduced his master to her, she wondered how she should greet this important man. She bobbed her head in deference and asked the two visitors to sit down while she busied herself pouring wine for them, nervously apologizing for the plain and simple cups.

Hearing the familiar voice of Drubaal, Ruth came out of the bedroom. She stopped short when she saw Ibrahim sitting there and turned to go back into the room, afraid.

Ibrahim's voice stopped her. He said gruffly "Ruth, come here child." He watched as her feet involuntarily moved towards him. As she stood before him, he looked her up and down, saying "I am pleased to see that you are well." He took a deep breath. "Drubaal told me you had a daughter. I would very much like to see her."

Anxiety written all over her face, Ruth looked at her former master, afraid that he might hurt her baby. She relaxed a little when he assured her he meant no harm to her or her child, and went into the bedroom to fetch her. When she returned holding the baby close to her, Ibrahim held out his arms, asking if he could hold the child. She gently passed her daughter to the older man, who pushed back the shawl and looked into her little face. The baby looked up at him with large, luminous eyes fringed with thick, dark lashes. Ibrahim felt the ice in his heart slowly begin to melt. He murmured softly, "She is beautiful. Such lovely, dark eyes, just like my darling Farrah." A tear formed in the corner of his eye and he tickled the baby under her tiny chin, bringing forth gurgles of delight. He looked up at Ruth and asked, "Tell me, have you given her a name yet?"

Ruth shook her head. "No, not yet, but I thought Mary would be a good name." Ruth looked at the older woman, who stared back at her in surprise.

Without taking his eyes off the baby lying contentedly in his arms, Ibrahim said "Would you do me the honour of also naming the child after my beloved niece?"

Astounded by this request, Ruth was lost for words. After a long moment of silence, she said humbly. "Master, I too loved my mistress. If it should please you, may I name the baby Mary-Farrah?"

Ibrahim was visibly overcome. "Yes. That is an admirable choice." He handed the baby back to her mother and stood up. "I think it is time we returned to the fortress, Drubaal." He smiled at Ruth and said, "But I will visit you again." Turning to Mary, he said "If that is possible, Mary?"

Mary replied quickly, "You are welcome in this house any time, sir. Perhaps when you call again Peter and my son will be here, I'm sure they will be pleased to meet you."

Ibrahim nodded. "Drubaal has spoken to me of your son and of the man called Peter. I would be very interested to speak to them, Peter in particular. He seems a remarkable man." The two men walked towards the door. Ibrahim turned and said "Until we meet again." With that he and Drubaal left the house as a stunned Ruth and Mary looked on.

Back in his room in the Antonia, Ibrahim carefully picked up the casket containing his niece's ashes. Tears filled his eyes as he looked at it. "My beloved Farrah, I am an old man now with no children of my own," he said. "I despaired of your name dying with you. Now your name will live on. For this I must thank Ruth. I have treated her badly, yet she has repaid me with a wonderful gift."

He had been angry at Drubaal's insistence that he should see Ruth and the baby and for repeating the same fantastic story of mother and child having been brought back from the dead by this man called Peter. He had thought of dismissing him, but grudgingly remembered the faithful service the Carthaginian had given him over the years, so he had finally given up arguing about it and decided to see the girl for himself, to tell her he had no further need of her and that she was free to go wherever she wanted, thus putting an end to the whole tiresome business. But things had not turned out that way. He wondered what it was about that house and that baby that had changed his mind. He only knew that when he had entered the house a feeling of peace had settled over him, a peace he had not felt for a long time. At first he had scoffed at the story of the magical saving of Ruth and the baby; now he wasn't so sure. If the people living there did practice magic, it was not evil but good. He was impatient to see Peter to find out more.

Now that Ibrahim had made his peace with Ruth, he visited her again with an eager Drubaal, and delighted in holding the baby. On the third occasion he met Peter, who smiled at the visitors and said jovially, "Come in. You are welcome. I'm sorry the rest of our group aren't here for you to meet, they are away, visiting different areas of Judaea and Galilee." He didn't add that they were telling the story of Jesus to the people who lived in every village in those regions.

Impatient to know, Ibrahim asked Peter about Ruth's miraculous recovery and the saving of the child. Peter's answer staggered him. It was not magic that had saved them but the love and power of someone he called the Lord Jesus. When Ibrahim asked for more information, Peter took just a moment to decide he was trustworthy and gladly gave it.

When Peter finished his story, Ibrahim sat quietly, trying to absorb the amazing stories he'd just been told. After a while he looked at Peter and said, "In truth, my friend, I don't know what to think." He sighed. "I understand you Jews worship one deity, whereas in my country we worship many, but I would like to know more about this Jesus whom you call Lord and the Son of your God." He was glad when Peter said he would happily speak to him more about his time serving Jesus and an agreement was made that he should return to the house for this purpose. In fact, Ibrahim returned several more times and gradually, he began to believe.

On one visit, Ibrahim looked grave. Ruth asked him if anything was wrong, and his answer amazed her.

"I have refused the Emperor's honour of becoming a Roman Citizen," he said. "I am loyal to King Aretas and I will obey only him. This has not gone down well with Governor Pilate and has made it embarrassing for me to remain here. Besides, Jerusalem holds too many painful memories for me. Now that ben-Ezra is no longer a threat, I am anxious to return to my homeland." He took a deep breath. "In any case, it is time for me to supervise the placing of my niece's remains in the family tomb so she may be reunited with the rest of her family. In a few days' time, a caravan is leaving Jerusalem for Nabatea. I have made arrangements to travel with it." He looked intently at Ruth and asked softly, "Ruth, will you and the child return with me as members of my family?"

He could see Ruth was stunned, and smiled. "I do not require an answer now, but I ask you to think about my request. I will send Drubaal to you tomorrow for your answer."

John Mark was taken aback by the Sheikh's offer. He looked earnestly at Ruth, knowing that if she accepted the offer he would be devastated.

Ruth saw John Mark's questioning look. All kind of thoughts were racing through her mind. Should she go with the Sheikh? What about John Mark? She was sure she had a future with him. It was plain to see that he loved her, and she was beginning to return that love. She would miss Mary, Peter and the other Disciples too, but the Sheikh also meant a lot to her. She looked at his hunched shoulders and sunken eyes as he sat on the bench opposite, and her heart went out to him. The death of her mistress had almost destroyed him; how could she abandon him? What to do? She needed time to think.

"I will give you my answer when Drubaal comes tomorrow," she said. The Sheikh nodded, then got up stiffly from the bench, acknowledged Peter, John Mark and Mary and, with Drubaal in tow, left the house.

Peter covered Ruth's hand with his own and spoke gravely. "Ruth, the decision must be yours. If you decide to go with the Sheikh, remember you will always be welcome in this house and much loved by those in it. It is such a big decision. I ask you to pray for guidance to make the right choice."

Tears stung Ruth's eyes. She could barely look at John Mark's grimly hopeful face, knowing it would be a wrench to leave him, to leave them all. She also knew she would spend a sleepless night desperately trying to reach the right decision.

# CHAPTER TWENTY-FIVE

Ruth spent a fretful night tossing and turning, her mind in turmoil, praying again and again, asking for guidance as to which path she should follow. As dawn began to break, she suddenly smelt the faint fragrance of flowers permeate the air, and heard a voice speak to her. She put her hands to her head and covered her ears, crying out "Who are you?" Shaking with fear, she looked around the room; there was no one there. The voice spoke again. 'Ruth, Ruth, I have need of you. Will you spread the Word to those who have not yet heard?' She had never met Jesus, never heard his voice when he was alive, so how could she know if it was the Lord speaking to her now? Was she dreaming? She wrestled with this strange, terrifying message. Why would the Lord Jesus need her, a humble servant girl with a child conceived in sin, to spread the news about Him?

Then the words of Jesus' mother Mary came flooding back to her: 'You have been chosen by my Son to work for His great purpose." John Mark had told her that after the birth of little Mary-Farrah she had died and that Peter had asked the Lord to bring her back to life – a request that had been miraculously answered. Why? Was it for His great purpose, as Mary had foretold? If the voice in her head was that of Jesus, then she must put her trust in Him and go wherever He sent her. She made her decision, knowing it was the right one.

She got up from her bed and found Peter sitting quietly at the table, praying. When she told him what had happened, he nodded and said "There is no doubt in my mind that it was the Lord who spoke to you, Ruth. You are blessed indeed. He has chosen you for a reason. If it is His wish that you travel to Nabatea and perhaps beyond, then you must go."

Ruth bowed her head. "Then I will obey the Lord's command. I will go to Nabatea."

Hearing the disturbance, Mary and John Mark had got up from their beds and followed Ruth into the room. They heard Ruth and Peter's conversation. Ruth's decision left John Mark crestfallen. So Ruth had made her choice: she was going to Nabatea with the Sheikh.

Peter, seeing his friends standing there and the look of misery on the young man's face, stood up and motioned Mary to leave Ruth and John Mark alone so they could speak privately.

Knowing her decision had upset John Mark, Ruth could barely look him in the face. She touched his arm and said sadly, "I'm sorry, John Mark, but I have to go. I can't lose this feeling that I am being called to work for the Lord Jesus. I don't know what He wants me to do or where I may have to go after Nabatea, all I know is, I have to put my trust in Him. I know He will guide my footsteps."

John Mark tried hard to smile. "I understand, Ruth. You know I will always love you. All I ask is, when you go away, please don't forget me."

Tears began to roll down Ruth's cheeks. "I will always love you, John Mark. I will never forget you, even if my journey takes me to the ends of the earth."

He kissed her tear-soaked face. How could he argue against what the Lord had decided?

A short time later Drubaal arrived and Ruth gave him her answer. "I would very much like to travel to Nabatea with the Sheikh and with you, my friend. Please tell the Sheikh I honour him and thank him for accepting me into his family."

Drubaal was overjoyed and whooped in delight. Hearing this, Peter and Mary came back into the room. Mary's heart was heavy; she had grown to love Ruth and baby Mary-Farrah. Looking at her son and seeing his barely-concealed distress, she took his hand in an effort to comfort him.

Peter looked at Drubaal and said, "Take good care of her, Drubaal."

Drubaal nodded, then returned to the Sheikh with the good news.

As soon as Flavius heard that the Sheikh was leaving, he went to see him. "I have been told you are returning to Nabatea, Sheikh Ibrahim," he said, noting the older man's look of resentment. He knew the Sheikh blamed him for Farrah's death, something he had blamed himself for many times. He had been stupidly careless and it had cost Farrah her life.

"That is correct," Ibrahim replied. "It is time for me to go home. I am too old to play the spy now." He let out a deep sigh. "There is also the matter of my niece – it is time she was laid to rest with her family. Besides, as I'm sure you must know, I have declined the Emperor's offer of Roman citizenship, which would make things awkward for me here now."

He pre-empted the question on Flavius' lips by saying, "You're wondering if my Farrah would have accepted this offer." He shrugged. "Perhaps she would have, for you, but unfortunately, we will never know now." He saw Flavius' face redden and softened his tone. "I know how much you loved her, Tribune, and I am sure she returned that love, even though a marriage between you would have been impossible." He raised his hand in a placatory gesture. "I mean no offence to you, but my people are a proud people and are not usually given in marriage to those from other countries, particularly to Romans, whose first allegiance is to their Emperor. Our King does not approve of that – and neither do I."

Flavius felt hurt by this statement, but told himself that aristocratic Romans felt exactly the same way about mixed marriages. He knew the difficulty he himself might have faced. He saw the dark shadows under the older man's eyes and knew he was worn out by all of his troubles. It was for the best that he did return to his homeland. He stood at attention and said, "Sheikh Ibrahim, it has been an honour to know you. I wish you a safe journey back to Nabatea."

Ibrahim touched his mouth and forehead with his fingers in a stiff salute of goodbye. Flavius returned the salute in Roman fashion, turned on his heel and left the room.

The next morning, Flavius and Marcus, as part of Pilate's entourage, began the journey back to Caesarea.

# CHAPTER TWENTY-SIX

As soon as he had some free time, Flavius visited the home of Cornelius. He handed Saturn over to Cornelius' Greek manservant, Andros, then approached the house.

"Welcome, Tribune." Martha gave a quick curtsy, then led him inside. Laughter came from one of the rooms followed by the sound of Julia's excited voice. "There's much excitement," said a beaming Martha, "Mistress Julia's wedding is in two days' time."

Flavius smiled. "Yes, I know. It seems Marcus is just as excited. He's told half the garrison." At that moment Julia came rushing out of the room, followed by two of her friends. Not seeing Flavius, she almost bumped into him. Flavius smiled at the look of surprise on her face.

"Oh, Tribune Flavius. I didn't know you were here," she said breathlessly.

"I've only just arrived." He studied her face. "It's good to see you looking so happy, Julia."

Julia smiled radiantly at him. "I am happy and I'm glad to see you safe and well, Tribune. How long will you be in Caesarea?"

He shrugged. "Until Governor Pilate decides to travel again."

"If it is possible, I would like it very much if you could come to my wedding," she said coyly.

He smiled. "If Marcus doesn't mind and my duties allow, I would love to come. Thank you for inviting me." He knew Marcus would not object, because of the unspoken pact they had made.

Just then Cornelius appeared from the garden. He came straight up to Flavius and clasped his arm enthusiastically, then, with an apology to his daughter, led him into the dining room and asked him about his time back in Jerusalem. Flavius told him about the battles and Julius' bravery in saving the life of Drubaal, saying he was the bodyguard of a very important person. He decided to leave out the circumstances of Farrah's death. He then went on to describe the captured prisoners' executions. When he told Cornelius about Antonius' crooked dealings and his subsequent banishment to the mines, Cornelius heaved a sigh of relief.

"Good riddance," he said harshly. "The Legions have no need of men like him, although I fear there are many others like him."

"Yes, I'm afraid Sejanus has left us a legacy of corruption and greed among some of the officer hierarchy."

Cornelius nodded. "I thank the gods that Sejanus is dead, but I hear the Emperor is still taking his anger out on his followers. One of our new legionaries, recently come from Rome, told me the streets are running with blood."

Flavius blanched, remembering how his father had pretended to support Sejanus to keep his estates and make sure his family survived. Fortunately for them all, the Emperor Tiberius had forgiven him. He hoped the Emperor still favoured his father. He tried desperately to banish the thought from his mind and changed the subject. "The new Senior Tribune, Paullus, is expected to arrive here tomorrow with fresh troops," he said. "I wonder what he will be like."

"Let's pray he's a decent officer," Cornelius said, hopefully.

There followed a brief silence, then Flavius said "It appears that all is ready for Julia's wedding."

Cornelius smiled. "Yes. I've never seen my daughter so excited. I hear her singing in the garden, although she doesn't know it. My one wish is that she is happy in her married life. You know I wasn't sure about young Marcus, but lately he seems to be a changed man, more mature."

Flavius thought that taking part in the battle against ben-Ezra and the carnage he had witnessed had surely changed Marcus; he knew it had changed him. He smiled, saying "I'm sure he will make Julia a good husband."

Cornelius nodded, then looked at Flavius and said unexpectedly, "I know you are a Tribune Laticlavius, sir, and will serve for a short time in the Legions before you enter the Senate, as is your right, but how much longer will you serve in Judaea and Caesarea?"

Flavius calculated in his mind, then said, "I've been in Palestine for almost a year, and with the year I spent with the First Italica Legion in Rome, my two-year stint in the army is almost up, although Pilate has asked me to stay on." He sighed. "I don't know how much longer Pilate will expect me to stay on as a member of his staff, but one day soon I will have to join the ranks of Senators."

"Excuse me Tribune, but are you not pleased about the prospect of entering the Senate?" Cornelius asked carefully, not wishing to embarrass Flavius.

Flavius' reply came without hesitation. "No, I'm not. Politics bores me. My younger brother, Marius, is more suited to that particular career. He's always got his nose in one scroll or another to do with law or politics. Of course, with my being the elder son and heir, it falls to me to follow my father, a fact that makes Marius jealous, even though he knows my heart is not in it. If only I could pass this particular inheritance on to him. I am more suited to army life and travelling."

"That I understand." Cornelius smiled. "As you know, even at my age, although I'm no longer an active soldier, I am still part of a Legion." He felt sympathy for Flavius, knowing how trapped and frustrated he must feel. "Of course, it's good that Governor Pilate is keeping you on his staff for a while longer, as your father is still a member of the Senate. Perhaps you can stay with the Governor indefinitely."

Flavius smiled sadly. "Perhaps, but personally I don't think so. It is inevitable that my father will expect me to enter the Senate soon. Even Pilate can't upset the ancient order of things."

"Could you delay your return home, after your duties here are finished? It might be better if you don't return to Rome until things there settle down."

Flavius grimaced, but did not answer. Cornelius saw the look on his face and regretted mentioning it.

Flavius was aware of his rudeness, and somewhat embarrassed, he said apologetically, "I'm sorry, but I have to go. Pilate is holding another of his interminable receptions tonight and wants me there as Port Official. He's worried that the newly-increased port duties will not go down well with the merchants."

Cornelius stroked his chin and said, "No, they probably won't. The merchants are a touchy lot."

Flavius sighed. "I am also to greet Paullus on his arrival."

"Well, I hope everything goes well and that there's no trouble for you."

Cornelius went outside with Flavius and watched as he mounted Saturn. Before the Tribune rode away, he said jovially, "I look forward to seeing you at the wedding,

Tribune. And please don't worry on my behalf, I will heed your advice about the new Tribune."

# CHAPTER TWENTY-SEVEN

As Ruth gathered her sparse belongings, Mary dressed the baby ready for the long journey ahead. She looked at her tiny face and when she saw the large, dark eyes looking back at her, she could not stop her tears from flowing. She wiped them away with the back of her hand and tried desperately to hide her feelings in front of Ruth. She then wrapped Mary-Farrah in a soft blanket and handed the baby to her mother.

Ruth turned and saw Drubaal's massive frame standing in the doorway. It was time to go. She embraced Mary, saying in a choked voice, "Thank you for all the kindness you have shown me, Mary. I don't know what I would have done without you."

Afraid her voice would break with emotion, Mary nodded and kissed Ruth on the forehead as a mother would a beloved child who was about to leave the family home.

Ruth turned to Peter, who had been standing watching, and said humbly, "Peter, I cannot find the words to thank you enough for what you have done for me and for Mary-Farrah."

Peter took her hand and smiled, feeling a fierce pride in Ruth for her decision to obey the Lord's will. He knew only too well the dangers that awaited her when she began to spread the news of Jesus in a foreign land. Looking deep into Ruth's eyes, he said "What you are doing is a courageous thing, Ruth. You will always be in our prayers. Who knows, if the Lord wills it, perhaps we will all be together again one day soon."

Drubaal looked down, embarrassed. Peter and Mary turned away as John Mark went to her. Ruth saw the anguish on his face and felt tears welling up in her eyes.

"Ruth, you know I will always love you. If things don't work out for you in your new land, remember I will always be here waiting."

She reached up and kissed his cheek, her voice trembling as she said "I know, John Mark. I love you too. One day we will meet again, I'm sure of it."

Drubaal bowed to the small group who had become his friends and said, "I will take care of her." Then to Ruth, "The caravan is ready to leave. My master awaits you."

Unable to bear the tension, Ruth turned to Drubaal. "I am ready," she said, struggling to keep her voice steady.

He stood aside as with one last look, Ruth smiled at the

people she had grown to love, then with her baby safely in her arms, turned and left the house with Drubaal. John Mark followed them out into the street. With a heavy heart, he watched as Drubaal lifted Ruth onto his horse, then handed Mary-Farrah to her. Ruth immediately clutched her baby to her chest, and Drubaal mounted up behind her. Making sure mother and child were safely settled, he gave a quick salute to John Mark, then urged his horse on. As they slowly rode away, John Mark whispered, "May the Lord be with you, my darling Ruth." He let out a deep sigh, then went back into the house, closing the door behind him.

When they reached the caravan, Ruth was astounded. She had never seen so many camels in one place, and the noise was deafening. They snorted, bellowed and stamped their feet on the hard ground as though impatient to go, and the pungent smell of the beasts filled her nostrils. One camel turned its head to look straight at her and she stepped back in fear as it bared its teeth at her. The camel drover brought his stick down on to the camel's flanks and spoke to it in a harsh voice until it turned its head back again to face forward. Ruth breathed a sigh of relief.

Sheikh Ibrahim was all smiles as he greeted Ruth and the baby. He held Mary-Farrah in his arms, looking lovingly at her, as Ruth climbed into a horse-drawn covered carriage. She marvelled at the sheer luxury of the interior of the vehicle. It was lined in costly silken material and decked out with thick cushions. There was also a small cloth cot which had been fashioned for Mary-Farrah to lie in. This would make the long journey more comfortable for both mother and child.

Once Ruth had settled back into the plump, richly-embroidered cushions, the Sheikh handed the baby to her. As Ruth gently placed the baby into the cot, her eyes went to an object wrapped in silk, secured in a corner of the carriage. She looked questioningly at Ibrahim.

"The silk is wrapped around the cedar wood box containing my niece's ashes," he said gravely. "I thought that as you took such great care of your mistress in life, you might wish to take care of her on her last journey home."

Ruth tried hard to quell her tears. "You do me a great honour, Sheikh Ibrahim. I am happy to be of final service to my mistress. Thank you."

Ibrahim nodded. He was glad to be leaving this troubled land and going home. He let down the material which covered the entrance to the carriage, giving Ruth and Mary-Farrah privacy, then climbed up onto his magnificent white Arabian stallion. Drubaal steered his horse beside the Sheikh, ready, as always, to protect his master. Ibrahim's guards surrounded them both. The drovers walked up and down, checking that the camels were properly hitched and the goods the animals carried were fastened securely. The mounted and armed caravan guards took their positions up and down the length of the camel-train. When the leader of the caravan saluted that all was ready, Ibrahim gave the order for it to begin its long journey home. With deafening bellows from the camels, the cavalcade moved off.

In the carriage Ruth leaned over and looked at Mary-Farrah, now fast asleep in her little cot. Satisfied the child was settled, she lay back on the cushions and closed her eyes. From now on they were in the hands of the Sheikh and the Lord Jesus.


The harbour was filled with merchants impatient to have their goods loaded onto the merchant ships waiting in the port, as well as the troops waiting for a trireme to dock. The trireme carried the new Senior Tribune, together with legionaries from other garrisons sent to replace some of those from the Caesarea garrison.

The trireme's Captain yelled out orders as the ship manoeuvered smoothly into the dock. Soon all was ready for its passengers to disembark. Flavius watched as a heavily-built man wearing the uniform of a Tribune walked down the gangplank and stepped off the ship. He looked around the quayside and upon seeing Flavius, a fellow Tribune, walked across to him and said pompously "I am Tribune Gnaeus Aeneas Paullus, and you are...?"

Flavius pulled himself up to his full height, not liking the new officer's tone. "I am Tribune Flavius Quinctilius Silvanus, a Tribune of the Governor's personal staff." He gave a brief, stiff nod of his head. "Welcome to Caesarea, Tribune Paullus, Governor Pilate is expecting you."

"Good. Then would someone lead me to the Governor's

office? I must report my arrival and give him the latest dispatches from Rome."

Flavius turned to a junior officer and said, "Please escort the Tribune to Governor Pilate." The officer saluted and ordered two of his accompanying legionaries to take care of the Tribune's luggage. As Paullus waited impatiently for the legionaries to collect his luggage, he looked around the busy port and said grimly, "Is it always like this?"

Flavius tried not to laugh at the bewildered expression on the new Senior Tribune's face. "No, not always. One of the crew of a merchant ship told me storms in the Western Tyrrhenian Sea a few days back delayed several supply and troop ships sailing from Ostia and other western ports, so now the late ships are all arriving at once."

"We managed to catch the last remnants of that storm when we were finally able to set sail. It has not been pleasant." Paullus suddenly turned his attention to one of the legionaries who was struggling with a heavy bundle of luggage and moving, in his opinion, far too slowly. He shouted, "You there!" He bristled as the legionary ignored him and continued to struggle. "I said, you there!" Paullus walked swiftly to the legionary and stopped before him, his hand on his sword hilt and said menacingly, "When I speak to you, you acknowledge me."

The legionary quickly placed the luggage on the ground and nervously saluted. Flavius saw the frightened look on the young legionary's face as Paullus roared angrily, "Be careful, you idiot. That is my personal luggage you have there. If anything is damaged I will hold you personally responsible. Now, pick it up!"

As the man picked up the luggage, Paullus shouted orders to the legionaries who had accompanied him on the ship. They quickly lined up behind him. He then turned back to the junior officer and said impatiently "Come on, man. What are we waiting for?" Following the young officer, the new Tribune and his guard marched smartly off the quayside towards the Governor's residence.

Laurentius was standing by and had seen and heard the Tribune. He approached Flavius and said with contempt in his voice, "Huh! So that's the new Tribune is it?" He's heading for all kinds of trouble if he carries on like this. I'm glad he didn't speak to me the way he spoke to that young legionary. It wouldn't do my career any good being arrested for punching a senior officer."

Flavius smiled. "I agree Laurentius, it's definitely not worth ruining your life for somebody like that."

Laurentius grinned, then walked over to the Captain of the trireme and produced his check-list, which they checked through together.

Flavius noted the arrogant-looking Captain and disliked him on sight. There was something in the way he looked at Laurentius that set his teeth on edge. Still, the Captain meant nothing to him; he didn't have to deal personally with him. He turned his attention to other matters on the quayside and forgot about him.

The day passed quickly as ship after ship arrived in port and was successfully unloaded, and in some cases reloaded, with goods to be taken back to Ostia or other Roman-held ports when the tide had turned the next morning. Flavius was relieved that so far, the merchants had not caused any trouble. Perhaps it was the sight of the extra legionaries that had forestalled any action. Whatever the reason, his duty would thankfully soon be over for the day.

Pilate welcomed Paullus and the new Tribune handed over the dispatch bag to him. Pilate laid it on his desk, then called for a guard to escort Paullus to his quarters. He waved a hand airily as Paullus saluted him, then, after Paullus had gone, he looked through the dispatch bag. It contained the usual reports and news from Rome. He hesitated as he saw a sealed scroll addressed to Flavius. It was different from the usual communications. He didn't recognise the handwriting and he wondered who it was from. He sent for a legionary.

Flavius was glad when his duty was finished. He was tired and hot, but thought a bathing session would help to freshen him and ease his aching muscles. He hoped Paullus would not be at the baths, as he had no desire to enter into conversation with him.

As he entered Pilate's palace, a legionary approached him and saluted, saying, "Governor Pilate wishes to see you immediately, Tribune." Flavius sighed, then nodded. The legionary escorted him to Pilate's office.

As Flavius entered the Governor's office, Pilate got up from behind his desk. He held out a rolled scroll to Flavius, saying "I've just received the latest dispatches from Rome. This one's for you."

Flavius took it, quickly scanning the seal on the outside of the scroll. He did not recognise it. Knowing that since the Antonius affair, Pilate had grown paranoid about communications, Flavius said "Permission to read it, sir?" Seeing Pilate's quizzical look Flavius explained, "I don't know who has written this, sir, and I would like to read it in your presence in case something is wrong."

"Permission granted, Tribune," came the swift reply.

Flavius read the communication. He couldn't take in what he was reading. His father was dead? He'd never had a day's illness in his life. He had always been such a strong and robust man. And why had the scroll been sent by his father's friend, Senator Claudius, and not his mother or brother? Something had happened, he was sure. But what?

Pilate saw Flavius' face grow ashen and the younger man's body sway slightly. His voice held a note of concern as he asked, "Is anything wrong, Flavius?"

Flavius swallowed hard. "I'm afraid so, sir. This scroll is from a Senator friend of my father. He writes that my father has recently died. He doesn't give any details but passes on a request from my mother that I should be allowed to return to Rome as soon as possible."

Pilate's shock was evident. "My dear boy, please accept my deepest sympathy. I've always respected your father.

He was a good man and a brilliant Senator, and I am sad for your mother. It's obvious she needs you at her side at this present time. I will grant you as much leave as you require." He returned to his desk. "The trireme that brought Paullus here is returning to Ostia on the morning tide. I suggest you accompany the legionaries who are also returning. I will arrange passage for you." He hurriedly wrote out a signed order to the ship's Captain and an extended leave pass to show to the authorities in Ostia, then handed both to Flavius.

Lost for words, Flavius nodded in reply. "Why don't you go to the baths, then have a good meal?" Pilate continued. "You don't have much equipment to sort out, so packing your essentials shouldn't take long. The ship will be leaving early in the morning. Try to get a good night's sleep, you need to be ready to deal with whatever awaits you in Rome."

Flavius saluted and said, "Thank you Governor Pilate." Pilate sighed as Flavius left the room. He had grown fond of the young man and was sorry he had received such shocking news. For a brief moment he too wondered about Senator Silvanus' sudden death, but he was sure his son would get to the bottom of it.

At the baths, Flavius remembered that he was supposed to be attending Julia's wedding the next day. He did not have time to send them a message and Marcus had been granted a few days' leave before the marriage. He knew Cornelius and Julia would be disappointed, but perhaps he could write to them when things were settled at home. It was his mother he had to think of now.

# CHAPTER TWENTY-EIGHT

"Wake up, mistress." Julia opened her eyes to see a smiling Martha looking down at her. "It's time to get ready." Julia pulled a face and scolded her, saying "You let me oversleep."

Martha knew Julia was only pretending to be angry and said, "Yes, mistress. After all, it's not every day a girl gets married."

Julia stretched her arms above her head and smiled. Today was her wedding day. Soon she would be married to Marcus, the man she loved above all others, except for her father; part of her did not want to leave him. She knew that with Julius far away in Jerusalem, and now her imminent departure from the family home, he would be alone except for Martha and Andros. She resolved that she would visit him as often as she could and would never leave him on his own for too long.

She threw back the covers and sat on the edge of her bed as Martha carefully removed the crimson net which had held her hair in place overnight. "Oh, Martha, I am so happy," she purred.

"I think you should eat something, mistress. It will be hours before you have your wedding banquet, and we don't want you passing out on your big day."

"Oh, Martha, don't fuss. I'm so excited I don't think I could eat a thing," she replied. But Martha would not be moved and she brought Julia a small platter of honey cakes and a goblet of foaming goat's milk to give her strength. Afterwards, satisfied that Julia had finished all of it, she led the bride-to-be off to bathe.

The floral scented water was soothing and as she sponged Julia down, Martha could see her begin to relax. She smiled to herself at the memory of Julia as a child, when she would clean the dirt off her after she had naughtily disobeyed her mother and played on the wet and grubby seashore, presenting her mother with sea-shells she had found there. Martha carefully wrapped Julia in a fluffy towel and dried her, then massaged her body with sweet-smelling oils.

Julia stood still as Martha dressed her in a white hemless woollen tunic, then put a girdle of white wool around her small waist, tying it with a double knot; this was the ancient sign of purity and would be undone by her husband on the wedding night. Julia fought back tears, knowing the girdle should be tied by the bride's mother.

Oh, if only her mother had lived to see this day!

Martha arranged a large saffron-coloured rectangular woollen cloth over the dress, then put saffron-coloured sandals on Julia's feet. Placing a metal collar around her neck, she then fixed six pads of artificial hair, separated by narrow bands, into her hair. She put a flaming orange veil over Julia's elaborate hairstyle which covered the upper part of her face, finishing by fixing a wreath of myrtle and orange blossom over the veil.

Martha wiped away a tear as she gazed proudly at Julia. "You look so beautiful, so like your dear mother. Marcus is a very lucky man."

Julia's Matron of Honour arrived with the bridesmaids, numbering ten, who would also act as witnesses at the ceremony. On seeing Julia, they expressed their approval.

Cornelius entered the room. He stood for a moment taking in the sight of his beautiful daughter, then said proudly, "How lovely you look, my dear." Smiling, he held out his arm for her to rest her hand on, saying "Come, Marcus and his friends have arrived. It's time."

Followed by a beaming Martha, the Matron of Honour and giggling bridesmaids, Julia and her proud father entered the room where Marcus and his friends from the garrison were waiting. Marcus was stunned by Julia's beauty. Although his parents had not travelled from Rome to attend the ceremony, Marcus' father had given permission for the marriage; although Cornelius was of the equestrian class, a slightly lower class than Marcus' parents, he came from an illustrious and historic background. Julia's mother had been a patrician who, Julia had once told him, had defied class and married for love. A fleeting moment of guilt crossed Marcus' mind when he remembered the outrageous things he had done whilst this vision of sweet loveliness walking towards him had patiently waited. She clearly still loved him, despite the inconsiderate way he had sometimes treated her. He vowed never to leave her side again.

Julia looked lovingly at her husband-to-be and a thrill of delight swept through her. How handsome he looked in his crisp white toga with a wreath of flowers circling his head.

The wedding party, including Martha, Andros and several neighbours, moved off to the family altar where sacrifices to the household and family gods were made. The interpreter of omens examined the entrails of the sacrifices, pronouncing that the auspices were favourable. Then, in the atrium of the family home, Julia's Matron of Honour took Julia's right hand and joined it to Marcus' right hand. The priest intoned the sacred words and gazing into one another's eyes, the couple exchanged their vows, sealing them with a kiss.

Now that the official ceremony was over, the guests burst into congratulations and good wishes, all saying loudly, "May happiness wait upon you."

Julia wondered why Flavius had not come. Perhaps his duties would not allow it. She dismissed that thought as she entered the main room of her family home, delighted to see the table groaning with delicacies and the wine vats filled to overflowing. "You have done magnificently, Martha," she said, hugging Martha in appreciation of her efforts to put on a good show to uphold family pride.

Martha replied modestly, "I didn't do this all on my own. I had the help of some local tradesmen." Julia smiled, and was led off by Marcus to speak to some of the guests.

Cornelius invited the guests to help themselves to the food, while Andros continuously poured the wine into wine cups eagerly held out by Marcus' friends. The pretty bridesmaids soon found themselves besieged by the young officers present, who spent much of the evening flirting with them and persuading them to agree to romantic assignations.

The wedding feast lasted until nightfall. The food tables and wine barrels were now empty, and it was time for the couple to depart. With Julia carrying a spindle signifying her womanly skills, the procession, led by flute players and followed by five torch bearers, made its way to the house Marcus had bought in the city, staffed by a burly doorkeeper and a young serving girl for Julia. On the way, Julia dropped one of the three coins she carried onto the ground for the gods of the crossroads. Later she would give one to Marcus as an emblem of the dowry she brought him, saving the third for an offering to her new household gods.

Much to Martha's disgust and the delight of the giggling bridesmaids, Marcus' friends began to bellow out lewd songs. Martha had never heard such ribaldry and tutted as the words of the songs grew ever more licentious. As they walked on, Marcus threw nuts to the children who had gathered around them, in memory of his childhood when he had played with childish toys. It was also a good omen for future happiness and fertility. Then he and his friends split from the procession and hurried on to his house, ready to greet his new bride there.

Julia was surprised and delighted when she saw her new home, but felt a pang of regret when she turned to her father and saw his face. She knew he was struggling with seeing his only daughter leave home to begin a new life.

She went to him, and he held her for a brief moment, reassuring her that he was happy for her and nodding his approval before urging her to return to her husband. Julia took a small jar of oil carried by Martha and anointed the door posts of the house with it, then bound bands of wool around them, symbolically making herself the mistress of the house. Marcus lifted Julia up into his arms ready to cross the threshold of their new home, as it was believed that evil spirits dwelt on the threshold of a property waiting to curse newlyweds. If the bride was lifted over them, they could not enter her body through the soles of her feet.

Marcus half-turned to face his friends as they cheered, uttering more ribald comments and wishing them a happy and fruitful wedding night. Marcus carried his new bride into the house, closing the door behind him with the back of his foot.

Happily tired out by the day's events, Cornelius, Martha, Andros, and those neighbours who had followed the procession turned away and began their journey home. Meanwhile Marcus' fellow officers went roistering down to the nearest tavern to continue the celebrations and to drink to their friend and his beautiful wife's lusty coupling in the marriage bed. They slapped each other on the back and made vulgar jokes in embarrassingly loud, inebriated voices.

Cornelius sat in the garden, alone with his memories. In his mind's eye he saw Julia and Julius as small children running around the pots of flowers and shrubs, shrieking with laughter at their childish game as Helena warned them to be careful. Then later, also in this garden, had come the moment when Julius had told him he wanted to join the legions. At first, he had been afraid for his son. He had seen too many battles and did not want his son to have to experience the blood and gore he remembered so well, but knowing Julius' mind was made up and wanting to do his duty for the Emperor, he reluctantly agreed to let him go. He had hoped Julius would be stationed here in Caesarea and was disappointed when he was sent to the garrison in Jerusalem.

He remembered an older Julia sitting on the stone seat, opposite where he now sat, discussing the latest handsome young hero with her young lady friends and commenting on fashion and hairstyles. It was here that Marcus had first asked for Julia's hand in marriage. At first he had not been keen, but then, seeing Julia's look of love at the young officer, he had relented and given his consent.

Now all was silence. He looked up at the twinkling stars lighting up the dark sky and wondered if his beloved Helena was looking down on him. What would she have said about her only daughter's marriage? Would she have approved, knowing what her own actions had been in marrying him? If only she were here now. Life was sometimes so cruel. He was happy for Julia, but he had never felt so alone. With a deep sigh he returned to the house and retired to bed.

# CHAPTER TWENTY-NINE

Flavius recognised most of the junior officers and legionaries waiting to board the trireme and returned their salutes. He stared at the impressive warship riding at anchor in the harbour and saw, just below the water-line, the early morning sunlight reflecting off the huge bronze-sheathed ram on the prow. He looked upwards at the mainmast and the sailors busy in the rigging, checking the furled sails, then at the smaller sail on the prow and finally at the three banks of oars where he knew skilled oarsmen were waiting for their instructions.

Seeing Flavius standing on the quayside, Laurentius walked over to him. He greeted him with a salute and a smile. "Have a safe journey, Tribune. I pray Neptune will be kind to you on your voyage. Hopefully that summer storm has passed us by."

Flavius returned his smile. "I hope so too."

Laurentius saluted again, saying "Excuse me, sir, I have to oversee the loading of supplies onto the trireme." Flavius watched him walk towards the piles of goods waiting on the quayside with a group of sailors standing ready to load them onto the ship.

Because of his rank, Flavius was the first passenger to go on board. Leading Saturn by the reins, he was duly met by the Centurion of the Marines who stood at attention and saluted him, saying "Hello Tribune, sir."

Flavius was astounded "Rufio! What are the chances...?"

Rufio smiled "This is now my regular run, sir, but with a different Captain." He looked at Flavius, noting the lines of tension around his mouth and the haunted look in his eyes. All he said was, "You survived Judaea, sir. The gods must have protected you."

Flavius gave a wan smile. "Yes and no, Rufio." He saw Rufio's quizzical look. "When there is time, perhaps I will tell you about it."

"Whenever you're ready, Tribune."

As the other junior officers and legionaries boarded, Flavius looked around the deck. "Do you have proper provision for the transport of my horse?"

Before the Centurion could reply, an older man joined them. His weather-beaten face wore a scowl as he looked Flavius up and down. Flavius recognised him as the Captain to whom Laurentius had spoken the day before. On closer inspection, Flavius disliked the man even more.

The Centurion introduced the Captain. "Sir, this is Captain Alessandro Decimus Silva, master of this trireme"

Silva looked at Saturn. "That's a magnificent horse you have there, Tribune."

"Yes, and I want him to stay that way." Flavius gave the Captain a stern look.

Silva returned Flavius' look and said gruffly, "I think you will find, Tribune, that our cavalry facilities will meet your standards." He turned to Rufio. "Get one of your marines to take care of the Tribune's horse."

Rufio shouted for one of the marines, who quickly appeared before him. "Eolus, make sure the Tribune's horse is safely installed."

"Yes, Centurion." The marine saluted and, under the watchful eye of Flavius, took hold of the reins and led Saturn away.

Silva turned to Flavius. "If you wish to satisfy yourself that your horse will be safe, Tribune, you have my permission to follow Eolus. Then perhaps you would like to inspect your cabin, I'm sure it will meet your demands. Tribune Paullus gave no complaint to me."

"Yes, I think I will," replied Flavius.

Silva had noticed the broad purple band on the bottom of Flavius' tunic. It signified a Tribune Laticlavius, an aristocratic would-be politician who used the army only to pursue their political ambitions, one who served for only two years then dashed back to their pleasures as fast as their well-shod feet could carry them. He narrowed his eyes as he thought of the danger and hardship he had faced during his many years at sea and gave Flavius a withering look, his expression failing to hide his obvious contempt. He snorted in derision, then turned away to give orders to those of his crew charged with directing the rest of the legionaries returning to Ostia to their places.

Flavius ignored the Captain and followed the marine, Eolus. Saturn was installed in one of the pens used for the transportation of cavalry horses. He was the only horse on board, although the many empty pens showed the ship could carry several more when required.

"You see, Tribune, sir, we are used to transporting horses," said Eolus. "I'm sure your beauty here will reach our destination safe and sound."

Flavius nodded, biting back his anger at being addressed in such a familiar way by a lower ranked marine, but he could see that Saturn would be safe here.

At first, Saturn had other ideas. He restlessly tossed his mane and reared up, stamping his hooves down again and again, not liking the confined space. Flavius soothed him with calming words and the horse eventually settled. Flavius turned to Eolus. "I'm willing to pay for special care and decent fodder for him."

Eolus smiled, showing uneven, stained teeth. "There's no need for that, Tribune. Governor Pilate had instructions issued to Captain Silva yesterday. High quality fodder is already on board. The Governor obviously knows how much you value your horse, sir." He looked at Saturn, then at Flavius. "Don't worry, Tribune. I'm used to handling horses, it will be my privilege to personally take care of such a special animal. You don't see a horse like this every day."

Flavius nodded, grateful that Pilate had thought of Saturn's comfort. "Very well, but I too will be keeping an eye on him," he replied.

Flavius heard instructions being bellowed to the crew, and the sound of sudden hurried movement on deck. The ship must be about to set sail. This was soon confirmed as he heard the steady rhythm of the drumbeat coming from below decks, and began to feel a sudden shift beneath his feet as the oarsmen demonstrated their skill at manoeuvering the ship out of the harbour. The trireme left the harbour and began to move out into the open sea.

Flavius held on to Saturn's stall as the trireme began to roll. The horse became restless again and Flavius soothed him, saying "Be patient, we are going home." The trireme steadied and the oarsmen, sweating at their task, propelled the warship onwards.

# CHAPTER THIRTY

The voyage seemed interminable to Flavius. They had been blessed with fair winds and good weather, but although the trireme cut easily through the waves, speeding up the journey, time could not pass quickly enough for him. He was anxious to get home. He checked on Saturn every day and was satisfied that Eolus was keeping his word. Saturn was well fed and in good health. He avoided the surly Captain whenever he could, although contact could not always be avoided.

Sometimes he would keep to the small cabin recently vacated by Paullus, or, if Rufio was not busy, he would talk with him. He discovered Rufio had been born in Rome and was a member of the equestrian class. This did not bother Flavius, as he found Rufio's company pleasant and he enjoyed listening to his stories about life at sea, battles with pirates and recent events in Rome, as well as gossip picked up in Ostia's taverns. He also concluded that Rufio was not fond of Silva and seemed glad that, given his age, the Captain's career would soon be over.

Flavius also enjoyed watching the legionaries on deck, playing dice or knuckle bones, and listening to the good-natured camaraderie of the men. It was good to see the soldiers at ease and enjoying themselves instead of being on constant alert for trouble. Like him, they were happy for any light relief to pass the tedium of the journey, although some could not get used to the ship's roll and spent a good deal of time leaning over the rail. He would also watch as Rufio, his voice harsh and authoritative, put his marines through their paces every morning. He was impressed by Rufio's disciplined commands and was fascinated by the difference between training to fight at sea and the training of land-based legionaries. From the stories Rufio had told him about their many sea battles it was obvious to Flavius that repetitive training was of paramount importance for survival at sea.

They were now several days out from Caesarea. It had been a hot, uncomfortable day so soldiers and crew alike gave thanks when the sun, the god Apollo, drove his fiery chariot towards the horizon and disappeared into the depths of the sea. Soon the goddess Luna arose in his place, casting her silvery pathway over the dark waves. A favourable wind blew up and the mainsail was unfurled, giving the rowers a brief respite from their labours. With the helmsman's steady hand on the tiller, the wind-driven mainsail carried the ship onwards.

Flavius stood on deck looking out at the seemingly endless sea with the waves rising and falling against the hull. There was no sign of any other ship; they were alone in the vast expanse of water.

He suddenly became aware of Rufio standing beside him. Rufio stepped forward and saluted

"Sir. Permission to speak, sir."

Flavius nodded, then turned to face Rufio, who asked, "Is everything all right, Tribune?"

Flavius replied sadly, "I am well Rufio, just regretful." As he scanned Flavius' face, Rufio could see the dark shadows beneath the senior officer's eyes and the taut lines around his mouth and instinctively knew that the time had come for Flavius to tell him what had happened in Judaea. "If you are ready to talk, Tribune, I'm listening," was all he said.

Flavius gave a deep sigh and nodded, feeling the need to unburden himself of the sorry tale.

Rufio listened without saying a word as Flavius told him all that had happened over the past few months: about the religious turmoil, the battles with ben-Ezra and his gang and the subsequent grisly executions he'd been put in charge of – and about his lost love, killed through his carelessness.

Rufio shook his head. "By the gods, sir, you have had terrible experiences, especially for your first mission."

When Flavius didn't reply, Rufio quietly walked away, leaving Flavius standing looking mournfully out to sea.

The telling of his tale to another did not comfort Flavius. Rather he was overwhelmed by guilt and loneliness and the remembrance of all that had happened since he had first come to Judaea. It reminded him how immature he had been then, how arrogant and hedonistic.

He remembered the day he had first seen the magnificent Temple in Jerusalem and the crush of people storming out of the Temple Precinct into the city, dragging a young man along with them, and the horror of watching that man being stoned to death. Then that same night, going to the tavern with Philo, who, because of his stupidity, had died needlessly. It was at that tavern that he had seen the mysterious dancing girl, a girl who proved to be so much more than she seemed, and one he would love for the rest of his days.

He suppressed a shudder. The battle at Beth-Horon Pass and its aftermath would haunt him forever. Now all he had to remind him of her was the golden amulet she had given him. He felt for the amulet, which he wore constantly around his neck. She said it would protect him from five dangerous things; well, he had survived the battle but she had died. Guilt engulfed him. She had passed her protection on to him. Heartbroken, he cried out "Farrah!" For a brief moment in time, her name lingered on the breeze, and then it was gone.

He pulled himself up; life had to go on. Now he had

to think about his family and the mystery of his father's sudden death. Weariness swept over him, but he knew sleep was impossible. He stood staring at the sea until the goddess Aurora slowly manifested her golden-pink beauty in the eastern sky. The wind dropped and the sound of the oarsmen's drumbeat resumed.

The day passed with the same tedium for Flavius. By evening he was weary, with a headache he could not shake off. Tonight he would retire to his cabin, lie down on the cot and try to sleep.

The sun was climbing in the sky when Flavius suddenly awoke to the sound of shouted commands and sudden activity up on deck. He heard a voice booming from the masthead: "Land ho!" Thank the gods, he thought, they must be close to Ostia. He got up and quickly dressed himself, anxious to see the harbour.

Standing on deck, he was amazed to see many ships vying for position to try to reach the dockside. He counted two biremes and two massive merchant ships waiting, as well as a smaller merchant ship that had just docked and was being unloaded. He frowned. It looked as if it would take a considerable time to complete his journey. Frustrated that they were so close to port and yet could not dock, he brought his fist down onto the rail. He heard a gruff voice behind him say sarcastically, "Even you haven't the power to change this, Tribune. You'll just have to put up with it."

Flavius turned and saw Silva standing there. He

wanted to hit him, but with a great effort, he restrained himself and watched grim-faced as the grinning Captain walked away.

Rufio had seen Flavius hit the rail and had heard Silva's comments. Seeing the angry expression on Flavius's face, he approached him. "I'm sorry we can't land yet, sir, but I'm afraid it's always like this," he said. Flavius turned and gave Rufio a stern look. Undaunted, Rufio continued his explanation. "Ships arrive here from most of the Empire, some even larger than that big merchant ship over there." He pointed to the largest merchant ship riding at anchor out at sea. "That's the *Aurelia*, sir. She's a grain carrier ship and a regular visitor here. She must have just returned from Egypt. Her crew will have to unload well over three hundred tons of grain today. Given the *Aurelia*'s size, the grain will have to be transferred to smaller craft as the ship's too big to enter the port."

Flavius' knuckles grew white as he angrily gripped the rail and gave full vent to his frustration. "Body of Bacchus! We will be here for hours!" he shouted.

Rufio felt sympathy for Flavius. To have sailed this far without any trouble and then to be so close to his destination and not be able to complete the trip was enough to make anyone angry. He offered some hope. "Not necessarily, sir. As soon as those biremes move away, we'll manoeuvre around her and dock." He looked at the legionaries from Caesarea gathering their equipment together ready for the order to disembark. They seemed unconcerned by the wait.

"The legionaries don't appear to be worried about docking, sir."

Flavius turned his head to look at them and said coldly, "They're used to it. All legionaries, whatever their rank, know that the Legions' motto is 'hurry up and wait'. Once they have cleared the port authorities and reported to the Port Commander at the Castrum, they'll face a further wait to find out where they will be sent next. Hopefully not somewhere worse than Judaea, if that is possible."

Rufio smiled. "Waiting is a condition I know only too well, sir, be it for tides or summer storm delays." With that, he saluted and went off to ready his marines for landing.

Eventually, after an interminable wait, the trireme bypassed the biremes and swung expertly along the dockside. Relieved that the voyage was over, Flavius went to Saturn's pen, where Eolus was waiting for him. Eolus saluted and smiled. "Your horse is safe and well, Tribune."

Flavius satisfied himself that this was true and nodded, relieved. He turned to Eolus and said "Thank you for your care. It is appreciated."

Flavius waited until the troops had disembarked, then led Saturn onto the deck. Ignoring Flavius, Silva carried on giving orders to the crew. Rufio, however, stood at attention before him and saluted, saying, "Well, sir, we got here safe and sound. I hope the journey was not too uncomfortable for you."

Flavius returned the salute. "It could have been a lot worse, Rufio. Nevertheless, I am glad to be here in Ostia. I want to thank you for helping me pass the time – and for listening to my woeful tale and not judging me."

"It has been a pleasure, Tribune. As for judging you – after what you've been through sir, no one could ever do that." He stood tall and added, "Perhaps we may meet again one day."

Flavius smiled wanly. "Who knows, maybe one day we will. We must wait and see what the gods have in store for us."

"Yes, sir." Rufio saluted again. He felt Silva's eyes on him, and turned to see the Captain glaring at him. "If you will excuse me, sir, I must attend to my duties." With one final salute, Rufio turned and walked towards the Captain.

Flavius handed over Saturn's reins to a legionary, then stood for a while in the entrance of the port garrison. He watched as the legionaries who had accompanied him on the voyage were shunted to another part of the garrison to wait for further orders about their next destination. He silently wished them luck and hoped they would not be sent to yet another troublesome part of the Empire.

He entered the garrison and asked a burly legionary where he might find the Port Commander. The legionary, seeing his rank, stood stiffly to attention and saluted, saying crisply "If you will follow me, Tribune."

Flavius followed the legionary until he stopped outside a massive wooden and bronze door. He knocked loudly. A voice from inside answered, "Enter."

The legionary opened the door and stepped inside. "Commander, sir. A Tribune wishes to see you."

"Send him in," came the terse order.

The legionary stood aside as Flavius entered the room, then, saluting both officers, he left the room and stood guarding the door.

Flavius looked around the room. Apart from a desk and a chair there was no other furniture. The middle-aged Port Commander rose up from the chair and walked towards Flavius. Saluting, he said, "Tribune, you asked to see me?"

"Yes, Commander. I have a pass from the Governor of Judaea granting me a quick departure from Ostia to return to Rome where I have urgent, private business to attend to." He pulled the pass out of his bag and gave it to the Commander, who studied it carefully, then said "It seems in order." The Commander moved back behind his desk, still holding the pass. He looked directly at Flavius and said, "Well, Tribune Silvanus, may I ask how Governor Pilate is involved in your private business? Is it a matter of state?"

Flavius thought quickly and came up with an answer. "I'm sorry, Commander I can't reveal the full facts of the Governor's involvement, only that it concerns a member of his family to whom I am also related." Flavius hoped that would satisfy the Commander's curiosity.

The Commander thought for a moment then said warily, "You say your business is urgent?"

Flavius nodded, trying to keep his growing annoyance

from showing. "Yes, Commander."

"Well then, I'd best let you get on your way." His smile was stilted as he handed the pass back to a relieved Flavius, saying "Have a safe journey back to Rome."

Flavius returned the Commander's salute and left the room. As soon as he had gone, the Commander took a scroll and wrote on it: 'The one you are waiting for has arrived.' He rolled the scroll, sealing it with his seal, then called the legionary back into the room, barking out "Send a cavalryman to me!" A few minutes later, a cavalry officer arrived. He took the proffered scroll from the Commander, who said sternly "This communication is of the utmost importance. See that it is placed in the hands of Calpurnius Aquila, and only him, as soon as possible."

From his office window, the Commander watched as the rider mounted his horse and galloped across the courtyard, forcing Flavius aside. Flavius swore under his breath at the rider's carelessness, then mounted an agitated Saturn. As they rode out of the fortress, Saturn tossed his beautiful mane, relieved to be on firm ground again. Then at his master's command, he picked up speed until horse and rider were galloping along the Via Ostiensis: the road to Rome.